TANYA BIRD

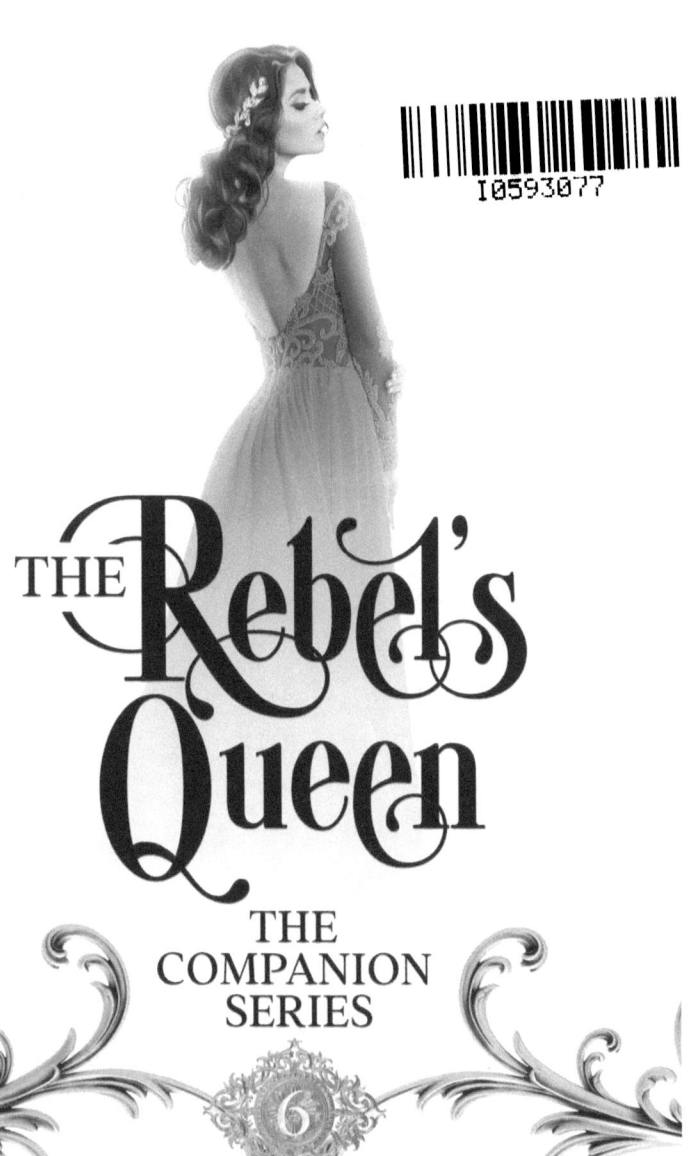

THE Rebel's Queen

THE COMPANION SERIES

6

For my readers.
You wanted more Cora. I give you more Cora.

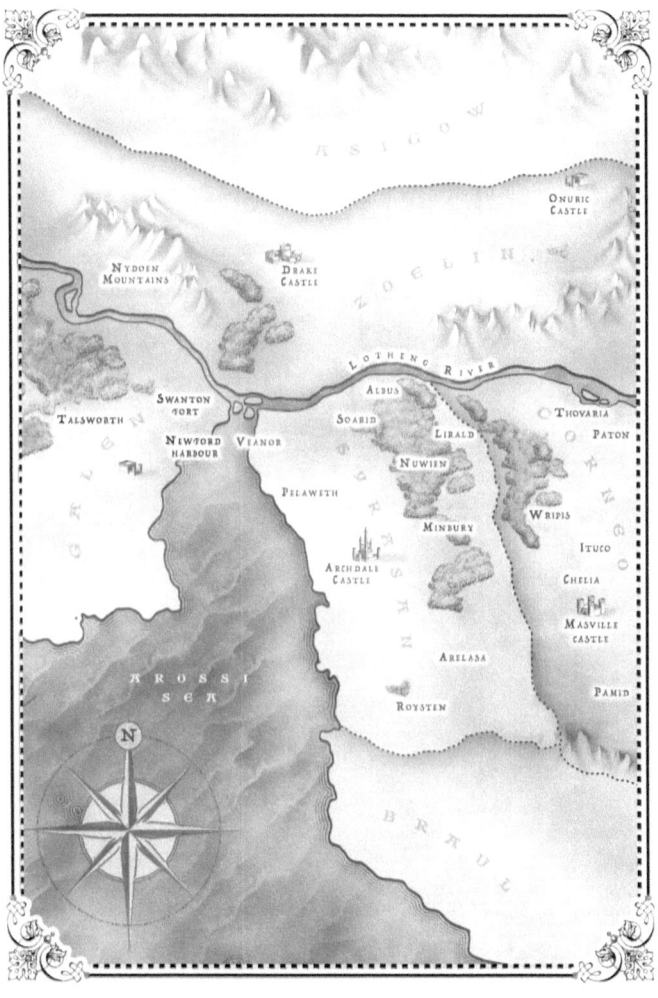

PROLOGUE

*B*rom watched the archers atop the wall, their arrows nocked, drawn—and pointed at him. He glanced over his shoulder to where his own small army of men waited out of shooting range, hands resting on the hilts of their swords. Two empty carts sat behind them, dusted with fresh snow and ready to be loaded. Brom's eyes returned to the soldiers, weapons steady in their hands. He was very much *within* shooting range. An act of faith. It would be a shame to die after such a long and painful negotiation.

A crow cawed and took flight as the gate split down the middle, revealing a sliver of what awaited him on the other side.

'Want me to come with you?' Carac asked.

Brom glanced sideways at him. 'Won't do much good.'

'Might give you a chance to escape if the need arises.'

Brom exhaled through his nose. 'There's no escaping him right now.' He nudged his horse with his heels. 'Wait here.'

The shuffle of small feet reached him through the widening gap. His eyes narrowed on the cluster of children huddled between two guards, looking suitably wary. Their ages ranged from six to fourteen. The older ones feigned confidence well enough while the younger ones failed miserably. One even tried to turn back. He was confusing familiar with safe. An older boy caught him by the arm, shoving him forwards. Brom looked past them to where Jayr sat on horseback, watching him with a dark expression.

His brother.

His king.

The man who wished him dead.

'That is far enough,' Jayr called out.

Brom stopped his horse a few paces from the gate, dismounted, and waited for the children to reach him. The arrows above followed his every move.

'This is all of them?' Brom asked one of the guards.

'One more to come,' he replied, glancing over his shoulder.

Brom followed his line of sight to a cloaked woman holding a young boy. Arms and legs wrapped her tightly. Even at that distance, Brom could hear the child crying. It was Queen Cora —better known as the Ice Queen. She met his gaze, unflinching, as she held the boy's head against her shoulder. Brom snuck a glance at Jayr. The king's eyes held a warning for him.

Cora stopped a few feet away, slightly out of breath from the effort of carrying the young boy through two feet of fresh snowfall. They regarded each other for a moment.

'Your Majesty,' he said, breaking the silence between them. He focused on the boy. 'Who do we have here?'

'He cannot walk.' The words came out with a puff of steam.

Brom looked him over. 'Why's that?'

'He injured his ankle.'

'How?'

She swallowed. 'Training, I think.'

'Ah.' Brom closed the distance between them, and the arrows followed him once more.

'He is also scared,' Cora added. 'Perhaps he could ride with you.' She whispered the last part.

Brom searched her face for a moment. She was striking close up, with those green eyes and that porcelain skin. Lashes and lips for days. 'Are you the one who wrote me?'

Her eyes moved between his. 'That would be a betrayal to my husband.'

She did not say no. Not that it mattered—it was the same outcome regardless of who the informant was—yet for some strange reason, he wanted to know if it was her. The person had known things he suspected only a queen could know, like just how far a king can be pushed in a negotiation. He decided not to interrogate her while her husband was watching.

He was reaching for the boy when he noticed a bruise on her left cheek. It reached all the way to her eye. She had done her best to cover the mark with powder. 'What happened to your face?'

He should have just taken the boy, said nothing.

She peeled arms from her neck. 'Take him.' Her tone was cold.

Brom settled the sniffling boy against his chest, looking at her the whole time. 'You have a fall?'

'Something like that.' Her hand went to the child's back. 'Brom is going to take you somewhere safe. You can trust him.'

Her voice was soft and reassuring when she addressed the child. Brom had no idea what to make of her. 'He can ride with me.'

She nodded, meeting his gaze once more. He was at least

a foot and a half taller than her, but she was not the slightest bit intimidated.

'He will buy more,' she said.

He squinted. 'Boys?'

The slightest nod from her.

Brom stepped back, and her bright eyes followed him like the arrows. 'Then I guess I'll wait for that anonymous letter.' He winked, looked one more time at the mark on her face, and went to leave.

'His name is Perrin, by the way,' she said, stopping him. 'He does not talk much.'

Her expression had softened considerably. Anyone would have thought she was sorry to see the boy go.

'Cora!' Jayr's voice cut through the still air like a blade. 'Inside. Now.'

She looked over her shoulder, acknowledging her husband with a nod, then back at Brom.

He regarded her for the longest time before speaking. 'He's not allowed to hit you, you know. He could lose his crown.'

Something resembling amusement passed over her face. 'And who is going to take it from him? You?' She glanced a final time at Perrin, then turned and trudged back through the gate.

CHAPTER 1

*H*er cheek burned, and her ear rang. She tried to focus, but light danced in her vision. Striking a queen was forbidden. She knew it. Jayr knew it. Every guard standing idly by knew it. But he did it anyway. Jayr played by his own rules nowadays.

The sound of her bodyguard's boots pounding on the marble floor made her raise her hand. The footsteps stopped. Shame prevented her from looking up. Lief was the only man in the kingdom foolish enough to go up against his own king in order to protect her, and that protection was reciprocated. She would not let him risk his own life. This was her mess, her fault.

Pushing herself up onto her feet, she brought a trembling hand to her face. She would not cry in front of Jayr, refused to feed his power. There were four feet between them now. If only she had been ready for it, she would have ensured her feet never moved at all. She finally lifted her gaze to him, watched as he brushed a hand over his shaved head. He hated himself in those moments, but not enough to stop doing it.

'See what you drive me to?' His voice was raised.

Her hands betrayed her, shaking violently. She clasped them in front of her. 'You *dare* hit the queen of Zoelin.'

Jayr closed the distance between them. She made sure her feet stuck this time, even when he thrust a folded-up piece of parchment at her face.

'You *wrote* him.'

Cora had written to Brom many times over the previous few months. Despite taking every precaution, Jayr's growing paranoia had pushed his controlling nature to an entirely new level. He was not only having her watched but all those in her service. He was unhinged—and holding on to his crown by a thread. The problem was, the tighter he held on, the more mistakes he made.

'You bought more children from Asigow. Did you think our people would sit by while you grew your collection at Onuric Castle?'

He stepped closer, making himself as tall as possible. She held her breath, never looking away. Cursing, he stepped back, linking his hands on top of his head as he tried to calm himself.

'I won't explain myself to you. Buying soldiers is the fastest way to grow our army.'

'But you are not buying soldiers, are you? You are buying *children.*'

'Whose future would have been no brighter had they remained in Asigow.'

'Why not focus on mending relations with your neighbours instead of building defences that will make no difference?'

'And how do you know they will make no difference? Did my brother tell you in one of his letters?'

She could see his hands balling into fists, his frustration building once more. 'You are forcing Brom's hand.'

'And you are holding it!'

6

She took an involuntary step back. 'I cannot have this same argument over and over.'

'Neither can I, so I suggest you walk away.' His gaze flicked to her reddened cheek. 'Have Sarey put ice on your face. I do not need more people talking.'

Heat coursed through her, anger with nowhere to go. 'What *will* people think of you?'

'That sarcastic mouth of yours is going to get you into a lot of trouble one day.'

'Oh, I think that ship has sailed.' She turned away, eyes going to Lief, who looked ready to tackle the king to the ground. She shook her head ever so slightly.

'I will see you at dinner,' Jayr said to her back.

'I am not hungry.' She was already walking away.

'You had better be there, or I will come to your room and drag you there by your hair.'

She closed her eyes, her pace even and back straight so he would not suspect how close she was to breaking. Lief followed, silent for now. Cora did not stop until she reached her quarters. The guard waiting at the door opened it without a word. Only then did she turn to face her bodyguard.

'You should've let me do my job,' he said, his jaw working.

She could feel her eye swelling. 'There is nothing you can do, and I will not give that man the pleasure of taking your head. He will consider it another win, and he has had enough of those.' She pressed her lips together when they began to tremble. 'I am going to change, and then I am going for a ride. Have someone saddle my horse.'

'What about dinner?'

'I already told Jayr I am not hungry.'

Lief looked off down the corridor as he ran a hand down his inked face. He bit back the words on the edge of his tongue and gave a small bow before marching off, his wide frame filling the corridor. Cora pushed the door shut and leaned her forehead on it.

'What happened?' Sarey asked behind her.

Cora turned to face her lady-in-waiting. Just one lady. Her trust only stretched so far.

Sarey's eyes narrowed on Cora's cheek, and she rushed forwards to take a closer look.

'Jayr?'

Cora gave her a look that suggested she should know the answer. 'He is in a mood.' When Sarey reached out to touch her, Cora pushed her hand away. 'Do not fuss. It will fade. They always fade.' She stepped past, went to the chair by the fireplace, and sank down into it. The split in her dress revealed a long, polished leg.

'Your face is swelling.'

Cora stared at the flames. The heat was stifling. She had always thought she would struggle with Zoelin's weather, being perched on a mountain in freezing temperatures under relentless snowfall, but there was something cleansing about the air at that altitude. When outdoors, she liked to watch the air leave her mouth in puffs of steam, every breath a kind of exorcism.

'I'll fetch some snow for your face,' Sarey said, moving for the door.

'I need my riding boots and a cloak.'

Sarey stopped. 'Riding boots?'

Cora pushed herself up from the chair. If she remained there any longer, she might start to feel sorry for herself. 'Yes. I am going for a ride.'

Sarey glanced at the large window. 'But it'll be dark soon, and the king has requested you dine with him.'

'Yes. He is going to be *so* disappointed. I am sure he will find comfort between the legs of one of his many whores.'

Sarey hesitated before going to fetch Cora's boots. 'I thought you scared them all off.'

'I did, but he is always finding new ones who do not know any better.'

'You'll make everything much worse if you don't show up tonight.'

Cora's head throbbed. 'How much worse can it get?' She unpinned her dark hair and let it fall about her shoulders, trying to ease the headache. Her hair had taken three years to grow after Jayr had hacked it off. He was very big on teaching her lessons. *Such* a pity they never stuck.

Sarey kneeled in front of her with the boots. 'Must we find out?' She rose. 'I'm coming with you.'

'No. It is bad enough Lief is forced to follow behind. At least he will not talk.'

Sarey knew better than to be offended. 'And what would you like me to say to your husband when he storms through here looking for you later?'

Cora turned so Sarey could wrap the cloak around her. 'Tell him I am indisposed.'

'*Indisposed*? Oh, he'll love that. Anyone would think you have a death wish.'

Cora closed her eyes. The relief might be nice.

Her eyes snapped open at the thought. *No.* She would not let her mind go there.

'Perhaps you'd be better off taking a long walk,' Sarey suggested gently. 'You know what the king says about your long rides—'

Cora spun around. 'Remind me. What does he say?' Her tone was sharper than she had intended.

Sarey's expression was full of pity. 'I don't agree with him. I'm just trying to protect you.'

'My fertility has nothing to do with me riding or not riding.'

'*I* know that.'

'Then be quiet. There is always something I am doing wrong. Wrong food, not enough sleep, too much sleep, stress, wine. Pray harder, and harder still. The sooner everyone accepts I am barren, the sooner they will move on from their disappointment.' And the sooner she could move on from hers.

Sarey took hold of her hands. 'Are you sure you don't want me to come with you?'

Cora felt a pang of remorse. 'No.' She forced a small smile in place of an apology.

Sarey sighed. 'You're allowed to feel angry—about everything.'

Cora swallowed and looked away. 'He had a letter I wrote to Brom.'

'You mean one of the letters *I* scribed?'

Cora pulled her hands free. 'Brom is on his own now. Jayr will be watching me very closely, and I have no idea who I can trust. At the moment, that list stands at you and Lief.'

Sarey nodded, thoughtful. 'Brom will find out what the king is up to one way or another—if he doesn't know already.'

'He has supporters right across the kingdom now.'

It had been two months since the rebel and his men had surrounded the castle and made their demands. Two months since Jayr had realised what he was truly up against. The siege had been his tipping point. Cora had watched him from the open window as he exited the castle, feeling oddly calm at the prospect of him not returning. Then he had ridden back through the gates an hour later, and she had felt crushing disappointment followed by shame. She had held the wall for balance, suspecting she was truly losing her mind. If her husband had not returned, Brom's men would have stormed the castle and stripped her of her crown, and without that crown, she was just a vulnerable princess in a foreign kingdom.

'Perhaps you should play submissive wife for a while. At least until things calm down,' Sarey said, pulling her from her thoughts.

Cora headed for the door. 'Now where is the fun in that?'

'He's getting worse. You must see that.'

She certainly felt it. The previous shoving, hair pulling, and holding of her wrists too tightly all seemed rather civil compared to their more recent fights. Handing those children over to his brother had done irreparable damage to Jayr's ego. 'I have to go before I lose light.'

'At least let me paint your face to cover the mark before you go.'

Cora shook her head. 'I am done covering up that man's sins. It is time those loyal to him saw their king's handiwork.'

Lief was waiting outside when she opened the door. She stepped past him without saying anything. Boots followed her along the corridor, down the steps, and outside. Cora made her way to the mounting yard in front of the stables, where Ida was saddled and waiting for her. The mare emitted a low whinny as Cora approached.

'Hello, my love,' she said, stepping up to the mare and stroking her face with one gloved hand. 'Ready to escape for a while?'

She took the reins from the groom, her gaze falling briefly to the scar on the mare's neck. When the groom moved forwards to help her, she shook her head, and he immediately stepped back.

A few minutes later, they approached the gate, but it did not open in front of her like usual. A bad feeling rose like bile in her throat as she neared the guard. He was standing in the middle of the road like a physical barrier. He did not even bow when she reached him.

Lief trotted past her before she had a chance to speak.

'Bow before your queen.' His tone resembled a growl.

The guard took a small step back from the horse, then bowed. 'Her Majesty's not to pass through the gates. King's orders.'

Cora looked up at the men lining the top of the wall, all watching, all armed. 'My husband must have given a reason for such orders.'

'Not that I'm permitted to share, Your Majesty.'

Lief's hand went to the hilt of his sword, but he did not draw it, instead looking to her for instructions. He could probably get her out if she really needed him to. He had the skills and strength. But to what end?

Another guard came to stand beside the other man, and Ida laid her ears back in warning. Cora patted the mare's neck. 'You know, it is rather late. Perhaps I will leave my ride until tomorrow.' She directed her words at Lief, keeping her tone casual for the sake of the guards.

The bodyguard let go of his sword, glaring at the men before swinging his horse around.

Cora turned away also, pushing the mare into a canter and sending a spray of muddy snow into the air behind her. She did not follow the path but rather rode along the base of the wall, out of sight of the castle. The cold air stung her eyes, and her ears ached. She inhaled deeply, inviting the frosty air to numb her insides. If Jayr thought holding her prisoner would improve her mood, he was a slow learner.

'Do not follow me!' she shouted over her shoulder to Lief before picking up speed.

He immediately pulled up his horse, watching her until she was out of sight.

Cora went behind the fruit trees lining the east wall, stopping beneath the cover of branches. Ida snorted and stepped sideways, eager to resume galloping.

Cora's breathing turned to gasps, and her throat burned. 'Easy,' she said, trying not to let her anxiety transfer to the mare. Folding over, she buried her face in Ida's mane, tensing every muscle in her body to hold in the tears—but it was no good. A hand flew up to cover her mouth, and her body shook with silent sobs. She remained that way for some time until she finally stilled and her breathing returned to normal. Straightening, she drew some long breaths and wiped at her face, wincing when her hand passed over the fresh bruise. She looked up when she felt fresh tears arrive, a trick she had learned over the years.

No more.

Every tear was a tiny victory for Jayr.

She sat there, breathing and staring, hating and hurting, until she stopped feeling anything at all. That was much easier. She looked around then, praying no one had seen the outburst. Satisfied, she turned in the direction of the stables.

It was time to soldier up and return to the marital frontline.

CHAPTER 2

*R*elaxing the arm was key in managing the pain of the needle. Every time Brom flinched, Droet would pause, wiping the blood from the wound and studying his work.

'When a man needles another, he learns something of his brothers.'

Droet was the oldest member of the Valter tribe. He was also Carac's grandfather and the man who had welcomed Brom into his home all those years back. Carac liked to point out that his arrival had also been the beginning of his grandfather's mental decline. It was true that the grandor's mind was not what it used to be. At seventy-eight, the sharing of wisdom came in the form of confused ramblings. He still had a steady ink hand though.

The sun was setting behind the huts, and the older boys had built a fire big enough to warm the entire village. The tribe sat cross-legged around it, the women with tired children nestled in their laps, all watching the ritual. Pup was curled up against Brom's legs, whining every time he tensed. The wolf was finely tuned to emotions.

'A mark of courage,' Droet said, dipping two fingers into the pot of black powder and rubbing it over the fresh wound.

Brom looked down at the mark. 'Courage for what?'

The old man's eyes met his briefly. 'It's not an easy thing to fight blood.'

'I've been fighting Jayr since I could walk.'

Droet chuckled, his long beard twitching with the action. 'It's time for Jayr's reign to come to an end. You must be ready.'

Brom knew he was right, he was just struggling to accept it. 'He bought more children from Asigow. He's housing them at Onuric Castle.'

'We knew he would. The mind is furnished with bad ideas.'

Another saying that had evolved over time.

There was a childish part of Brom that had hoped Jayr would be miraculously reformed by the siege. Six days they had surrounded Drake Castle, making it clear they would not leave until the Asigow children were handed over. Jayr had sent a legion of men out to deal with him, a flexing of muscle. None of them had returned. Once the king had realised he was going to have to sacrifice more men or risk starving to death, he had finally agreed to meet.

The meeting had gone as expected. Jayr knew the entire kingdom was watching, that further conflict would only expose him. People would see him for who he was. The children had been handed over, and months had passed before Brom learned that he was still buying soldiers, housing and training them at Onuric Castle in the East. It seemed to be the place for all his dark dealings.

'Did the queen write you?' Droet asked without looking up.

'Not recently. She's gone quiet.'

Droet nodded. 'There's great risk for her.'

Brom thought back to his encounter with her. He had thought a lot about it in the months since. She had presented herself so stoically, living up to her reputation. The queen with the iron will and frozen heart. He wondered if she had arrived at Drake Castle that way or had evolved out of necessity. Somehow, she had coexisted with Jayr in the confines of that castle for three years.

His thoughts were interrupted when Carac slumped down beside him, wine sloshing out of his cup as he landed. He rubbed Pup's head, scratching behind her missing ear in that spot that made her foot tap. 'Don't tell me you're still talking about the Ice Queen.'

'A strong woman is a dark ocean without shores,' Droet said, eyes on his work.

Carac and Brom exchanged a smile.

'I think our rebel has a thing for her,' Carac said, eyeing his friend. 'She's a snake disguised as a goddess.'

'The people like her,' Droet said.

Carac nodded. 'Because her balls are bigger than Jayr's. They're intrigued.'

Brom's lips formed a disapproving line. 'Careful. She's still your queen.'

Carac stifled a yawn. 'For now. The second Jayr's gone, she's out of there.'

'Harsh.' For some strange reason, Brom felt the need to defend her. 'She's proved herself as a queen. She's loyal to Zoelin.'

'But not to her poor husband.'

'The poor husband you wish dead?'

Carac shrugged. 'I'm allowed to wish him dead. I'm not married to him.'

Droet looked up. 'I've heard many good things about her.'

Carac rolled his eyes, but Brom waited for him to continue.

'She's quietly generous.'

'What does "quietly generous" mean?' Carac asked.

Droet wiped at the wound with a cloth. 'She helps people.'

Carac scoffed at that. 'All queens help people. It's part of the job.'

The elder continued working. 'She doesn't make a big display of her generosity. I think she'd prefer no one knew.'

Another scoff from Carac. 'Because they might suspect her of having a beating heart?'

A smile flickered on Droet's face. 'She sends gifts, food, and coin to families in need. Always discreet.'

Carac dropped his empty cup in the dirt. 'How do you know it's her?'

'One can recognise emotion if one understands the shift of seasons.'

Carac frowned at the nonsense response, then looked to Brom. 'Look at you, eating all this up. The woman carries one injured boy out of a castle and suddenly you think she's doing the work of God. She's the same spoilt princess you heard stories about when your father was still on the throne. She hasn't changed.'

'I never said she'd changed. I said she might be misunderstood.'

Carac laughed while Droet placed his tools down and stretched out his back.

'All finished.'

Carac narrowed his eyes on the fresh ink. 'Is that the mark of a king? A little premature, don't you think?' Though he winked at Brom when he said it.

Droet gestured for Brom to come closer, taking hold of his face with both hands and pressing their foreheads together. 'The crown awaits you.'

'Hope it's patient,' Brom replied.

Droet laughed and patted his cheek—much too hard.

'Your grandfather would be very proud. If he were alive, he'd tell you so.'

Brom's chest tightened at the mention of his grandfather. Pup sat up and looked at him, sensing the shift in mood. He rubbed her head and looked down at her exposed teeth. Her lip had been torn off when wolves had come for the goats. She was more of a pet nowadays. No good at protecting anything.

The women gathered around the fire began to sing, marking the end of the ritual.

'When are you going to act?' Carac asked, keeping his voice low. 'How many more children must cross the border before you realise your brother can't be redeemed?'

It was a fair question. 'I don't hesitate for his sake but for what his death will mean for everyone else. Am I to slaughter all loyal to him? What of his advisors? His army? My sister for that matter.'

'His army will become your army. As for your sister, she's been locked away at Onuric Castle far too long. People will show their true colours soon enough. They're likely as keen to be rid of him as the rest of us.' He paused. 'Or perhaps your hesitation has more to do with a certain displaced queen.'

Brom looked away. 'She doesn't deserve to be tarnished by Jayr.'

'One brief conversation and suddenly you think you know her.' Carac was grinning.

'Call it a feeling.'

'Oh, I know it's a *feeling*.' Carac bumped him with his shoulder. 'Well, when you're king, you can decide what happens to her.'

Brom blinked away the image of those green eyes assessing him. 'Her family will likely want her back in Syrasan—unharmed.'

'Sounds reasonable,' Carac replied.

Droet laughed and tutted. 'Or you could *marry* her.'

Carac choked on his own laughter. 'Marry her? Why on earth would he do that to himself?'

Droet looked up at the sky. 'She's glue.'

'Ah, I think that's enough bad advice from you today.' Carac shook his head.

'That's how you fix a divided kingdom,' Droet added, looking straight at Brom. 'She's a cunning woman.'

Carac nodded in agreement. 'Exactly.'

'With experience in the role,' Droet added.

'She's also rumoured to have claws like a cat,' Carac said.

Droet went on. 'Her brother is the king of Syrasan, her uncle the king of Galen.'

Brom could not ignore those last points. 'But what of trust?'

Droet's eyes smiled. 'Well, she's not led you astray yet.'

'Worth noting that she hasn't produced an heir,' Carac said. 'Three years they've been married.'

Droet patted Brom's arm. 'A woman's womb needs sun to blossom.'

Brom tried to think of what he might have meant to say but came up blank. 'So I take my brother's throne, his army, his castles, and his *wife?*'

Carac shook his head. 'You'd be mad to take her on. I heard she once cut off the hair of one of your brother's mistresses and had it made into a wig.'

'Let's not get ahead of ourselves. As it stands, she's married to my brother, who's still very much alive.'

Carac regarded him for a moment. 'His reign is up. You know that, right?'

Brom ran a hand down his face and looked back at the fire as the song came to an end. 'I know.'

CHAPTER 3

Cora managed to avoid her husband until the following evening, when he sent two guards to her quarters to collect her for dinner. She had requested food be brought to her room, but Jayr had invited some people to dine at the castle and was insisting she attend.

'He said to wear something appropriate or he will cover you with the table linen,' said one of the guards.

It would not be the first time. Sighing, she asked, 'Who are the guests?'

The guard rattled off half a dozen names. Some of them lords from Corneo, a few grandors from Asigow. It was likely to do with the ongoing Companion trade that Jayr continued to facilitate.

'I need to dress. I will be down soon.'

Once the men had left, Cora turned to Sarey. 'I hate him.'

'I know.' Sarey went into the other room to select a dress, and Cora followed. 'Just give him what he wants, then leave early with a headache.'

Cora poured herself some more wine from the table by

the window. She had barely had time to sober up from the night prior. She felt Sarey's disapproving gaze on her.

'Arriving intoxicated isn't going to improve his mood.'

Cora emptied the cup before going to dress. 'No, but it will improve mine.'

Once her face was painted and her hair pulled back into a tight braid, she threw on a few pieces of random jewellery and declared herself ready. Lief was waiting outside for her. She nodded a greeting as she stepped past him, Sarey following behind.

When they arrived at the great hall, Cora waited to be announced before entering. The guests split down the middle, all turning to watch her, the men's gazes lingering just a fraction too long. Jayr could not blame her this time, as the velvet dress covered everything except her hands. She barely cared what she wore nowadays. The revealing dresses had served a purpose when she had come of age and had wanted to rebel. They had also served in annoying Jayr for a while. But nowadays she dressed for power, not attention, choosing high-collared gowns, dark paint, bold lips, and heeled boots for extra height.

Jayr stood in front of the high table, waiting for her to reach him. She took in his smug expression, the one she had grown to resent so deeply. He would punish her for standing him up the night prior.

She came to a stop in front of him, curtsying. 'Husband.'

His eyes moved over her. 'My queen.'

She looked around the room. 'What is the occasion this time?'

'Must I need an occasion?'

Her eyes returned to him. 'You are the king. You can do as you please.'

Jayr offered his arm and led her up to her chair at the high table. Lief went to stand in his usual spot against the wall, and Sarey stood a few feet behind the queen, hands folded in front of her as she watched the room.

'I hear you enjoyed a relaxing day in your quarters,' Jayr said, one corner of his mouth lifting.

Cora went to reach for the wine but realised there was no goblet in front of her, only a cup filled with water. 'You cannot keep me locked inside this castle forever, you know. I am your wife, not your prisoner.'

'Of course I can.'

She turned her head, eyes burning in his direction. 'You must have a short memory. Have you forgotten that when we play these games, you never win?'

'But neither do you, and that is a win of sorts.' He reached down and retrieved a small wooden box, placing it on the table.

Cora's stomach clenched as she recognised the box. 'Absolutely not.'

'I thought I would honour you with some ink.'

She rolled her eyes. 'You just want to stab me with needles.'

Jayr took her hand, squeezing it much too tightly. 'It is an honour.'

She brought her face closer to his and whispered, 'It is a punishment, an excuse to hurt me.'

He kept hold of her hand. 'You know, if I did not need Syrasan and Galen as allies right now, I would throw you from the closest window and marry someone of use.' He released her hand. 'Someone fertile.'

They said horrible things to each other all the time, but that last part felt like a punch to the stomach. 'I would happily jump from that window if it would not please you so much.' She glanced over her shoulder at Sarey. 'Please get me a drink.'

'There is water right in front of you,' Jayr said, pushing her cup closer.

She turned to look at him. 'I do not want water.'

He levelled her with a cold stare. 'That is too bad, because that is all I am allowing this evening.'

Only three years into her life sentence. How was that possible? She wanted to cry, scratch his face, throw a chair at him, scream until her lungs gave out, but she did none of those things. She turned back to the room instead.

'I am going to speak with our guests,' Jayr said. 'You can join me.'

She did not have it in her to stand, walk, smile, talk. 'I will join you in a moment.' She reached for the cup of water and brought it to her lips, watching him over the rim.

'Fine.' He rose and left the table. 'Behave.'

The moment he stepped down, Cora reached for his goblet, but as she brought it to her lips, a hand caught her arm.

'Don't,' Sarey said. 'You'll only anger him more.'

Cora tugged her arm free, and the wine sloshed up the side of the cup and spilled onto her hand. 'Now look what you've—'

Her eyes went to her hand, which was stinging. She placed the cup down and reached for a napkin. The skin came away when she wiped it. Sarey sucked in a breath, then picked up the cup of water and threw it over the hand. Cora shot up from her chair as her skin continued to burn, her heart drumming away in her chest as she comprehended what had just happened.

'What is it now?' Jayr asked, stopping in front of the high table. When he registered her expression, his gaze fell to her hand. It did not take him long to put the pieces together.

The drink was poisoned.

'Guards!'

The entire room fell silent and looked in their direction. Cora edged back from the table, her mind racing. She heard Lief's boots, but she did not turn, because her vision snagged on a man approaching her husband from behind. She saw a dagger drop from the man's sleeve into his hand. She opened her mouth to warn Jayr, but before anything came out, the man thrust the knife into her husband's neck.

Cora felt like she had been plunged into icy water as she stared into Jayr's wide eyes. His hands went to his neck, as though holding in some of the blood would help him in that moment. Cora's went over her mouth, holding in a scream. Then she was pulled backwards, her vision blocked by Lief's large frame. Sarey's arms went around her, holding tightly. Cora was frozen in place.

Weapons were drawn, and guests fled. She heard something hit the ground, and someone shouted, 'Long live King Bro—' Guards were upon him before the name passed his lips.

'Start moving,' Lief said, ushering the women towards the door.

Screams rang out around them. Somehow Cora's feet worked, despite having no feeling in them. She searched for Jayr amid the chaos and found him still and bleeding out on the floor, his killer on the ground behind him.

The king was dead.

Her *husband* was dead.

CHAPTER 4

The castle gates opened, and Cora watched from atop the steps as her mother's wagon rolled through, its red flag flying. Tyron, her brother, was on horseback, trotting alongside it. They were there for her, to offer support and ensure she was safe during her regency. Cora swallowed down the emotion rising at the sight of them. She needed to be stronger than that.

'I'll be away for a few days,' Pollux said beside her. 'I have some business to tend to, and I'm sure your brother would prefer I not be here.'

Cora glanced up at her advisor. He had served Jayr the entire time he was on the throne. As much as she had grown to despise her husband, it seemed appropriate that at least one person mourn him. 'You have business at a time like this?'

'Personal business.'

She faced forwards again. 'Princess Tasia is due to arrive today to farewell her brother and king.'

'I'll return in time for the funeral tomorrow.'

The funeral. The day Jayr's body would be burned, his ashes returned to the earth. Much better than having his corpse a few doors down, slowly decomposing. 'Is there any word from Brom?'

'He'll be here for the funeral also.'

Cora felt a surge of annoyance. 'Why did you not tell me he had written?'

Pollux looked down at her, unblinking. 'You're grieving, Your Majesty. I didn't wish to burden you.'

'I am regent until Brom's coronation. That is Zoelin law, is it not?'

He looked away. 'That's right.'

'Then treat me as such. I am quite capable of performing my role, no matter how deep the grief.' They both knew her grief was not that deep. It was the shock of his death that rocked her, and a deep concern for her future. In a few days, she would be displaced—queen of nothing, a barren widow with no prospects. 'I thought it might be nice to have our soldiers welcome their new king. Queen-regent or not, our army will look to you for leadership in the interim.'

'Of course.'

Her eyes returned to him. 'That is all, grandor.'

He bowed, and she watched him walk off. At least he was being compliant. It seemed the man's loyalty to Zoelin outweighed his loyalty to Jayr.

Her gaze landed briefly on Lief, who eyed the advisor as he passed. Always so suspicious.

Drawing a breath, Cora descended the steps with her head high and hands folded neatly in front of her. No need for her family to know she had barely eaten or slept since her husband's assassination. Whenever she closed her eyes, she saw Jayr's face at the moment the weapon was plunged into his neck. The detail she recalled was extraordinary and disturbing. Thank goodness for Sarey—keeper of her sanity.

'Sister,' Tyron said, dismounting and going to her.

Neither was big on public displays of affection, but this time her brother pulled her to him and held tightly for a moment. She stood stiff in his arms, determined not to cry.

'Thank you for coming,' she said before pulling away.

'I was hardly going to leave you here alone with a known rapist.'

He was referring to Pollux. Tyron had never been able to move past the fact that his wife, a former Companion, had once been gifted to the man. According to Cora's spies, the evening had gotten very out of hand. She had seen the bruises herself but had never asked Tyron for details because she knew the memory of that night still pained him. Pandarus had casually brought up the event once, telling her that the Companion had been uncooperative—that she had failed at her role. Cora made a point of not getting involved with the Companions because she could not risk caring.

A servant moved forwards to open the carriage door, and a moment later Eldoris stepped down, looking around before her eyes landed on Cora. She rushed forwards, enveloping her daughter in her arms. 'Thank God,' she breathed.

Cora patted her mother's back before withdrawing. 'There is no need to fuss.'

Eldoris took her in, the way a mother does. 'You are thinner. Have you been eating? Sleeping?' No amount of paint could hide the dark circles. Eldoris's eyes narrowed. 'Is that a bruise?'

Or the ugly mark Jayr had left on her face. It had turned a pleasant shade of yellow. 'I fell off my horse.' She could see her mother did not believe her. 'Let us go inside. I know how you despise our weather.'

Eldoris took her arm as they began to walk. 'What a mess. We will bury your husband, remain for the coronation, then get you out of here.'

Cora blinked slowly. 'And where am I to go?'

'Home, of course. Your husband was killed before your eyes. You need time to process these events.'

Cora lifted her face to the sky, missing the snow. The warm season was only just beginning.

'It is very important you remain sober over the next few days. Everyone will be watching you.'

Cora groaned. 'For God's sake, Mother. We have not even gotten inside yet.' She pulled her arm free, needing space.

Eldoris leaned in, keeping her voice down. 'You tend to self-destruct in times of crisis. I suggest you let Pollux handle things in the interim.'

Cora's entire body twitched with irritation. 'He is my advisor. Do you really expect me to abandon my people? Two days after losing their king?'

Eldoris looked around before speaking. 'They are hardly grieving.'

They found Sarey waiting for them at the top, and Cora let out a big sigh of relief. 'Please show my brother and mother to their quarters. I am going to take a walk.'

Eldoris glanced at Tyron. 'Cora—'

'You can address me as Your Majesty in public,' Cora said, backing away. 'I am still queen for a few more days.'

Eldoris watched Cora with an expression of pity. *Pity.*

'This way, Your Majesty, my lord,' Sarey said, gesturing towards the door.

Cora was already walking away, listening for the sound of Lief's boots behind her. Instead, Tyron jogged up beside her.

'Cora.'

'Go rest.'

He matched her stride for stride as they descended the steps. 'She is just worried about you.'

'Well, those are her feelings to manage. I have enough on

my plate right now.' When Tyron did not reply, she glanced sideways at him. 'What? No lecture?'

'You have never listened to me before. I cannot imagine you will start now.' He paused. 'Aldara sends her condolences.'

Cora rolled her eyes. 'Bet she could not wipe the smile off her face. She hated him more than anyone.'

'She felt the same relief we all did. The same relief you no doubt feel.'

Cora pulled up sharply and turned to face him. 'You know nothing of what I feel. He was my husband.'

Tyron crossed his arms. 'Your lies are wasted on me. I have spent enough time here over the years to know the real story, time away from my own family—'

'I did not ask you to.'

'Because I lived in fear he would kill you.'

She looked down, saying nothing for the longest time. It was true. He had found excuses to visit and had watched them together most carefully. He had been opposed to the match from the beginning while knowing he was partly responsible for it. Marrying Jayr had been one of the few selfless acts she could recall doing in her life, and it had cost her dearly.

'I imagined his death so many times.' It was a whispered confession. 'Every bloody and violent detail.' She looked up. 'Perhaps you think I orchestrated it.'

He shook his head. 'I think I know you a little better than that. I should never have let the wedding go ahead.'

'It was my choice, and I stand by it.'

Tyron's gaze fell to the bruise on her face. 'I did not realise how bad things had gotten. He is lucky he is already dead.'

Cora drew a breath. 'Fear changes people.'

Tyron watched her for a moment. 'I am here for you. Just tell me what you need.'

She pressed her lips together. 'What do you think of Zoelin's new king?'

'I think he is a good man by all accounts. Trustworthy. I know he wants better for his people.'

'They deserve better than Jayr.' She stood hugging herself, feeling the cold in that moment. 'I do not know what I am supposed to do next.'

'Return to Archdale Castle. You do not need to have all the answers now.'

They continued walking, making their way down to the stables. Cora led them to Ida's stall, but the mare did not come to her because Tyron was with her. She did not trust men.

'One good thing to come out of all this,' Cora said. 'My wedding gift.'

Tyron looked the mare over, saying nothing of the unsightly scars.

'Three years married to a monster and nothing to show for it except a mare that is more unstable than me. Not even one failed pregnancy to speak of.'

Tyron leaned against the stall door. 'You know, it took Lord Yuri and Lady Hali a long time before they had their daughter.'

She glanced at him. 'That man is old enough to be her father. I am surprised he could perform his duties at all.'

Tyron rubbed his forehead. 'There is the old Cora.'

'I am simply pointing out that their story is more uncomfortable than inspiring.' She turned to him, her expression sincere. 'Thank you for coming. I know it is a big thing for you to leave your pregnant wife.'

'Aldara. Her name is Aldara, and she insisted I go. Despite

what you think, she cares about you, even when you still refuse to use her name all these years later.'

'I use her name.'

'You have moved on from "the Companion", I will give you that.' He drew a breath. 'Keep your head high and your mind sharp. Call it a gut feeling, but I think we are in for a few surprises over the next few days.'

CHAPTER 5

*E*ldoris fiddled with the collar of Cora's gown, the skin between her eyebrows pinched in concentration.

'For goodness' sake, Mother,' Cora said, losing patience and stepping back. 'No one is going to be looking that closely at my gown.'

'Every detail matters at a time like this.'

'The man has spent the last ten years rolling about in the mud, climbing trees, and whatever else those mountain people do. He is in no position to judge me.'

'Really, Cora.'

The door to the bedchamber opened, and Sarey walked in. 'They're less than a mile out. Anything I can do to help?'

Cora ignored the nerves starting in her belly. 'Did Pollux prepare the army as instructed?'

'Four hundred men wait in formation.'

'Are you sure that is a good idea?' Eldoris asked. 'Brom might read it as confrontational.'

Cora waved her off. 'He will arrive with his own men.

Anyway, he should know I am protected, in case he gets any ideas.'

'He is not going to behead you in the courtyard if that is what you are thinking,' Eldoris said, attempting humour.

'You do not know that.'

Eldoris looked her daughter over, all the way from her crown to her jewelled slippers. 'You have never looked more beautiful.'

Cora adjusted her crown, a headache already starting from the weight. 'I am not going for beautiful, I am going for powerful. Beauty is only helpful *before* a marriage, not after the man is dead.'

Sarey smiled down at her feet.

'You do not want to scare Brom,' Eldoris said. 'He will have some say in what becomes of you now. If you wish to return to Syrasan, some charm might be helpful.'

'Charm will not work on him. He is all honour and loyalty.' Cora waved a hand. 'Or so I have heard from others. Perhaps I should have worn a low neckline to truly judge his character.'

Eldoris stepped up and held Cora's face. 'Play your role, survive the next few days, and then we can all return to Syrasan together.' She let go and stepped back. 'You have many Galen cousins who would be happy to take you as a wife. In fact, Borin already has children from his first marriage. Two sons. His wife died quite tragically last year when her horse rolled on her. He has a lovely manor in the South.'

Cora wanted to cover her ears. The idea of being married off to a cousin, prepared to overlook her inability to produce children, was unbearable.

Sarey offered her a sympathetic smile. 'Let us go and welcome the future king of Zoelin.'

Outside, Cora was warmed by the sight of hundreds of

soldiers waiting in formation. They wore blue vests, held a shield in their left hand and a spear in their right. A sword sat at their hip. She spotted Pollux at the top of the steps and went to stand with him.

'Your Majesty.' He kept his eyes on the trees, where Brom would appear at any moment. 'You can let me handle the new king. He'll understand your absence.'

Cora drew a tired breath. 'You served my husband a long time. How does it feel to welcome the man he spent years trying to wipe out?'

He continued to watch the trees. 'My loyalty is not to one man but to my kingdom. The people want Brom on the throne, and everyone living within these walls wants happy people.'

Because Jayr was a man with a lot of acquaintances and few friends, she believed him. In fact, she could not think of one person he had shared a genuine connection with—not even his wife. Relationships were just transactions.

The sound of footsteps made Cora turn. Tyron strode towards them, his gaze flicking briefly to Pollux. He could only tolerate the man's presence for a few minutes at a time.

'Sister,' Tyron said, coming to a stop on the other side of her. He did not even acknowledge Pollux, and the advisor did not care.

'Brother.' Cora nodded towards the trees. 'Here they come.'

Three men on horseback emerged: Brom, another broad-shouldered man, and an older man who looked like he would need a lie-down upon arrival. She watched the trees behind them, waiting, but no more horses appeared. 'Where is his army?'

The three of them waited.

'Perhaps he did not feel the need to bring one,' Tyron said.

'I thought you said he is smart.'

Tyron glanced at her. 'Perhaps he did not want to appear threatening.'

Pollux looked around. 'Or his warriors are hiding in the trees with arrows trained on us.'

Cora shifted.

'No one is pointing arrows at us,' Tyron said, glaring at the advisor. 'Brom is a peaceful man unless he has cause not to be. Then watch out.'

The gates opened, and Cora's gaze drifted to the soldiers waiting below. She suddenly felt silly for putting on a big display for a man who was not one for shows. The soldiers split down the middle to let the men through. The larger man looked somewhat cautious as he passed by them.

Pollux headed off down the steps to meet them, and Cora leaned closer to her brother. 'Who are the men with him?'

'I believe the older man is Droet, elder of the Valter tribe. The other man may be his grandson, a friend of Brom's since childhood.'

Cora watched as Brom slipped from the saddle and thanked the groom. Jayr would have tossed the reins in his general direction. She continued to watch the new king, noting his calm expression and easy stance. She tried to relax her own hands, which were clasped in front of her. Brom was definitely the more handsome of the two brothers with that strong jaw of his. His hair and beard were shaved short, his nose slightly crooked, likely broken many times. He wore a simple wool vest, trousers with loose threads, and boots in desperate need of a clean. Not a hint of royalty about him. 'He is awfully smug, just strolling unprotected through the gates after murdering his brother and king.'

Tyron looked at her. 'You do not even know if he was behind it. Many people wished Jayr dead.'

'Yes, but only one gets a crown at the end.' Her eyes met Brom's at that exact moment, and she fell silent. He regarded her with warm curiosity before turning to say something to Droet. Cora's heart beat a little harder in her chest.

'Are you all right?' Tyron asked.

She looked at him. 'What?'

He angled his head as he took in her expression. 'I said, are you all right? You are allowed to feel nervous.'

Her gaze returned to Brom, taking in his tall frame covered in lean muscle. 'I am not nervous.'

The new king climbed the steps with a casual stride, his shoulders relaxed as he looked around. Pollux spoke as they walked, but Brom kept turning back to see how Droet was managing the steps. His other companion caught up and took the old man's arm. Only then did Brom face forwards, eyes meeting Cora's once more. Every time they did that, her lungs seemed to falter. Perhaps she was nervous. That made sense. He would ultimately decide what became of her after the coronation.

While there were definitely some physical similarities between Brom and Jayr, Brom's features were softer, his mouth fuller. His eyes were the exact same shade of brown, but they were rounder, giving a friendlier appearance. Those eyes moved over her so discreetly, she might have missed it had she blinked—but she did not blink.

'Your Majesty,' he said when he reached her, giving a small bow.

She nodded and gestured to Tyron. 'My brother, Prince Tyron of Syrasan.' The men shook hands. 'You have met my advisor, Grandor Pollux.'

Brom glanced briefly at the man. 'Hope it wasn't your advice to buy an army of foreign children.'

Cora did not know him well enough to tell if he was serious. Perhaps he had a dark sense of humour—like her. The old man thought it was a joke, judging by the way he laughed. Not the sanest noise.

'I can only advise,' Pollux said. 'Unfortunately, your brother wasn't always open to advice.'

Brom returned his attention to Cora, gaze flicking down to the bruise. 'You have another fall?'

She wondered if that was supposed to be another joke. 'I fell off my horse.'

He nodded slowly. 'Hope it wasn't too traumatic.'

'You know what was traumatic? Seeing my husband get stabbed through the neck in your name. Oh, and I came very close to drinking the poisoned wine you kindly organised for the gathering.' Her thumb instinctively moved over the burn on her hand, and the movement caught his eye. He reached for her hand and studied the wound. She willed her lungs to work.

'Might leave a scar,' he said, letting go.

She covered it with her other hand. 'How would you prefer to be addressed in the lead-up to your coronation?'

He looked behind to the soldiers lined up below. 'Brom is fine. I appreciate the welcome party, by the way.' There was a hint of amusement in his eyes when he looked back at her. He gestured to his companions. 'This is Droet, elder of the Valter tribe, and his grandson, Carac.'

Carac bowed, but not very low. His disinterest was blatant.

Droet stepped forwards to take her hand. He smiled widely, revealing yellow teeth.

'Virtue is nothing but one's desire drowned,' he told her.

Cora looked to Brom for an explanation, but he just shook his head. Droet was studying the ink on her hand, then ran his thumb over the burn.

'His death marks you,' he said, looking up at her.

Cora withdrew her hand as if he had torn the scab from it.

Droet tutted, his bright eyes on her. 'A king who marks

the face of a queen knows no honour.'

Brom placed a hand on Droet's shoulder, silencing him. That surprised her. Surely he would want to revel in his brother's shortfalls for as long as possible.

'Would you like to pay your respects to your brother?' Cora was aware of everyone looking at her.

He nodded. 'Yes, thank you.'

At least he had better manners than Jayr. She turned and led the way inside, and Lief followed behind. Brom lengthened his stride to catch up with her.

'I'd prefer not to have an audience,' he said.

'Can I trust you not to kill him a second time?' Cora asked without looking at him.

'To be fair, I didn't kill him the first time.'

She rolled her eyes. 'One of your many admirers, then. We will wait for you in the hall.'

'Not you.'

She met his gaze. 'You wish me to come in with you?'

'I thought it might give us a chance to speak.'

Her eyes went to the sword at his hip. 'Fine. You can leave your weapons with my guard.'

He laughed quietly. 'I'm not one to kill a widow standing over her husband's deathbed.'

'You can understand why I might be sceptical given all that has happened.' She looked back at those following to see if they were listening. Tyron was speaking with Carac, Pollux walking behind them. She faced forwards again.

'I'm surprised you didn't write me about the new arrivals at Onuric Castle,' he whispered.

She moved closer. 'Do you think me a traitor?'

'Yes. I happen to like that about you.'

She increased the distance between them. 'I saw him die, you know. And now I see it every time I enter the hall.'

'I'm sorry for that.'

'Stop.' She glared in his direction. 'He was killed in your name, so you can save your empty apology.'

'He may have been killed in my name but not on my order.'

She rolled her eyes.

'I admit, I would've been forced to act eventually.' He was silent a moment. 'But not in your home—in battle.'

'*So* noble.' He held back so she could go ahead of him up the stairs. When they reached Jayr's quarters, Cora turned to the others. 'I will take Brom in. You can all wait for us in the throne room.'

Tyron looked between the two of them. 'Lief can go with you.'

Cora shook her head. 'Lief is going to keep Brom's weapons nice and safe.' She looked up at Brom, waiting.

A high-pitched chuckle rang out from Droet. He rocked on his heels, thoroughly entertained.

Brom held her gaze as he unbelted his sword, unstrapped his dagger, and then lifted his vest to retrieve another hidden beneath it. She made a point of not looking down for the last part.

'This way,' she said.

The air was cold inside. They needed it cold to preserve the body. Cora paused in the doorway of the bedchamber, still not used to the sight of her husband that way. She kept expecting him to sit up and call out to her. It was reassuring that he was in the exact position as the last time she had seen him.

She stepped aside to let Brom enter, then remained by the door. He walked over to the bed, brushing a finger down his nose. Jayr had been cleaned up, sewn up, and dressed in his best. Brom's gaze swept the length of him. He was unreadable at that distance. She let out a breath and went to stand on the other side of the bed, looking everywhere but down.

'I'm sorry you had to witness his death,' Brom said.

Of all the things he could have said, she had not been expecting that. 'Not too sorry, I am sure.'

He regarded her for a moment. 'You really do speak your mind, don't you?'

'Yes, I really do.'

'Good.' Brom nodded and crossed his arms. 'Good.'

Cora folded her hands in front of her. 'What is it you wanted to say that you did not want the others to hear?'

'And direct.' A lazy smile came and went on his face. 'Like it or not, I'm soon to be the new king of Zoelin. If you had produced an heir, things would have been different.'

She made a conscious effort not to move. 'Yes. Though you would have likely come for my son too.'

'That would've depended on the infant's politics.'

He did have a dark sense of humour. 'Go on.'

'I thought we could ask each other questions. You can go first if you like.'

She was immediately suspicious. 'Questions about what?'

'Anything you like.'

She tilted her head. 'Am I expected to trust your responses?'

He grinned. 'I heard you read people rather well. Surely you'll know if I'm lying.'

She looked down at Jayr for a moment. 'All right. How did you manipulate an entire kingdom into supporting you?'

'I manipulated no one,' he replied without hesitation. 'My actions were always honest, but I think in the end, Jayr made too many mistakes. They're trusting me to fix them.' He paused. 'My turn. Is it true you anonymously gift my family's coin to people in need around the kingdom?'

She lifted her chin. 'Why do you ask?'

'Yes or no.'

'Yes. There is still plenty left if that is what you are worried about.'

'I don't care about the coin. I'm just trying to make out your character. I've heard so many conflicting reports. Some say you matched my brother in temperament.'

She lifted one shoulder. 'I would say he was outmatched in that regard.'

One corner of Brom's mouth rose. 'Your turn.'

She thought for a moment. 'Have all the Asigow children we handed over been returned to their families in Asigow?'

'No.'

'No?'

'Some of them have no one to return to, so they've remained in the Nydoen Mountains.'

'As what?'

'As children. And that was two questions, but I'll let it slide.'

Cora crossed her arms. 'Did you really choose to leave when Jayr took the throne, or did he cast you out?'

'I left.'

'Because you disagreed with his politics?'

'I believe it's my turn.'

She noted the playful glint in his eyes. 'You are a real stickler for the rules.'

He nodded. 'Why did you marry Jayr when your own family counselled against it?'

The question caught her off guard. She thought about what answer to give, suspecting he would see through her lies also. 'Partly to aid the alliance between our kingdoms and partly as a form of rebellion. I wanted to make one choice for myself.' She paused. 'It was the first useful thing I ever did, and possibly the most foolish.' More words had spilled out than she intended. She swallowed.

There was no judgement from Brom. He just nodded, like

he understood. 'Did you know who you were marrying?'

He was really asking the tough questions. 'I thought I could handle him, even change him.'

'And did you?'

She stared at the corpse. 'That is two questions.' She thought about what to ask next. 'What will you do differently than your brother, besides not buying children?'

His expression turned thoughtful. 'It's time to remind people what we stand for. Any business that isn't in line with our kingdom's values is finished as far as I'm concerned.'

Her eyes met his. 'Are you prepared to kill people to make that happen?'

'That's two questions, but I'll allow it.' He offered a small smile. 'Yes. I'll kill to rid this kingdom of greed and filth.'

Time would tell.

She waited for his next question.

'Did you love Jayr?'

She wondered why he cared either way. 'I tried to. Can you love a monster?'

'Is that your question for me?'

She *almost* smiled but caught herself. 'No.' She stared long and hard at him. 'What are you expecting me to do once you are king?'

His expression did not change. 'I think people will expect you to retire to Onuric Castle, keep company with my sister there. But I would like my sister to come here.'

His response surprised her. 'I think Tasia would like that. Your brother wanted to keep her there until she married, but that seems to be taking a rather long time.'

'Jayr had a way of repelling suitors. I expect you want to return to Syrasan with your family.'

That was the last thing she wanted, but she could not tell him that. 'That would be the sensible thing to do.'

His expression turned serious. He opened his mouth to

speak, closed it, and then tried again. 'Or you could stay here.'

Her brow creased. 'And play the role of sad widow?'

He searched her eyes. 'As queen.'

Her hands fell to her sides. 'What?'

'As my wife.'

She continued to stare, trying to understand. 'Your wife?' There was a long silence. 'Why?' For once she was lost for words, and *why* seemed to encompass everything she needed from him in that moment.

'You're understandably surprised.'

She did not know what she was. Of all the places her mind had gone, it had never gone there. 'I am trying to understand your motive. Is this some sort of sick revenge on your brother?'

'No.'

'Then what?'

He looked uncomfortable for the first time. 'Droet suggested it.'

'The crazy old man?'

'He's not *that* crazy, and it's not the worst idea he's had.'

She blinked. 'Not the worst idea?'

'It solves a lot of problems for both of us.'

Her mind raced. 'You are going to have to explain that to me. What exactly does it solve?'

He hesitated. 'The union keeps the alliance with Syrasan and Zoelin alive. You get to keep your crown. Plus it's a good bridge between old and new. Of course, we would need to wait until after the funeral. And the coronation. What do you think?'

Her mouth was so dry she doubted her ability to speak. 'About marrying you?'

'I admit, this isn't the most romantic setting for a proposal.'

Her gaze returned to the bed. 'You literally just proposed over my husband's corpse.'

'If I thought you were genuinely grieving, I would've waited.'

'Big of you.' She shook her head. 'Perhaps you have not heard the rumours.'

'What rumours?'

'I am barren.' She watched for his reaction, but he only shrugged.

'Did a physician tell you that?'

'Three years lying with a man and not one pregnancy to show for it tells me that.'

He thought for a moment. 'I have other children to worry about right now anyway.'

She searched his eyes for lies, finding none. 'I will not spend the rest of my life apologising for your disappointment.'

'I'm not asking you to.'

'I have a cousin. Lots of cousins, actually.' She cleared her throat. 'But one in particular is widowed with children. Sons. Two of them. He does not need what you need.'

Brom leaned on one foot. 'Right now, I need a queen, a partner, someone to help me navigate this court. I need someone who won't shy away from the hard parts. And the Zoelin people seem to like you.'

She laughed. 'You do not know me. If you could see me through your brother's eyes for just a moment, you would abandon this notion at once.'

He looked her straight in the eye. 'I've no interest in seeing through his eyes. I'm quite capable of drawing my own conclusions.'

No. The answer was no. She could not marry the man responsible for her husband's death. So why was she not telling him that instead of indulging him? 'I am wondering what sort of fantasy you have created in that mind of yours. You are a fool if you think this match will be anything but a disaster.'

He shifted his weight. 'How can you be so sure?'

'Experience.'

'With Jayr? Who cared nothing for your happiness?'

No one had ever spoken of her happiness during such a transaction. 'Do not pretend to care about my feelings.' Her tone was sharper than she had intended.

He looked genuinely confused. 'This only works if you're happy and willing.'

His sincerity unsettled her. 'My experience with kings is that they are too preoccupied with their own needs to care about anyone else.'

'And what's your experience with mountain rebels?'

She stared at him. 'I know them to be smooth talkers.'

He laughed at that. 'You know, I really think this could work. As long as you're prepared to play nice and work with me.'

She looked down at Jayr, her heart beating faster at the realisation that she was considering it. 'Men want to look at me, not marry me.'

'Is that what my brother told you?'

'That is what *my* brothers have told me.'

'And did you cry?'

She set her cold eyes on him. 'Tears only give men ammunition to use against me later.'

His expression bordered on pity. 'Not all men are like that.'

He would not last five minutes as king. Perhaps he did need her. Someone to balance out all that kindness, all those good deeds.

She spent a moment imagining herself on his arm, being introduced as his wife. She tried to picture eating a meal together and discussing their day. She even went as far as imagining them in bed together. It would likely be very sensible, bordering on bland. She had only ever known Jayr in that regard, a dangerous push-and-pull of power stemming from a need to punish one another. Nothing could shock her now. No quirks, kinks, or outbursts. Nothing Brom could say or do would be worse than the things her husband had said to her most days. Brom would be a stroll amid the flowers in comparison.

'You will not hit me,' she said, a warning in her voice. 'Or keep me confined.'

Brom nodded. 'I would never hit a woman. And what reason would I have for confining you?'

'Power.'

Another nod. 'You are free to come and go as you please.'

Her shoulders fell a few inches. 'I am very resilient, but I will not be silent next time a man strikes me or locks me up.'

'Marry me and there won't be a next time. I'll protect you as I would my own sister.'

His words were no doubt meant to ease her mind, but they only raised her suspicion. 'I am struggling to find faults in you.'

'Smart girl like you will find them soon enough.'

More silence as she thought. She could barely believe what she was about to say. 'You will need to ask Pandarus's permission.' She pressed her lips together. 'Are you sure about this? The beauty does not run very deep.'

He watched her with those soft eyes of his, his head dipped slightly. 'We all have ugly parts.'

At least he could never say he was not warned. 'Are you done paying your respects to your brother?'

A nod. 'Yes. I think we're done here.'

Cora glanced a final time at Jayr. 'Then let us go break the happy news.'

The queen's mother and brother were seated opposite Pollux, Carac, and Droet at the table in the throne room. Brom stood with Cora, taking in the shocked expressions. Droet was grinning, Carac staring silently at the table. At least he was not objecting.

Pollux was perched on the end of his chair looking utterly confused.

'Married?' He struggled to keep the surprise from his voice.

Brom had suggested they tell people individually, but Cora had wanted to witness honest reactions.

'After the coronation,' Brom said. He really hoped he was doing the right thing. Droet was hardly the most reliable source of counsel, but if he were being honest, it was not only the elder's influence. She had been in his thoughts for months, ever since he saw her come through those gates holding a child far too old to be carried. She could have sent a servant in her place, but the boy had been afraid, and despite her indifferent face, she had cared very much. She was a beautiful contradiction.

Eldoris had a hand pressed to her chest. It was probably a good thing she was already seated. 'And you agreed?' She was looking only at Cora.

The queen lifted her chin. 'Yes. It solves a lot of problems.'

He liked that she was using his line from earlier.

'A step up from the widowed cousin, is it not?' Cora added.

Droet laughed, drawing everyone's attention. 'Love is not water but fish.'

Carac placed his hands on the table. 'I think my grandfather speaks for all of us.'

'Not helping,' Brom said with a shake of his head.

'Of course we are pleased,' Eldoris said, sounding genuine.

Cora was still looking at her brother. 'Have you nothing else to say on the matter?'

Tyron hesitated. 'It is a good outcome that benefits both kingdoms.'

'But?' Brom asked.

Tyron exhaled. 'May I speak frankly?'

'Of course. I prefer that to hushed conversations behind my back.'

Tyron nodded. 'Most of what we know of you is hearsay. My sister has just come from a very destructive relationship.'

'You are the one who told me Brom was a good man by all accounts,' Cora said.

Tyron blinked. 'So you will marry a man on hearsay? Perhaps you could court for a period first.'

The concerned older brother. Brom could respect that.

Cora responded. 'When was the last time you heard of a king and queen courting?'

Eldoris spoke up at that. 'Your father and I courted.'

'Is that supposed to support his argument?'

Brom's gaze went to Cora. She might have been one of

the most beautiful creatures he had ever laid eyes on, but she was going to be a handful.

'You will have to get Pandarus's blessing,' Tyron said.

Cora looked out the window. 'He will be thrilled that I am someone else's problem once more.'

Interestingly, no one refuted that.

Brom was not looking forward to meeting the king of Syrasan. The man was rumoured to have quite the ego.

'Brom,' Pollux said, 'may we speak privately?'

'About what?' Brom replied flatly.

Pollux glanced at Tyron, who was glaring in his direction. 'About the matter at hand.'

'If there's something you wish to add, speak in front of your queen.' He could feel Cora looking at him.

Pollux gave a resigned nod. 'Have you considered the need for an heir?'

Tyron shot up from his chair, hands curled into fists.

'Walk it off, brother,' Cora said. 'It is a valid question.'

So there was bad blood between the two men. Brom would have to ask Cora about that later.

Tyron pushed his chair back and walked out of the room. Eldoris rose slowly and went after him.

'Perhaps you would care to elaborate,' Cora said to Pollux as soon as the others had left.

'King Tuyon of Asigow has unwed sisters. That's a big opportunity for a new king.'

Brom shook his head. 'I've no interest in aligning with King Tuyon.'

'That's unwise given how vulnerable we are right now.' Pollux looked around. 'A kingdom going through big change is like a newborn lamb. The eagles are circling. We don't have the luxury of considering feelings.'

Cora straightened. 'No one is talking about feelings,

Grandor. Ours is not a love match.' She stared unblinking at him.

'I'm also thinking of the queen's safety,' the advisor added. 'Like it or not, she's aligned with Jayr in the people's eyes. Some won't be happy.'

'You were also aligned with Jayr,' Cora said.

She was articulate and sharp, which gave Brom hope that the match might actually work.

'She's going to give you hell,' Droet said, grinning madly, 'but I like her.'

Carac tapped a finger on his arm as he continued to stare at the table.

'What have you to say on the subject, Carac?' Cora asked, picking up on his body language.

The warrior raised his eyes, his blatant disapproval written all over his face. 'I support my king in whatever he decides.'

Cora stared at him for a moment. 'I see.' She turned to Brom. 'If we are done here, I would like to go for a ride.'

Apparently they were done discussing the matter. He looked over to where her guard stood by the wall, a man built like a castle who had barely taken his eyes off Brom since he arrived. Judging by the state of Cora's face, it seemed the man had a right to be cautious. 'Not alone, I hope.'

'With my lady-in-waiting.'

It felt like a test. They stood awkwardly for a moment, Carac and Pollux watching them and Droet humming a tune quietly to himself.

'Of course. I'll write to King Pandarus.'

'Good.' She glanced at the others before adding, 'I shall see you later.' She turned to Pollux. 'Ensure the guards know I am going out. I do not want any problems at the gate.'

'Why would you have problems?' Brom asked.

Pollux spoke up at that. 'The queen has been confined to the grounds in the past for various reasons.'

'Such as?'

'My husband's various whims,' Cora said, running a thumb over her burn. 'But never mind. The gates will open every time now, as per our agreement.'

Another test. 'Of course. Enjoy your ride.'

She looked very pleased with herself. 'Thank you.'

CHAPTER 7

*T*he women walked their mares beneath tall pines on icy ground, Lief trailing some distance behind them. Cora was still trying to process the enormous decision she had made. She could have asked for more time, spent a few days discussing it with her family. Instead, she had agreed within minutes, like an impulsive child.

'So,' Sarey said, breaking the silence, 'a royal wedding.'

Cora recoiled inwardly. 'Let us just get through the funeral first.'

'I still can't believe he proposed.'

Neither could she. 'It was purely political.'

'Despite all the stories floating around.'

'I think you have made your point.'

'Maybe the gossip never reached him.'

Cora gave her a tired stare. 'I am confident Carac passed on all of the relevant information judging by his open contempt towards me.'

'He's just looking out for his friend. He'll change his mind in time.'

'Are you honestly suggesting his opinion of me will improve when he knows me better?'

Sarey faced forwards. 'Probably not, but only because you show people the worst of yourself.'

'As opposed to all the sweet parts?'

Sarey was silent a moment. 'I know I'm not supposed to have an opinion—'

'Then swallow it and be quiet.'

'However,' she continued, undeterred, 'I'm quite surprised you agreed. He might be a king, but he's basically a stranger.'

True, they barely knew each other. And yet Brom did not feel like a stranger. 'His reasoning made sense.'

Sarey gave her a coy smile. 'I'm sure the fact that he's a handsome warrior never entered your mind.'

'Jayr was handsome, and look how that turned out.'

'Nevertheless, he didn't have Brom's smile and superior morals.'

'You sound ridiculous.'

Sarey laughed. 'You just need some time to recover from your previous marriage. Then you'll see. Despite what you think, you deserve this.'

'Another life sentence?'

'A sane, *kind* husband. Just try not to scare him off before you exchange vows.'

Cora's gloved hand went to the silver line on Ida's neck. The mare had another one on her chest, two on her rump, and one above her eye. Cora closed her eyes at the memory. The horse had been so head-shy after the ordeal, it had taken months to get a bridle near her. Cora had not let Jayr into her bedchamber for weeks. She had even considered poisoning him. Nothing too serious. A few weeks spent in the garderobe with a cramping bowel would have been adequate. Perhaps it was an indication of her own kindness that she had refrained.

Sarey looked over her shoulder at Lief. 'You've been very quiet about all of this. What do you think of our new king's smile?'

The bodyguard shrugged. 'Not my place to have an opinion.'

Sarey turned back around. 'Well, he's no fun. Anyway, while I'm surprised you agreed, I think he's a nice, sensible choice.'

Cora glanced across at her friend. 'Nice and sensible are alternative words for dull.'

'Most people would welcome dull after an experience like yours. *Nice* men don't hit their wives, throw drinks in their faces, set their favourite gowns alight—'

'Point taken.' Cora could not bear to let her finish.

'You must think of this as a new start. No more games. No tests designed to drive him away.'

The queen looked heavenwards. 'If he is driven away by a few simple tests, then I am afraid he was never up to the task to begin with.'

Sarey moved her horse closer. 'That's the thing. You shouldn't be a *task*.'

The sound of horses approaching at a gallop made the three of them look to the trees ahead. Cora heard Lief's sword leave its sheath as he moved in front of her. A moment later, five horses burst through the trees. It was Princess Tasia surrounded by four of her guards.

'Halt!' Lief shouted.

The party came to a skidding stop around ten feet from them, the guards drawing their weapons.

Cora's eyes locked with the princess, and she could see something was wrong. 'Move aside,' she instructed, nudging her mare forwards. 'What is going on?'

The guards recognised Cora and relaxed.

'Your Majesty,' one of the men said, bowing his head. 'We

need to get the princess to Drake Castle immediately, for her safety.'

Cora looked to Tasia for an explanation.

'King Tuyon took Onuric,' Tasia said, her voice laced with fatigue.

'I do not understand.'

'He crossed the border in the East, with his army. They forced their way inside and tore down our banners.'

Fear moved like liquid down Cora's spine. It was the perfect time for the Asigow king to make a move. Before the coronation, while the kingdom was at its most vulnerable. 'And he just let you go?'

Tasia pushed damp curls off her face. 'We left via the tunnel—just in time. They may have followed. I do not know.' She glanced nervously over her shoulder.

Cora looked past her to the trees, then swung her horse around. 'Come. I will take you to Brom.'

Brom marched through the ice-crusted courtyard, body angled against the sharp wind. It had arrived with his sister. He spotted her beneath the archway, familiar, and yet when she looked at him, he saw a stranger. She was not a child anymore. Gone was the sister of his youth.

Tasia watched his approach, her expression guarded, conflicted. She had removed her gloves, and her hands hung at her sides. 'Brother.'

He stopped a few feet away, his gaze sweeping the length of her. 'Are you all right?'

She nodded.

'They didn't hurt you?'

'They did not have the chance.'

Her cool eyes never left his. It was hard to imagine they

had once been inseparable as children. 'What does he want?'

'I did not wait around to find out. We barely had time to collect our horses.' She exhaled. 'He is testing you. Jayr would have sent an army. He wants to see what you will do.'

Brom wet his lips, tasting the damp air. 'Well, violence isn't my first instinct.'

Tasia exhaled through her nose. 'No. Your first instinct is usually to run.' She swallowed.

He regarded her for a moment. 'You know I had to leave.'

'Ah, yes. You wanted to make the world a better place. Never mind about the rest of us left behind.'

'Jayr and I would've killed each other eventually.'

'You *did* kill him eventually.'

Her words landed like a punch to the stomach. There was no point in telling her he had not gotten around to it, that he had put it off for longer than was sensible. Someone else had gotten to their brother first.

'I never understood why you thought you deserved to escape and I did not.' She bit her top lip and looked away.

The pain in his gut travelled up to his chest. He had wanted to take her with him, but he knew Jayr would have come for her. It was one thing for him to turn his back on his king and quite another to drag her into his mess. 'I did what I thought was best.'

'For you.'

'No, for *you*.'

Her brow pinched. 'I do not recall discussing it.'

'You were a child.'

She laughed, but it was not a friendly noise. 'I see. You are selective with the children you are prepared to help.'

'Tasia—'

'It does not matter now. You have a new choice in front of you. Agree to whatever it is King Tuyon wants, or be prepared to fight a war you cannot win.' Her expression softened. 'No man in his right mind would go up against the Asigow army. Not even Jayr with all his pride and power.'

'Jayr was a man controlled by fear in the end.'

Tasia looked up at him, visibly exhausted. 'Tuyon will send for you eventually, and you will have no choice but to go to him. Take only a few trustworthy men. Hear him out, then pretend you need time to consider it, all the while knowing you will give him exactly what he wants.'

He was surprised by her response. 'You're afraid of him.'

'Everyone is afraid of him. You especially should be. Even with the support of the rebels, you do not have the men needed to say no to him.'

'There are no rebels anymore, only Zoelins.'

The faintest of smiles played on her lips. 'You always were idealistic.'

'And we have allies.'

She laughed again. 'What allies? Tuyon has acted now because he knows you have none.'

'Syrasan.'

She tutted. 'Did no one mention that King Pandarus despises you?'

'And Galen.'

'You are delirious. The friendship you share with the Galen captain does not extend to his king.'

He knew he had to tell her eventually. 'I'm going to marry.'

Nothing changed on her face. 'All right.'

'I'm going to marry Queen Cora.'

Tasia looked away, saying nothing for the longest time. 'That is a rather smart move, I suppose, though I am surprised she agreed to it. Thought she would be itching to leave this place.'

'Apparently not.'

Her gaze returned to him. 'Have you thought this

through? There is a reason why they call her the Ice Queen.'

'I know what they say about her.'

Tasia wore a worried look. 'She is actually an excellent queen—just a terrible wife.'

His hands went to rest on his hips. 'Why do you say that?'

'Because I have seen her help strangers, feed the starving, stand up to the smallest injustices. But I have also seen her scratch Jayr's face with her bare hands, throw things, and threaten to cut off his... manhood in his sleep. I have seen her so drunk she could not stand. I witnessed her bait Jayr until he could barely find his way through his own fury.' She paused for breath. 'Do you know she has never been sick in the entire time I have known her?'

'Isn't that a good thing? Don't we want a strong queen?'

Tasia looked far from impressed. 'Some say she is a witch.'

Brom looked away. He had heard all of the stories, but hearing them from his sister's mouth was something else. 'We could do with some dark magic on our side right now.'

Tasia did not laugh. 'Toxic people poison those they come in contact with.'

Brom shifted his weight to his other foot. 'I don't think Jayr was good for her.'

'Trust me, they were two peas in a pod.'

He wanted to believe she would be different with him.

'Perhaps you think you can tame her,' Tasia said. 'Sorry to disappoint you, but if Jayr did not succeed, you stand no chance. Do not be fooled by that beautiful face—our queen is a true mess.'

'We're all messes. Some people just hide it better than others.'

Tasia studied him. 'Listen to you. A moth to the flame.' She exhaled. 'Be careful with that one.'

His mouth turned up. 'Anyone would think you cared.'

She did not smile. 'Do not say you were not warned.'

CHAPTER 8

*S*leep did not come. Unsurprising given what Brom was facing. After the funeral, he would travel to Onuric Castle and confront King Tuyon. Cora had wanted to go, and as queen-regent, that was her right, but soon Brom would be king, and it was time for him to stand up.

'If he kills you, where does that leave us?' Tasia had asked at dinner the night before.

'He will not kill you,' Cora said. 'If you show up without an army, prepared to listen, no harm will come to you. He values his pride above all else.'

Tasia had leaned in and whispered, 'See? Excellent queen. Terrible wife.' Then she had gone back to largely ignoring him for the rest of the evening.

It seemed it was going to take a lot to earn her forgiveness. She had spent the last ten years resenting him. After their father had passed, Brom had stayed for Jayr's coronation, out of respect; then he had written a note to his brother, gone for a ride, and never returned.

Brom had watched the relationship between his father and the Nydoen people erode over the years. He knew when

Jayr took the throne he would have to make a choice. His grandfather's friends and family lived in those mountains, good people who had lost favour with the king because they did not share his greed. Brom had imagined a life without Jayr many times, but the cost of that choice had been Tasia.

The morning he left, he had gone to visit her in her bedchamber. She had been lying on the bed, legs swinging happily as she sketched with charcoal. She had looked up and smiled at him. It was the last time he had seen her smile.

Rubbing the memory from his eyes, he looked to the window where the darkness was finally relenting to the light. He dressed and decided to go down to the stables and take a look at the horses. The young groom was startled awake by his arrival. He leapt from his cot, bowed, then seemed unsure what to do next.

'Do you need a horse, Your Majesty?'

Your Majesty. It would take him some time to get used to being addressed so formally. He had been a king of sorts in the mountains but always treated like a warrior. The title was a tad premature, but he did not want to embarrass the boy by correcting him.

'Thought I'd take a look at my brother's famous collection.' Technically, they were his horses now.

The groom stepped out of the way, then went to retrieve a shovel and began working.

Brom wandered along the row of stalls, admiring the immaculately bred stallions, geldings, brood mares, and fillies. He stopped when he came upon a tall black mare bearing scars. Silver lines striped her head, neck, and body. Likely whip marks. He leaned against the door and studied the scars in the poor light. The mare moved to the other side of the stall, watching him cautiously.

'Boy,' he called to the groom.

The groom came at a run. 'Yes, Your Majesty?'

Brom nodded towards the mare. 'Whose horse is this?'

'Queen Cora's, Your Majesty.'

Cora's? He looked back at the horse. It was unheard of for a queen to ride a damaged animal. 'What happened to her?'

The boy shifted his weight, appearing nervous.

Brom's eyes returned to him. 'They look like whip marks.'

'They are.'

Brom narrowed his eyes. 'That your doing?'

The boy shook his head. 'No, Your Majesty. I'd lose a hand for marking the queen's horse.'

He did not want to ask the question, but he really needed to know the answer. 'The queen, then?'

'No, Queen Cora would never let a whip near the mare.'

'Who, then?'

The groom hesitated. 'King Jayr, Your Majesty.'

'Jayr?' Brom tried to recall his brother's training methods. Nothing that violent came to mind. 'Why?'

The boy was practically squirming. 'He was angry.'

Brom rested an arm on the stall door. 'Angry at the mare?'

'At the queen.' It came out like a whisper.

Brom sat with that information for a moment. 'And did the queen witness the... beating?'

'Her Majesty tried to stop him. She was down on her knees, begging at one point. Never seen anything like it. King Jayr whipped that horse until she was a bloody mess. Only time I've seen the queen cry.'

Brom's gaze returned to the mare. 'And what triggered the outburst?'

'I'm not privy to those things, Your Majesty. I only know they disagreed a lot.'

'You mean they fought?'

The boy closed his mouth and looked around before continuing. It was just the two of them in the stables. 'All the time.'

'How many times did he beat the horse?'

'Just the once that I'm aware of.'

The mare snorted and pounded the ground with her hoof. Brom noted the warning and stepped back from the door.

'She doesn't much like men, Your Majesty.'

Brom nodded. 'I see that. Tell me about the other fights you witnessed.' When the boy took a step away, Brom added, 'Nothing you tell me will come back to you. You have my word.'

The groom looked over his shoulder again, then exhaled. 'Most of their arguments took place behind closed doors, but there was another incident I remember clear as day. It was hard to watch.'

'What happened?'

The boy drew a breath. 'They were in the training yard, shouting and such. The king shoved her, and she lost her balance, fell. I went to help her up, but he yelled at me to stop.'

Brom could picture his brother's face in that moment. 'Did he go and help her up?'

'No.'

Brom gave himself a second. 'Go on.'

'The king marched over to her, grabbed her by the hair, and… pushed her face into the sand. He held her there while she struggled.'

Brom shuffled his feet. 'Where was her guard?'

'He intervened despite orders not to.'

'The king's orders?'

The groom shook his head. 'The queen's orders. She knew what King Jayr would do to anyone who came between them. She was protecting him.'

Another story contrasting popular opinion. 'What happened when the bodyguard intervened?'

'The guard pushed the king out of the way and just picked her up, carried her off. King Jayr shouted some things, threats. But none of it came to fruition. She has the same guard to this day.'

Cora's doing, no doubt. She had found a way to protect the guard from Jayr's wrath.

Brom took another step back from the door. 'Can you halter the mare for me? I want to have a proper look at her.'

The groom grabbed the halter hanging next to the door. He entered the stall and approached the mare slowly, taking his time as he slipped it on. Brom held the door open and watched the mare walk past. She sidestepped away from him.

'Easy, girl,' Brom said, extending a hand for her to sniff. He did not move, just stood there until she eventually lost interest. 'Is she safe to ride?'

'The queen basically broke her, with the help of her lady. She rides her most days, sometimes for hours.'

Brom took the lead, and the mare threw her head up. He waited for her to settle, all the while inspecting the scar above her eye. 'I'm surprised she can be ridden after such a beating.'

The groom nodded. 'The mare was useless for the longest time, but the queen came every day, sitting in the stall for hours.'

Patience was not a virtue he expected Cora to possess. Brom reached out a hand to stroke the mare's neck, and she stepped out of reach. They watched each other for a moment, and then the mare snorted.

'What are you doing?' came a familiar voice.

Brom searched the shadows, spotting Cora. She stood at the end of the row of stalls, eyes blazing in his direction. Lief was beside her, watching him with a matching expression. 'I was just asking about your mare.' He kept his voice low for the sake of the horse, which was already nervous.

Cora strode forwards, surprisingly graceful given her speed. She snatched the lead from Brom's hand. 'How dare you touch my horse without my permission.'

He did not need to ask why. He had heard the story, and the pain of that day was visible on her face. 'I came upon her and was curious about her injuries. That's all.'

Cora was breathing hard. 'She does not like men—and for good reason.'

Brom raised his hands to show he meant her no harm. 'All men?'

'*All men.*'

He attempted a smile. 'Perhaps she just needs to be around different men.'

Cora rolled her eyes. 'Just what every female wants, a man to tell her what she needs.'

He chuckled, causing the mare to flinch. 'Sorry, girl.' He reached out a hand again, and she laid her ears back. 'Is she safe to ride?'

'Quite. Careful, she bites.'

Brom let out a slow breath. 'You don't have to sound so pleased when you warn me.' At least her initial anger had been reduced to general annoyance. 'The queen requires a safe mount. Surely you can select another from this embarrassing collection.'

'The mare is perfectly safe when not provoked.'

His eyes creased at the corners. 'Provoked? I'm trying to pet her.'

Her gaze moved slowly over him. 'More muscle than sense, I see. She does not respond well to brute force.'

'Any sensible man knows you can't outmuscle a mare with this much fire in her.'

Cora reached up to stroke the mare's face. The horse remained perfectly still. 'Well, that does not stop your type trying.'

'My type?' Brom liked that she was at least talking to him instead of reprimanding him. 'I'm beginning to understand why you married Jayr.'

Cora looked up at him, doubtful. 'This should be good.'

'You like broken things.'

Her smug expression faltered, but she recovered quickly. 'Given the current state of your kingdom, and your recent choice of wife, it seems we have that in common.'

He smiled down at the ground, and when he looked up, he found her eyes a little lighter. 'When this mess is over, and we reach some semblance of normal, maybe we can go riding together.'

She searched his face for a moment. 'I shall discuss it with Ida.'

'Who's Ida?'

'My horse—who hates you.'

He looked at the mare. 'Her ears are forwards now. That's progress.'

'I still think it best you keep your hands away if you need your fingers.'

He could never tell what was going to come out of her mouth, but it was usually funny. His gaze fell to the queen's bare lips. It was the first time he had seen her face scrubbed clean. No paint, and not a jewel in sight. The expensive cloak wrapping her was the only indication of wealth. She was no less beautiful for it. Who needed jewels with those eyes?

'Point taken.' He glanced a final time at the mare. 'I think I'll go prepare for the funeral.'

When he went to step past her, she said, 'Brom.'

He stopped, his shoulder an inch from her, meeting her cool gaze.

'Do not go near her again. I will not be so nice next time.'

His eyebrows lifted. 'Wait. That was *nice*?'

Her eyes clouded. 'Leave my things alone and we will get along just fine.'

He stared at her for the longest time, expecting her to look away, to colour, to swallow, blink, react in some way. But she just watched him through a facade of frost. At least he hoped it was a facade, or he was in trouble.

'Noted.' Bowing his head, he stepped past her and left the stables.

CHAPTER 9

T he world looked even darker when viewed through a veil of black lace. Cora waited in the corridor for her mother to join her, drumming her fingers on her arm. Sarey was silent beside her.

'I can feel you looking at me,' Cora said. 'Stop waiting for me to implode.'

'It's not a small thing to send off one's husband.'

Cora glanced tiredly in her direction. 'I feel only relief at not having the corpse in the castle any longer.'

Sarey looked down at her feet. 'Perhaps that's why you were a little harsh this morning.'

'That maid almost set my room alight stoking the fire.'

'I'm not talking about the maid, though now that you mention it, threatening to brand her with a burning log was a bit much.'

'I did not see it through.'

Sarey looked up with that disapproving expression of hers. 'Not really the point, but I was actually referring to your encounter with Brom.'

'Oh, that.'

'Yes. That.'

'The man had his hands on my horse.'

'He was curious about her.'

'He is Jayr's brother. Do you blame me for being wary?'

Sarey sighed. 'They're nothing alike.'

Cora knew that, but the two still shared blood.

Eldoris's door opened, and the queen mother exited wearing a high-neck black gown, a harsh contrast against her Galen complexion.

'Let us get this over with,' Cora said.

Eldoris looked her daughter over. 'You look as though you have not slept.'

Cora drew a slow breath. 'How can you possibly tell that? I am wearing a veil.'

'I saw you walking outside this morning. It was barely light.'

'I was outside because it smells like death in here.' She began walking, and Eldoris followed.

'It is a strange thing to grieve a man you have mixed feelings for,' her mother continued. 'Trust me, I know.'

'There is nothing mixed about my feelings, Mother. You need not fret.'

They rounded the corner and headed for the stairs.

'People will be watching you carefully,' Eldoris said. 'If you appear too stoic, they may question why.'

Cora walked faster. 'I am not going to put on some emotional performance just to satisfy the gossips.'

Eldoris quickened her own pace. 'You must show people your softer side.'

'I do not have a softer side.'

'They have just lost their king.'

'And they are likely as relieved as I am.'

Eldoris cast a worried look in Cora's direction. 'It is also important for your future husband to see a different side of you.'

Cora stopped walking and lifted her veil. She looked from her mother to Sarey, eyes filled with accusation. 'You told her about this morning.'

Sarey pressed her lips together. 'Your mother enquired after you, and I answered. That's all.'

Cora resumed walking again. 'Traitor. I should have you whipped.' Of course, she would do no such thing. Sarey was the closest thing she had to family at Drake Castle.

Eldoris hurried to catch up again. 'All I will say on the matter—'

'Please do not feel the need to say anything at all.'

'—is do not push him away without good cause. You cannot punish him for the mistakes your husband made.'

Cora tugged the veil back over her face. 'I need to burn my first husband before I worry about the next one.'

Eldoris's mouth pinched. 'Really, Cora.'

They descended the steps and made their way outside, where snow was falling. It was unusual for that time of year. Perfect fat flakes floated down around them. Cora wanted to lift her veil again and turn her face up to the sky, enjoy the burn of the cold on her skin, but all eyes were on her as they approached the pyre where Jayr was laid out. Soldiers stood in rows behind, holding pikes. The absence of wind made the silence eerie.

Brom, Carac, Droet, and Tyron waited to one side. Tasia stood a few feet from them. On the opposite side were Pollux and other close acquaintances. Elders from nearby villages had also come to pay their respects, or perhaps ensure the rumours of his death were true. Cora went to stand between Brom and Tyron, suddenly grateful for the veil. Brom glanced down at her but said nothing.

Zoelin ceremonies were transitional rites intended to

give the deceased peace. There would be no outpouring of grief or beating of chests, only thoughtful silence and the smell of burning flesh. There were no parting words from an over-dressed priest, no speeches of any kind.

Pollux stepped forwards, torch in hand, and set fire to the pyre.

Cora looked around at the gathered crowd. Everyone was dry-eyed, even Tasia, proving the man was unlovable. Cora knew it better than anyone, because she had tried many times.

The heat from the flames melted the light dusting of snow caught in her veil. It was stifling, but she could not step back from it without drawing attention to herself. The wood crackled and popped, and she flinched at every noise. Brom glanced at her again, but she did not look back. There was only so much a veil could cover.

A moment later, Tyron took her hand and threaded it through his arm. She left it there as a sulphurous odour took over the air. It seemed to take forever for the body to burn. They stood there, in silence, for almost two hours, until finally there was nothing left except a low cloud of smoke, which she tried very hard not to inhale. Relief rolled over her when she realised he was finally gone from their world. Shame quickly followed.

Perhaps *she* was the monster.

She glanced over her shoulder at Sarey and Lief. She felt better knowing they were close by in case Jayr's spirit found a way to possess her at the last minute.

'Excuse me,' Brom said beside her.

Cora turned back as he walked over to a waiting messenger. The man's stern expression suggested it was bad news. Brom's face hardened as he listened. Cora thought about their exchange earlier that morning. She had given up on the idea of sleep and gone for a walk, ending up at the stables.

Ida had a way of levelling her, of bringing her out of her own head. The moment she had seen Brom standing with her horse, she had seen red. That was how her mind had been shaped over the years. She swung between defeat and barely contained rage. Yet that morning, Brom had disarmed her in a sense, proving there was middle ground between the extremes.

She focused on the fire in front of her. As much as her mother annoyed her with her never-ending criticism disguised as advice, Cora knew she was right about being watched. Some in attendance had been loyal to Jayr, and they would expect her to grieve. They would judge her harshly for marrying the man responsible for his death.

Carac wandered over to Brom, and the two men went inside, prompting Pollux to follow after them.

'How many years at Jayr's side, and he cannot even bother staying for the funeral,' Tyron said.

Her brother disapproved of everything Pollux did, so Cora just let the comment blow away with the smoke.

The rest of them remained where they were until the flames ceased, leaving only a pile of embers. Only then did the soldiers and elders disperse.

'News from Onuric?' Eldoris asked when only their party remained.

Cora looked in the direction of the castle. 'More than likely.'

Tasia walked past, nodding in her direction. Cora returned the gesture. They had always tolerated each other rather well. There was respect between them, but there was also truth. The princess had seen Cora at her worst more times than she could count.

'I should go in. It seems the men have forgotten that I am queen-regent until the coronation.'

'Want me to come in with you?' Tyron asked.

Cora shook her head. 'No. I do not require a translator. I speak fluent male.'

'Brom's sources say there are around two thousand Asigow warriors camping in and around Onuric Castle. Orange flags now hang from its walls,' Cora told her family that afternoon. She was seated in the solar with her mother. Tyron remained by the door, watching his feet.

'It is a good thing Brom has the mountain tribes onside.'

'The Asigow army still outnumber us, and there are plenty more soldiers where they came from.' Cora was having difficulty comprehending that number of men for a war that had not yet begun. She sniffed the air. 'I can still smell Jayr's ashes, despite changing.'

Tyron looked up. 'What is King Tuyon asking for?'

'Right now? An audience with Brom.'

Eldoris thought for a moment. 'Will he go before or after the coronation?'

'He is going tonight. We will hold the ceremony when he returns.' She reached for her cup and took a large drink of wine, closing her eyes as it warmed her.

'What sort of man makes a move on a kingdom when its king has not even been put to rest?' Eldoris asked.

'A smart one,' Tyron replied.

Eldoris looked at her daughter. 'You need to return to Syrasan with us.'

Cora's eyes snapped open, and she leaned forwards. 'I will do no such thing.'

'Be sensible.' Eldoris opened her hands in a plea. 'This kingdom is on the brink of war.'

'*My* kingdom. The queen-regent cannot just flee at the first sniff of trouble.'

'You said yourself that the people already see Brom as king. He is a good man. He will understand your decision.'

'You mean *your* decision.'

Eldoris drew in a breath. 'King Tuyon wants something Brom is not prepared to give. Why else would he take such drastic action?'

'I am not disagreeing with you.'

'Then leave with us.'

'I made a commitment.'

Eldoris sighed and clasped her hands together in her lap. 'If Brom is killed in the East, where will that leave you?'

'In exactly the same position. No crown, no prospects, and no control over my own life.'

Eldoris blinked. 'Please tell me this is not about control. If war comes to your door, what do you think King Tuyon is going to do to the woman who stands against him? He will use you as a pawn against *us*.'

'You are speaking as though Brom's death is inevitable. We do not even know what Tuyon wants yet.'

Tyron pushed off the door and wandered closer. 'Now would be the most sensible time to leave. If Brom does not return, men will grapple for his position—men with no right to it. It will get messy. You do not want to be caught up in that.'

Cora rose from her chair and went to the mantel above the fireplace, which was lined with vases. She picked one up, examining the faint lines only visible up close. Jayr had liked to break things when he was angry. *Her* things. Sentimental things. Most of them had been gifts given by women in villages they visited. He seemed to like the combination of flowers, water, and dangerous shards flying about the room. Cora would not let Sarey throw them out. She would sit at the small table by the window for hours and piece them back together with hide glue. There was immense satisfaction in displaying them.

Placing the vase back down, she turned back to her brother. 'So I am to run scared? Is that really your advice? Is that what you would do if you were in my position?' She crossed her arms, waiting for his reply.

Tyron cast an apologetic glance at their mother before speaking. 'No. I would stay, fulfil my role as regent, and honour the commitment made to the new king.'

Eldoris closed her eyes. 'Pandarus has not even agreed to the match yet.'

'But he will,' Tyron replied. 'The match is good for both kingdoms.'

'And we all know that trumps my personal safety,' Cora added dryly. 'The two of you should return to Syrasan while you still can. This is not your fight.'

Tyron looked worried. 'Cora—'

She held a hand up to silence him. 'Your wife is pregnant. If you leave her pining too long, she might come looking for you, and nobody wants that. Take Mother home while it is still safe to travel.'

Eldoris looked ready to argue.

'It has never been safer for me here,' Cora said, beating her to it. 'My biggest threat is now a pile of ashes.' Seeing her mother's distraught expression, she added, 'I am choosing to stay, and I understand the risks.'

'You are putting a lot of faith in Brom—a man you barely know,' Eldoris said.

Cora shook her head. 'You are wrong. I am putting faith in myself.'

Tyron and Eldoris exchanged a look.

'If anything happens to Brom, I will return and collect you,' Tyron said. 'There will be no argument about it. Understood?'

Cora knew if she did not agree, they would never leave, and she wanted them safely back in Syrasan. 'Of course. I will keep you updated as I have always done.'

Eldoris looked torn. 'How is it you trust the man so easily? One unsupervised conversation and next thing the two of you are getting married.'

She could not explain it because she barely understood it herself. 'I have good instincts about people.' That was the best she could offer them.

Eldoris moved forwards in her chair and took Cora's face in her hands. 'I pray your instincts are right.'

CHAPTER 10

*B*rom could feel Cora watching him as he tightened the girth of his saddle. When he glanced in her direction, he met those startling eyes of hers. He really wished his stomach would not lift in that way whenever it happened. It made him feel like an adolescent. 'If you want to return to Syrasan with your family, I understand. You're not a prisoner here.'

Cora looked over at Carac, who was eavesdropping. 'I am tiring of repeating myself to people. I am queen-regent until your coronation. I am not going anywhere.'

He smiled to himself as he secured the buckle. 'I admire your commitment.'

'Unless your wishes have changed. Perhaps someone got in your ear.' She looked in Carac's direction when she said that last part.

Brom turned to face her. He expected to see some vulnerability in that moment, but she stood tall and unblinking. 'My wishes haven't changed, but the risks have. I've no idea what will come from this meeting.'

'Whatever he asks for, give no answer. Just buy time.'

He regarded her a moment. 'That's what Tasia said.'

'Well, she is a smart woman.' Cora paused. 'The Zoelin people want you on the throne. It would be a shame to disappoint them.'

Excellent queen, terrible wife.

Brom slipped his foot into the stirrup and mounted. He looked down at her as he gathered the reins. 'If anything should happen to me, return to Syrasan. That's the safest place for you.'

Her eyes never left his. 'If anything should happen to you, know the kingdom is in good hands until a suitable replacement is found.'

Carac shook his head, and Cora glared in his direction.

'If you choose to stay, then you'll need to remain within the walls at all times,' Brom said, drawing her attention back to him. He was prepared for the possibility of her changing her mind. Her family would likely talk her out of staying. He understood the logic, but disappointment also accompanied the thought of her leaving.

'Like a prisoner?'

'It's not a punishment. It's for your safety.'

'Oh yes. It is *so* much safer inside these walls.'

The sarcasm was not lost on Brom. 'Just be safe.'

She was walking away before he finished getting the words out. He watched her until she was out of sight, or rather until Carac cleared his throat. Brom looked in his direction and found him shaking his head.

'If you could see yourself when that woman is around.'

Brom kicked his horse into a trot. '*That woman* is your queen. Show some respect.'

∾

The ride to Onuric Castle took longer than they had planned due to unexpected snowfall. They spent the night in Wetus, a small village of around one hundred people that marked the halfway point between the two castles. Brom was not sure how he would be received in that region, but the families were welcoming and addressed him formally.

The men were back in the saddle before the sun had even risen, disappearing into the thick fog. The only sound in the forest was the slush of hooves on the narrow path leading them higher into the mountains, until Onuric Castle finally appeared through the low cloud cover.

Brom stopped to take in the sight.

Onuric was over four hundred years old, built for practicality—sturdy and solemn. It was tucked away in the middle of nowhere, a place of dark secrets and alive with business dealings best suited to seclusion.

'What is the plan exactly?' Carac asked. They had barely spoken on the journey, reserving their energy for what lay ahead.

Brom looked around at the still trees. 'Now we wait.' He let go of the reins and raised his hands.

Carac sighed. 'Really?'

'We can go in peacefully or go in with swords drawn. Either way, it's Tuyon who decides if we get to leave.'

Carac reluctantly raised his hands just as horses emerged from the pines around them, seemingly from thin air. Asigow warriors sat upon them, their inked chests bare despite the frigid temperature. They formed a circle around the pair.

'I'm here to see King Tuyon,' Brom said, speaking their language.

One of the men moved closer. 'And who are you?'

'This is King Brom of Zoelin,' Carac said, his hard stare moving between the men.

The warrior looked between them. 'This way.'

The other men closed in around them, herding them towards the entrance like sheep. Brom raised his eyes to the warriors along the wall, all watching his approach. The man in front signalled to them, and a moment later, the portcullis rose. The noise cut through the air, and Brom and Carac exchanged a glance. They had no idea what awaited them on the other side.

Everything seemed to be in place, no sign of struggle or resistance. Anyone would have thought King Tuyon just strolled in and was offered refreshments upon arrival.

A groom came out to collect the horses, making no eye contact with the king. Brom noticed the ink on his hand. He was Zoelin.

The approach of heavy feet crunching in the icy snow made Brom look up.

'There he is,' King Tuyon said, his tone too friendly for the circumstances. 'The new king of Zoelin.'

Brom took in the broad, bearded man with his jewelled hands and cunning eyes. 'It's been a while.'

Tuyon stopped a few feet away. 'It has. I knew we'd meet again though. I saw your brother's death coming before you did.' He gestured to some guards on the ground, and they marched towards the pair.

Carac went for his sword, but Brom shook his head, raising his arms once more.

The warrior sighed. 'If I die without a weapon in my hand, I'm going to be very angry at you.'

The guards took all of their visible weapons, then all of their concealed ones. Carac cursed quietly the entire time.

Brom stared up at twenty-foot Asigow flags hanging from the walls. 'You've really made yourself at home.'

Tuyon laughed. 'You've got a much better sense of humour than your brother. Anyone ever told you that?'

Brom did not reply.

'Let's take a walk,' Tuyon said. 'Your friend can wait here with my friends.'

Brom did not want to leave Carac, but he also knew that if the king's intention was to kill him, there was little he could do to stop it. He gave Carac an apologetic look. 'Wait here.'

Carac's jaw tightened. 'Tell me you're joking.'

'Wait here.' His tone was firmer this time.

He followed after Tuyon, who led him to the path that encircled the castle. Fine stones had been placed atop the slush of melting ice.

'So, you finally got him,' Tuyon said.

Brom looked to the windows above them. 'I can't take the credit for Jayr's death. He had a number of enemies.'

'Probably for the better. In my experience, killing blood relations does come with a small crisis of conscience, and you don't need that when you're starting out.'

Brom squinted against the glare reflected off the ice. 'Tell me why you're here and what you want.'

Tuyon laughed. 'Not one for small talk, are you?' He looked Brom up and down. 'Or crowns for that matter. Thought you'd be wearing one by now.'

Brom drew a breath. 'We've barely had time to lay my brother to rest.'

'I understand your sister made it to the funeral.'

'No thanks to you.'

Tuyon just laughed again. 'You know, for the longest time, I thought I'd marry her.'

'And then you got a better offer?'

'Something like that.' Tuyon watched him for a moment. 'Your brother would have brought an army.'

'Would it have done him any good?'

'No.'

Brom was losing patience now. 'Why don't you tell me what you want, and then I can decide if I'm prepared to give it to you.'

Tuyon let out a contented sigh. 'I like you.'

'You have a strange way of showing it. Invading my kingdom and hanging your flags in my home. Don't have enough palaces in Asigow?'

Tuyon smiled at the ground. 'My ancestors once occupied these lands.'

Brom fought the urge to roll his eyes. 'You can spare me the history lesson. That war has already been fought—and won.'

'Always the peacekeeper.' Tuyon stretched his fingers. 'This castle plays a vital role in trade with Corneo.'

'What trade is that?'

'Wool, leather, Companions.'

Brom stopped walking and turned to face Tuyon. He knew about the Companion trade. It would be one of the first trades abolished under his rule, and it seemed Tuyon knew it.

'Your people handle the purchasing, housing, and mentoring. You send the women north when they're trained.'

Brom's brow creased. 'Trained?'

'They need certain skills to be of value.'

'Yes, I'm aware of that.'

'Not much good having women who don't speak our language.'

Brom studied him for a moment. 'It's my understanding that all trade between Zoelin and Corneo was supposed to have ceased a few years back.'

'King Pandarus has always made an exception for me.'

Brom stared hard at the man. In other words, Pandarus was powerless to stop him. All that power had long ago gone to Tuyon's head. 'So you want control over this castle and all that happens here, is that it?'

Tuyon regarded him. 'I suspect you'd sooner see your people wiped out than go against that conscience of yours.'

Cora's departing words came to mind. He wanted to say that he would have no hand in the trading of people moving forwards, but instead he said, 'I need to discuss the matter with my advisors. Apparently that's how things work when you're king.'

Tuyon nodded. 'I hope they help you see sense. I'd hate for your sound morals to be your undoing. I'd almost be sorry for it.'

Brom doubted that.

The pair resumed walking.

'For now,' Tuyon said, 'I think I'll spend some time in the land of my ancestors. Shame your sister couldn't join me as my guest.'

'You mean prisoner.'

A smile played on Tuyon's lips. 'Your sister was a prisoner here long before I came along. You can credit your brother for that.'

That was not easy to hear from his enemy. Jayr had done a superb job of isolating her until he could figure out a role for her in his never-ending game.

Tuyon reached into one of his trouser pockets and pulled out some folded parchment. 'I want these signed and returned to me by the end of the month.'

Brom stared down at them. 'What are they?'

'New terms of trade.'

Brom hesitated before taking them and shoving them inside his cloak without looking at them. 'And what happens if I don't sign them?'

Tuyon shook his head and looked around. 'Let's not think about that. Better to remain positive. Return them to me signed by the end of the month, and I take down these flags, pack up my men, and return to Asigow.'

Brom's jaw tightened. 'And I'm just supposed to trust you at your word?'

They rounded the south corner of the castle, and Brom's feet stopped. In front of them was a large cart with children packed in so tightly that limbs hung through the gaps in the wood. Pinched faces stared back at him.

Brom's eyebrows came together in a sharp line, his hands balling into fists. 'What's this?'

Tuyon continued strolling towards the cart, but Brom's feet were held in place by barely contained anger.

'These are Jayr's latest purchase from me.' He stopped a few yards from the cart and crossed his arms. 'But I suspect you already knew that.'

Anger rose like smoke inside Brom. 'Where are you taking them?'

Tuyon turned back to face him, taking in his rigid posture. 'You don't look very happy. Shame your brother isn't around to hash it out.'

Brom forced his hands open, trying to at least appear like he was in control of himself. He did not dare speak.

'Relax,' Tuyon said. 'I thought you could take them with you. Technically they're yours now, and I've no need for child soldiers. We fight with men where I come from.'

It was an olive branch of some sort—though one with thorns. 'You know how I feel about children being trained as soldiers.'

Tuyon continued to regard him. 'I can't control what happens to them once they're sold.'

'Then don't sell them. Change the law. Let them remain with their families.'

'These children are orphans.'

'You know what I mean.' Brom finally closed the distance

between them. 'They still have family, or at the very least tribes prepared to raise them.'

Tuyon only smiled. 'I'll take that feedback on board.' He clapped Brom on the shoulder. 'I know you don't respond well to threats, so consider this an offer. But the offer won't last forever, and I would hate for you to lose another castle.'

Brom imagined what it would feel like to shove him as hard as he could. 'I'm going to need more time.'

'You have until the end of the month, and not a day more.' He paused. 'Do we understand each other?'

Brom stretched his fingers out. While breaking Tuyon's face would relieve the pressure building inside of him, it would not help much else.

'Give my regards to your sister,' Tuyon said with a smirk before strolling away.

Brom watched him round the corner before looking back at the cart filled with children. Letting out a long breath, he went to them.

CHAPTER 11

*A*s the royal wagon pulled away, Tyron looked down at Cora from atop his horse.

'You sure about this?'

If she hesitated, he would never leave. 'For God's sake. Yes. Go.'

He exhaled. 'You should consider getting additional bodyguards. A lot can go wrong during these periods of transition.'

'Or maybe I will follow in your wife's footsteps and get myself a bow.'

'A bow will not do you any good at close range. Get a dagger.'

She had been joking, but his expression was serious. She stepped back from his horse. 'Say hello to the children for me.'

He bowed his head and forced a smile. 'See you soon.'

Cora watched them until they were out of sight, thinking about how Aldara had left her infant son and travelled to Corneo, worming her way inside that castle and living with her own monster. She had fought off men twice her size, knowing they could crush her at any moment. All in the name of love. Cora had thought it laughable, insane, until the waif of a thing had succeeded. No one had the heart to keep them apart after that—not even her.

Sarey walked up beside her. 'Would you like a tray brought up to your room, or will you be going for a ride?'

'Neither.' Cora turned to her. 'Have the behourde cleared.'

Sarey frowned. 'The behourde?'

'I am going to need some privacy to learn.'

Her lady shook her head, confused. 'Learn what?'

'How to use a dagger and sword.'

Sarey did not move. 'What?'

'Pollux spent many years in the army before becoming Jayr's advisor, did he not?'

'I believe so.'

Cora headed back inside. 'Have him meet me there. He can train me.'

Sarey let out an exasperated noise and hurried after her. 'Do you remember what happened last time you were caught with a weapon? The king had you confined to your quarters for two weeks.'

'Only because he thought I was going to cut his throat in his sleep.'

'Because you *told* him you were going to do it.'

She had said that once during a fight. He had broken a vase that day. It had taken Cora two days to piece it back together. 'Well, someone beat me to it.'

Lief fell into step behind her as she passed him.

'I refuse to be vulnerable because of my title, my gender, or the men I marry,' Cora said.

Sarey watched the ground as they walked. 'Pollux may not want to take up arms against you.'

'He will if I order him to do it. If he refuses, I'll have a finger or two removed.'

Sarey gave a resigned nod.

～

Cora had never seen Pollux uncomfortable in the entire time she had known him, but he was far from comfortable standing across from her holding that wooden sword.

'Perhaps we should wait for Brom to return and discuss it with him first,' Pollux said.

Cora gave him a tired look. 'Given that I am queen-regent, perhaps we can forego that unnecessary conversation.'

Pollux pointed to the skirt of her dress. 'It's hard to teach the basics when I can't even see your feet.'

Cora dropped her sword on the ground and hitched up the skirt of her dress, tying it in a knot around her thighs. Picking up her sword again, she said, 'Now can we begin?'

Sarey pressed her lips together to stop from smiling. Lief stood to one side with a disapproving expression on his face. Pollux released a resigned breath before moving to stand directly in front of her.

'Let's start with the basics. Right foot needs to be pointed at your opponent. Left is back at a right angle. Knees bent.'

Cora prided herself on being a fast learner and mirrored his stance to perfection.

'Ensure your knee stays over your ankle, and keep your back straight.'

'Am I holding the sword correctly?' Cora asked, extending it for him to see better.

He adjusted her grip. 'Right hand beneath the guard, left closest to the pommel.'

'Can I hit you now?'

Pollux gave her a lazy smile. 'Raise your sword like this.'

He lifted his weapon, ready to strike. 'And bring it down like this as you step forwards.' He demonstrated.

She tried, but he shifted his body and blocked the blow.

Cora stepped back, eyeing him. 'It is no fun when you defend yourself.'

'Again,' he said, shaking his head.

Cora positioned her feet, then raised her sword.

The following morning, Cora stood before the tall mirror admiring her reflection. She had spent her entire life in dresses, but she was due a rebellious moment.

'Brom will hear about this from someone,' Sarey said behind her.

Cora turned away from the mirror and snatched up her boots, waving Sarey off when she moved to help. 'Brom arrived here looking like he had spent the last few months sleeping with cattle in the mountains. He is in no position to offer fashion advice.'

They ran into Tasia as they exited the queen's quarters. She stopped in her tracks, eyes raking over Cora before giving the queen a confused look. 'What on earth are you wearing?'

Cora looked down at the tailored linen trousers the seamstress had reluctantly sewn for her. They were dark blue and high waisted, not to mention surprisingly flattering on her petite frame. 'Trousers.'

'I suppose the next logical question is why?'

Cora met her gaze once more. 'I am learning how to use weapons. My skirts get in the way.'

Tasia looked to Sarey for confirmation. 'Oh, you are serious.'

'You are welcome to join us.'

'Kind of you, but I prefer the solitude of my quarters. Excuse me.' Tasia resumed walking. 'Enjoy the fresh air, Your Majesty.'

Pollux was laying out the weapons when they arrived at the behourde. He straightened when he caught sight of her.

'Is this better?' Cora asked, coming to a stop in front of him. 'You cannot complain about not seeing my feet now.'

'If Jayr were alive, he'd send you straight back to your rooms to change.' Pollux picked up a sword and handed it to her.

Cora reached out one already blistered hand, enjoying the instant sting of the smooth wood against the wounds. She had surprised everyone by lasting four hours the day prior. Not the most patient of people, her urge to be instantly good at things was both a blessing and a curse. Every muscle in her body was aching. 'Let us begin.'

Pollux selected a weapon for himself. 'I think you're ready to move on to the next stage of training.'

'I was ready yesterday.'

Sarey snorted from her viewing spot. 'Ready to fall down. I had to peel your dress off you when we were done.'

'Well, now I have trousers.'

Lief shook his head, and Cora noticed.

'Do not start, bodyguard, or I shall have you replaced.'

Lief chuckled quietly, knowing she would do no such thing.

Cora adjusted her feet and grip on the weapon. 'Ready.'

It was five and a half hours later when Pollux dropped his sword on the ground and wiped his forehead with the back of his hand. Cora straightened, panting, sweating, and thoroughly high. It was the best she had felt in some time—maybe years. She liked the way her legs trembled and her skin burned hot. She liked the way loose threads of hair clung to her neck and face, the unbearable thirst. She loved all of it.

'With all due respect,' Pollux said, 'you're quite mad.'

'Am I?' Cora let her own weapon fall to the ground, panting. 'Or are you just soft?'

Sarey stifled a yawn before speaking. 'It has been hours, Your Majesty.'

'No one asked you to stay.' Cora stretched her fingers out and studied them. They were a mess of open wounds, oozing and bloody.

Lief grunted his disapproval when he caught sight of them. 'You're training too hard for someone with no conditioning.'

Cora continued to admire her hands. 'Will the wounds turn to calluses?' The thought was oddly exciting.

Lief nodded. 'The way you're going, you'll finish with bigger arms than me.'

She gave him a wicked grin. Before she could respond, another guard marched onto the sand towards them. Cora waited for him to reach her. 'What is it?'

'Our future king has returned, Your Majesty.'

She felt relief at hearing those words. 'Where is he?' She was already walking in that direction.

'Out front, Your Majesty.'

She nodded in reply.

Sarey ran to catch up with her. 'We need to get you out of those clothes.'

'I am wearing trousers, not having an affair. There is no need to cover it up.'

The four of them followed the path to the front of the castle, and the sound of children made Cora stop walking. Her eyes narrowed on the packed cart stopped at the bottom of the steps. Brom looked in her direction as he opened up the back and lowered it to the ground. She hated to admit it, but she liked the way his eyes warmed whenever they landed on her. His gaze dropped to the trousers as he straightened, and he frowned. She raised her chin a little and continued along the path towards him.

'You're still here,' Brom said when she reached him.

She watched as the first child stepped down from the cart. 'You returned much earlier than I was expecting. It was barely enough time to pack.'

Brom's eyes flicked to her again, even warmer than before. Her humour was delivered with such a straight face that most people missed it—but not him.

'We're going to have guests for a few days.'

'I see that.' She could barely believe how many children had been packed into such a small space. 'I gather these are the children Jayr purchased before his death?'

'Yes.'

'And King Tuyon just handed them over?'

Brom took hold of one of the smaller boys and helped him down. 'He's feeding me honey.'

'Better than poison, I suppose.' Cora could not know if the dig went over his head or if he chose to ignore it. Likely the latter.

She turned to the frozen children who stood huddled close together. 'You must all be hungry.' She spoke in Asigow, a language she was finally getting a handle on after three years of lessons. The boys looked between each other, then nodded. Crying drew her attention back to the cart, where a young boy remained huddled in the furthermost corner. When Brom went to reach for him, the child inhaled sharply and shrank back from his hand.

'It's all right,' Brom said. 'No one's going to hurt you.'

The child did not move.

Cora's chest tightened at the sight of the terrified boy. She stepped up into the cart. It was not high enough to stand up, so she got down on her hands and knees and crawled to him. She did not try to touch him, only sat beside him. 'Do you know who I am?'

He had his knees pulled up, arms wrapped tightly around them. He shook his head and wiped his nose with the back of his hand.

She gestured to Brom. 'What about him?'

The boy nodded. 'Brom.'

Cora shook her head. 'Not just Brom, *King* Brom.' When his eyes widened, she added, 'And do you know what he is famous for?'

The boy shook his head.

'For years now, he has been taking children from people who do not deserve them and giving them to people who will love them. How lucky that he found you.'

The boy's grip on his legs eased.

'What is your name?' Cora asked.

'Tanju.'

He looked no older than six, holding far too much pain in that tiny heart for one so young. His story was not uncommon: a child who had lost both of his parents only to become property of the empire. For the right price, King Tuyon would hand them over to anybody.

'Are you cold, Tanju?'

Another nod as he watched her cautiously.

'I know you must be hungry.'

No reply.

Cora leaned closer. 'What is your favourite thing to eat?'

He wet his lips. 'My mother's bread with blueberries in it. She'd cook it in the coals.'

'Sounds delicious, but I am afraid it is the wrong time of year for blueberries. Just between you and me though, our cook does magnificent things with pears. Perhaps we could go to the kitchen and put in a special request.'

The boy blinked and fat tears rolled down both cheeks. 'I want to go home.'

Cora had to look away for a moment. 'That might be possible, but you cannot stay out here in the meantime. You should come inside and eat pears with me for now.'

He thought very hard on that for a moment, then crawled into her lap. He was like an ice brick. She wrapped her arms around him, still hot from her training. They balanced each other's body temperature. 'Let us go and hassle the cook, shall we?'

Tanju sniffed and nodded.

Cora slid along the floor, and Brom took her arm, helping them both out of the cart. He kept hold of Cora even after her feet were steady on the ground.

'Want me to carry him?' Brom asked.

Tanju's legs tightened around her, giving her his answer. 'He is not that heavy.'

Sarey was already ushering the older boys up the steps. Lief was carrying one of the smaller boys who looked ready to fall down with fatigue.

Brom's hand moved to the small of her back. 'Do I want to know why your shirt is drenched?'

Cora began climbing the steps. 'Probably not.'

'Has it something to do with the men's trousers you're wearing?'

'These are *women's* trousers.'

'Women don't wear trousers.'

She looked up at him. He did not seem annoyed, only intrigued. 'I am always ahead of the trends.'

A tired laugh came from him.

Carac overtook them, his untrusting eyes landing briefly on her as he made his way up to his grandfather, who had wandered out of the castle to greet them. Droet waited at the top of the steps because they were a lot of effort for a man his age. Carac hugged him before continuing inside, his gait stiff from the long journey.

Droet clapped his hands together when Cora reached him. 'When the student is ready, the illusion becomes the master.'

Cora glanced at Brom, whose eyes shone with amusement.

'They say you have no heart,' Droet continued, 'but it beats for many.'

Cora adjusted her grip on the boy and glanced after Carac. 'I am guessing your grandson came up with the "you have no heart" part of that one.'

A high-pitched laugh erupted from the man as Cora passed him. She looked up at Brom, who was smiling at the ground now. How he had the energy to be amused, she had no idea. 'You should call upon your sister. She has barely left her quarters since you departed. I can sort out the children.'

Those warm eyes met hers once more. 'Then are you going to tell me why your hands are blistered?'

So he had noticed that. 'I would rather hear about what happened with Tuyon.'

'We can discuss both.'

He paused at the door to let her go first. His manners were effortless, even when there was no one around to witness them. She walked ahead of him, with Tanju's head resting on her shoulder and his eyes already sinking shut.

'You look good dressed as a man, by the way,' Brom said behind her.

She glanced over her shoulder without breaking stride. 'And you look good dressed as a beggar.'

His laughter followed her down the corridor.

CHAPTER 12

*A*fter Brom was done updating his sister, he wandered down to the kitchen to check on the children, but they were not there.

'In the hall, Your Majesty,' the cook told him.

Brom wandered to the great hall, where he found them seated at the long tables, trays of eggs and fruit in front of them and loaves of bread between. He leaned against the door and watched as Cora wandered between them, loading up their plates and encouraging the tired ones to eat. At some point she had changed into a dress. Pushing hair off her face, she bent to wake a boy who had fallen asleep at the table, her hand landing lightly on his back, rubbing small circles as she spoke. So much for not being maternal. He decided to go wash and return once the children were settled for the night.

It was dark when he got back, and the long tables had been replaced with cots. Most of the children were already asleep. He made his way up to Cora's quarters, where Sarey answered the door. She put a finger to her lips and led him through the solar to the bedchamber. His gaze drifted to the display of unusual vases on the mantel. When he looked closer, he could see they had been broken and glued back together.

'Do I want to know what that's about?'

Sarey shook her head. 'Probably not.'

He found Cora curled up in a ball atop her bed, sound asleep. She looked so young without her usual guarded expression.

'She could barely keep her eyes open,' Sarey whispered. 'But I can wake her if you like.'

He shook his head and reached inside his trousers for the papers Tuyon had given him. 'Let her sleep. Give her these when she wakes in the morning. We'll speak then.' He glanced at Cora as he turned away. He hardly knew her, and yet he was looking forward to a time when he might lie down beside her and watch her for as long as he liked.

Brom rose with the sun the following morning, sitting on the edge of his oversized bed in the same bedchamber he had slept in throughout his youth. He had no intention of moving into the king's quarters, where his brother's corpse had been when he arrived. He did not need the added luxury—or the memories, for that matter. He had survived just fine on a lumpy mattress, too short for his height, for years.

With his head in his hands, Tuyon's words replayed in his mind, taking on new meanings each time and slowly eroding his confidence. He had to stop thinking like a rebel and start thinking like a king. Jayr had been a natural ruler. Then he was supposed to have sons. The job was never supposed to fall to Brom.

Stretching his neck out, he made his way to the window, which overlooked the grounds. He spotted Cora already out walking, Lief's enormous frame trailing behind. He was carrying wooden swords, but what held Brom's attention was the fact that his soon-to-be wife was once again wearing trousers.

'What the hell are you up to?' he wondered aloud.

He stepped back from the window and went to wash and dress before going to investigate.

Brom found Cora in the behourde with Pollux. It looked like they were preparing to fight. He watched out of sight for a minute, wanting to make sure of what he was seeing before confronting her. Once they began sparring, he stepped into view. 'Want to tell me what's going on here?'

Pollux immediately stepped back from the queen, and Brom looked to Cora for an explanation. She cleared her throat before speaking.

'Grandor Pollux is teaching me how to use a sword.'

She said it like it was not the craziest thing that had ever come from a queen's mouth.

'He's teaching you how to *fight*?'

Pollux spoke up at that. 'Fighting is probably a strong word. Her Majesty just asked me to show her some basic manoeuvres.'

Cora looked offended by his response. 'Basic manoeuvres? I think we have well and truly covered the basics.'

Brom had no idea where to start with this one. 'And why do you want to learn how to use a sword?'

'So I can protect myself.'

'From what?'

She shrugged. 'Anything. Everything.'

'You've an entire army for that.'

'That army did not do my previous husband much good.'

'Nor did his fighting skills.' His gaze fell to her legs. 'I guess that explains the pants.'

'Dresses are not practical for combat.'

Brom squinted across the sand at her. 'Then let's hope your future assassins permit you time to change. Mind if I watch for a bit?'

She stiffened. 'Do you not have a coronation to prepare for?'

He moved out of the way. 'I have some time.'

She turned away from him. 'Fine with me.' Her fingers tightened around the wooden sword and she focused on Pollux, but the advisor hesitated.

'Perhaps we should do this another time, Your Majesty. We should all prepare for the coronation.'

Cora groaned. 'The only person who needs to prepare is the one getting a crown. Now focus. Pretend our new king is not loitering nearby trying to make me nervous.'

'Am I making you nervous?' Brom asked, his tone playful.

She glanced at him. 'Not at all.'

The pair began to spar, but Brom could see that Pollux was now holding back, and Cora was becoming increasingly frustrated.

'Stop letting me win,' she said, straightening.

Pollux circled her. 'Perhaps you're improving.'

'Not enough to beat you.' She gestured to Brom. 'Is it because he is here? He does not care if you hit me.'

'I do, actually,' Brom corrected. He stepped up and took the weapon from Pollux before facing her. Lief immediately became uneasy. 'You need to plant your feet firmer and move your body. Your constant shuffling is wasting valuable energy.' He expected her to reject his input and was surprised when she did not.

'Like this?' she asked, showing him the action.

'But don't let your knee go side to side. Back and forth only.'

She practiced that also before looking up at him. 'What else?'

He was surprised by how hungry she was to learn and wondered if she was driven by fear. The thought was an uncomfortable one. 'Leave us, please.'

Pollux appeared taken aback for a moment but then nodded before walking away.

Lief did not move.

'You don't have to worry about the queen's safety when I'm with her,' Brom told him.

Still, the bodyguard did not move.

'Leave us,' Cora said.

Only then did he leave. He could only imagine how much Jayr must have hated that.

'This is the part where you have a little rant, make threats, and I am forced to pretend I will change my behaviour.' She leaned on one foot, waiting.

That honesty was both refreshing and unsettling. 'It is? I might need some guidance on how this works. What exactly am I ranting about?'

'Half the fun is in the choosing. The swords, the trousers, or perhaps being alone with another man. I am sure you can think of *something*.'

It sounded like a joke, but her eyes told another story. 'Do I have cause to worry about you being alone with other men?'

'That depends on who you ask.'

'I'm asking you.'

She studied him a moment. 'No.'

He shrugged. 'Good.'

'*Good?*' Cora looked down at the sword in her hand. 'Hang on a minute. Is the casual act because you are intimidated by me now?'

'That's definitely the reason.'

She looked away when a smile tugged at her mouth, and he really wished she would not. Eventually her eyes returned to him, lighting up the behourde like an emerald sun.

'Jayr would have had me declawed by now. He threatened to once.'

He had not been expecting that response. 'And what did you say?'

'That unless he planned to have me *deteethed* also, he was no safer.'

Brom was not sure if he was shocked or impressed by her response. All right, shocked. Though what sort of man threatened to tear his wife's nails out? 'Why did he threaten such a thing?'

'Because I scratched his face.'

There was that honesty again. 'Why?'

'I barely remember.' Her gaze returned to him. 'You can be sure he deserved it though.'

He caught the mischievous glint in her eyes. 'I'd like to think we can fight without the theatrics.'

She tilted her head. 'You mean like grown-ups?'

He ignored the sarcasm. 'It's a rather long life together, and fingernails won't get you far with me.'

'I think it is a little premature to know that.' A smile played on her lips. 'Give me a few more days and we will be able to fight with swords.'

He laughed at that. 'Why don't we stick with words?'

'Words hurt most of all. Death via a thousand tiny cuts.'

Brom took a step towards her. 'I don't want to hurt you with words either.'

She searched his face. 'Even those words will hurt one day. I will think back to this conversation and hate myself for believing you.'

'That's the spirit.'

'You wanted honesty.'

'Let's just not fight, then. I promise to try if you do the same.'

She shook her head. 'Your brother promised me the world once.'

'Well, I'm not him, and I think you know that, or you wouldn't have agreed to marry me.'

She regarded him a moment. 'I gather from the fact that the coronation has been moved to this afternoon that you need to urgently secure your crown.'

He breathed out. 'Yes. Did you read the agreement I left last night?'

She nodded. 'Are you going to sign it?'

'Of course not. The only reason I'm here is because people are counting on me saying no.' When she did not reply, he went on. 'Listen. Normally in this situation, we'd wait an appropriate amount of time before marrying.'

'But you need to rush that also,' she finished.

He sighed. 'I wish I could give you more time.'

Her brow pinched as she thought, eyes never leaving his. 'You need soldiers. You plan on fighting King Tuyon, is that it?'

She did not miss much. 'I need to be ready in case it comes to that.'

'You may be forced to give him what he wants.'

'He doesn't get what he wants. Not this time.'

'You make it sound like we have a choice. Even with the support of the Syrasan army, you will not have enough men to defeat him.'

'Probably not. But with the support of the Galen army, we stand a chance.'

She exhaled. 'I cannot give you two armies. My uncle might be king of Galen, but his daughter is betrothed to King Tuyon. *Our* union will keep him neutral at best. I hope you were not counting on me to give you the impossible.'

'Perhaps I was being optimistic.'

'Or naive.'

A chuckle rose within him, despite the serious nature of their conversation. 'You know, I quite like the thought of marrying you sooner.'

Her face gave nothing away. 'Am I supposed to be flattered after you just admitted your motives?'

He had an urge to touch her in that moment, to run a finger down one flushed cheek. 'Can't I want both?'

'You are a king. You want everything by nature.'

He bit back another smile. 'I was warned that you're selfish and spoiled. No one told me you're funny.'

'I was told you are aloof and reckless.'

'Who told you that? Jayr? He's not a very reliable source.'

She waved off the suggestion. 'I trusted his opinions least of all. I have my own sources.'

'And what else did these sources say about me?'

She thought for a moment. 'That you are built like an ox but easy on the eye.'

'And do you agree?'

'That you resemble an ox? Yes.'

He laughed. 'You know, I've got no problem admitting I find you attractive.'

She watched him with those inquisitive eyes. 'My brothers used to say if I did not open my mouth, men might like me past the initial meeting.'

'Well, brothers can be brutal, as we both know.' He twisted the sword in his hand. 'Do you want to know what I find most attractive about you?'

'You are a man. I could hazard a guess.'

He suppressed a smile. 'You could barely lift that boy last night, but you carried him anyway.'

She looked like she did not believe him.

Reading her expression, he said, 'What? Strength is very attractive.'

She smiled, a real smile—and it was beautiful. For a fleeting moment, she forgot herself. Then it was gone. 'What will happen to the children who arrived last night?' she asked, moving the conversation along.

'We'll try to reunite them with family if we can locate them. Some will remain with families in the Nydoen Mountains. They're leaving this morning. It's the safest place for them right now.'

Cora looked disappointed. 'I suppose I just have to trust you know what you are doing.'

'And I'll try to do the same.' He nodded towards the sword in her hand. 'Learn to fight if it helps you feel more secure here. Wear trousers if you want.'

She stared at him for the longest time. Her expression was laden with distrust. Once again, he had the urge to reach out and touch her, to reassure her. But she had no reason to trust him yet.

'You know, I do not recall asking for your permission.' Cora stepped back from him. 'I should continue before the day slips away.'

He nodded. 'I should go get ready. First I'll claim my throne, and then I'm coming for my wife.' He winked before leaving her on the sand.

CHAPTER 13

It was the first time Cora had witnessed a Zoelin coronation. She wore a blue velvet gown with long sleeves and gold thread embroidered along the neckline and waist. It opened to the middle of her back, which she had managed to keep ink free thus far. Her hair was pulled tight and secured with a pearl comb, and her lips were painted a soft pink.

The ceremony took place outside in the courtyard between the castle and the tower. A blazing fire sat in the centre, the attending elders seated around it. Droet sat sipping wine and smiling at the flames. Carac was there also. He nodded in her direction instead of standing and bowing as he should have. She would have reprimanded him if she did not believe he had Brom's best interests at heart. Still, she was not going to indulge his bad manners. She faced forwards, ignoring his greeting entirely.

Nydoen warriors had arrived from the mountains, dressed in their best vests and armed as though they were going into battle for their king that afternoon. Cora went to sit in a chair that had been placed out of reach of the smoke.

She watched Brom greet each warrior as though they were friends. Perhaps they were. It had been a long time since Nydoen tribe members had been welcomed inside Drake Castle's walls. It made her hopeful for their future. She admired Brom's inclusive nature in that moment, the ease with which he conversed with people. She might have even been envious. Her strengths lay in pushing people away and finding fault in them.

'The men have not stopped looking at you since you arrived,' Sarey said quietly behind her.

The comment might have boosted her ego in the past. Nowadays, it only conjured an empty feeling inside.

Lief moved a step closer, his version of a warning.

'Easy, big man.' Cora rested her hands on the arms of her chair. 'They are just being men.'

Brom came to see her before the ceremony started, his liquid eyes moving over her as he approached. 'You look beautiful.'

The empty feeling dissipated, bringing some relief. That was the moment she realised she *wanted* his approval. 'I see you dressed up for the occasion.' Her eyes moved over the freshly dyed leather, new trousers, and boots so shiny she could practically see her reflection in them.

'Do I look like a king?'

'Depends which king you are mirroring. Jayr always wore a smug smile at these types of gatherings.'

He laughed at that. 'I'll see what I can muster up.'

She absorbed the laughter as if it were something that could be shared. 'Good luck.'

He winked at her as he turned away, as though they were conspirators. She supposed they were in a sense. Two people from powerful families conspiring for positive change in a kingdom long overdue. It warmed her to feel a part of something useful.

Tasia arrived, lowering herself into the chair beside Cora. 'What did I miss?'

Cora glanced at her, taking in her rigid posture. 'You are going to have to forgive him eventually, you know.'

'Forgive who?' Tasia said tiredly.

'Do not play the fool with me. Whatever it is you are so angry at Brom about. And no, I do not care to hear the details.'

Tasia drew a breath. 'That is rich advice from someone who holds a grudge longer than anyone I know.'

'You only know a handful of people because you have been locked away most of your life—but I thank you for the compliment.'

Tasia shook her head. 'I advised Brom not to marry you, you know.'

'You and many others.'

'Do you not want to know why?'

Cora turned to her tiredly. 'Do you honestly think I do not know what people say about me?'

'I told him you were an excellent queen and a terrible wife.'

Cora thought about that. 'That is a rather fair assessment.'

'Do you honestly not care that people think you are a cold-hearted drunk?'

'I absolutely would if I were *not* a cold-hearted drunk. Oh, that reminds me.' She looked over her shoulder at Sarey. 'Could you fetch me some wine? It appears I will be needing a steady supply.' She faced forwards again, folding her hands neatly in her lap as one of the elders led a black calf into the open space between them and Brom.

Tasia faced forwards again. 'I suppose you will have me banished now.'

The calf's throat was cut, and it bellowed before collapsing. The man slid the bowl beneath it to collect the blood.

'Why would I do that?' Cora asked, forcing herself to watch the ritual. One would think she would be desensitised to such things after three years. Though no one would suspect her discomfort looking at her.

'Because you can. It is what you do.'

Cora did not normally buy into other's drama, but she could sympathise with Tasia's situation. There was only one reason why a woman like her would lash out. Cora knew something of that. 'Tell Brom what you want. He will listen.'

'We are not exactly on good terms right now.'

'Tell him anyway.'

Tasia turned back to her. 'He is completely infatuated with you, which means you will have more say over my future than I will.'

Cora looked her straight in the eye. 'If you think I would suggest he take a strong, intelligent woman and hide her away from the rest of the world, then you do not know me as well as you think. You are a superb role model for young Zoelin women. You should be out there encouraging young girls to want better for themselves.' She faced forwards again. 'Do not confuse cold-hearted with spiteful. Besides, I like having someone around who is not afraid to speak their mind in my presence.'

Tasia was silent for the longest time. 'Please do not destroy him. He is not like Jayr. He does not know how to play your games, or even fight back, for that matter.'

'Then perhaps it is time he learned.' Where was that wine? She watched the bowl move between the men until it finally reached Brom. He sipped it before handing it to Droet.

The old man reached up and patted his cheek. 'A king's only failure is to ride with jesters.'

Cora and Tasia both smiled down at their laps. Droet reached for his box of ink supplies, the elders taking turns marking their king. The final result was a pattern on Brom's shoulder resembling a flowered crown. Jayr once had an almost identical mark on his back. She had dragged her fingernails over it many times. Where had all that intimacy gotten her? Not pregnant. Not loved.

Sarey returned with the wine and passed it to Cora. She emptied the cup and handed it back. When she looked over at Brom again, she found him watching her, no doubt trying to figure out how much truth there was to all those stories he had heard. Some of them would seem unbelievable, but most were true.

Droet rose to his feet and took the shiny gold crown handed to him. He sat it atop Brom's head with surprisingly steady hands. The ritual was followed by blessings and prayers Cora had never heard before. She watched the people around her, their serious expressions as they spoke the words. Brom was concentrating as though the phrases contained clues on how to rule a kingdom. She wondered how long it would take for his insecurities and fears to get the better of him.

'May King Brom of Zoelin guide and protect his people until his last breath,' Droet said, falling to his knees on the cold stone.

'At least that part made sense,' Tasia whispered.

Everyone got down on their knees, heads bowed. Some placed their palms on the frosty ground as they prayed aloud.

'Up you get,' Tasia said, rising.

Cora looked at her. 'What?'

'We must submit to our new king.'

She spoke the words as though it were the most normal thing in the world for a queen to kneel on filthy stone. Cora looked around and saw that everyone was indeed on the ground. Sarey laid a woollen blanket at her feet, and Cora reluctantly rose before gracefully going down on her knees. Tasia and Sarey knelt on either side of her.

'Long live King Jayr of Zoelin!' Droet said, throwing his arms up.

There was a collective intake of breath, and then their guests looked nervously around.

Tasia shook her head. 'Out of all the names he could have said.'

Carac rose and spoke into his grandfather's ear. Realising his mistake, Droet turned to Brom and took one of his hands in both of his, apologising. Brom was holding back a smile as he reassured the old man. Immediate forgiveness, like it was no big deal. He was not angry or embarrassed, as Jayr would have been.

Droet tried again. 'Long live King Brom of Zoelin!'

A chorus of voices echoed the sentiment. 'Long live King Brom of Zoelin!'

The kingdom had a new king, and Cora was no longer regent. In fact, she was nothing in that moment but a foreign widow. It should have hit hard. She had expected it to. But feeling anything other than pleased for Brom, and for the people who had waited so long for him, seemed unfair.

When her gaze caught his, he winked at her again, proving that even with the new crown, they remained conspirators. Her smile faded as she realised she was lowering her safety net for a man she barely knew. She needed to be smarter than that.

Breaking the connection, she bowed her head. 'Long live King Brom of Zoelin.'

CHAPTER 14

*C*ora handed her empty cup to Sarey as they walked along the corridor. Her lady tutted as she took it.

'Do not start,' Cora said.

'You could have at least waited until we arrived at the feast before making a mess of yourself.'

'You sound like my mother. I moved to another kingdom in order to avoid her lectures.'

Sarey chewed her lip as she looked Cora over. 'Are you sure about your choice of gown?'

Cora was wearing one of the dresses the seamstress remade after Jayr set fire to the original one in a jealous rage. At least he tore it off her body first. 'That is the second time you have asked me that. I gather you do not approve of my choice.'

'You look beautiful.'

'But? Go on. Too much skin on display? Too much breast? Leg? Too much temptation?'

'You had it made to prove a point to Jayr, and then you had it remade to prove another point. What point are you trying to prove now? Must you test him? Poke holes in a relationship that has barely begun? It's like you're waiting for him to trip, to prove all of your suspicions right.'

'Do not be ridiculous. My suspicions are always right.'

Sarey blew out a breath. 'You want to prove that behind Zoelin's new hero is just another jealous husband who tells you what to wear and hits you when you do not listen, is that it?'

Cora kept her eyes ahead. 'I want an honest glimpse of the man I am to marry. Is that really so unreasonable?'

'No king is going to react well to men leering at what's his. It's only natural he should want to protect you.'

'I do not need his protection.'

Sarey lowered her voice as they neared the great hall. 'You should really limit your wine intake from this point.'

'You should limit your opinions. And I know you water down the wine as the evening progresses.'

Sarey remained silent.

Cora stopped in the doorway of the hall, waiting to be introduced. Lief's boots came to a halt behind them. She angled her head as she looked around at the guests. 'I think I might like to dance this evening.'

Brom took in Cora's gown as she entered the room, her hips swaying and hands leisurely at her sides. It was basically one long piece of cream silk wrapping her neck, breasts, and crossing below her navel. The skirt was full-length at least. Ah, but there was a split. A very *high* split. Her hair was braided and tucked, secured with a seashell comb. Her lips were painted blood red, her arms decorated with gold cuffs, and her fingers covered in rings. She looked like she had just fallen from the heavens to test the will of every man in the room. Pure temptation. A visual representation of every sinful thought he had ever had in his life, the kind of woman he might have fantasised about when he was fifteen.

'Love begins with a single snowflake,' Droet said, appearing beside him.

Brom glanced at him. 'And ends in an avalanche?'

Droet's high-pitched laughter filled the space, drawing Carac's attention. The warrior broke off from his conversation and wandered over to join them. 'Here she comes, our gracious queen.' He turned to watch Cora walk towards them. 'You should tell her to change if you don't want trouble.'

Brom's eyes met Cora's, and he saw pure defiance. 'That's what she's expecting me to do.' She was like a lioness approaching, dangerous and poised. She stopped before them, and instead of curtsying, she scooped up a cup of wine off a passing tray meant for another. She gestured with a finger for them to wait while she drained it.

'Better,' she said, holding it out for a servant to take. 'Your Majesty. Grandor. Carac.' She said Carac's name with tired disinterest.

'You look nice,' Brom said, keeping his tone casual.

She studied him intently. If she was waiting for a bigger reaction, she would not get it from him.

'What better occasion to dress up than to celebrate our new king?' She turned to the servant. 'Get me another—and bring the jar.'

'Nice dress,' Carac said. 'Taking inspiration from Syrasan's Companions, I see.'

Her cool gaze slid to meet his. 'And you are taking inspiration from the homeless, I see. You know, I could have one of the servants bring a clean vest if you are feeling self-conscious.'

Brom glared at Carac before taking Cora's hand and pulling her away from the group. 'Come. Let's dance.'

'Do you even remember this dance? You are not in the mountains anymore.'

'Yes, I remember the dance.' Though he would be rusty for sure.

Droet chuckled happily behind them, and Carac rubbed at his jaw, visibly irritated.

Brom led Cora out into the centre of the room. No one else was dancing yet, so the guests moved aside to watch them. His large hand swallowed hers, his other going to her bare back. Her skin was impossibly silky beneath his calloused hands. His body reacted the way any man's would as he drew her closer.

The music began.

It had been a long time since he had danced in a hall with proper musicians. In the mountains, their celebrations had been less formal, more bare feet stomping dirt with sheets of smoke around them. He felt clumsy and oversized, but she followed his lead without missing a step.

'Want to tell me what's going on?' Brom asked as he turned her. 'Or am I supposed to guess?'

'Whatever do you mean?' She stepped left, then right.

He watched her. 'You come in dressed to kill, and then you took Carac's bait like an infant. The attention's off you, is that it?'

She stopped. 'Do you really think the attention is off me?'

She was so close he could smell the wine on her breath. He glanced around the room and saw that every man was indeed looking in her direction. They resumed dancing.

'You're testing me for some reason.' He brought his face closer to hers. 'Why? Honest answer, please.'

Her feet never faltered. 'I do not trust you.'

It was a start. 'So you thought you'd put on a revealing dress, get drunk, flirt with a few guests, and see what sort of rise you got out of me?'

She did not even blink. 'Everyone has a monster dormant inside of them. I prefer the ones I can see.'

'I'm not Jayr.'

Her feet stopped, and for a moment, he thought his words might have finally tripped her. But then he noticed a cool shine in her eyes. Her hips brushed his as she leaned in.

'*My* monster is unstable, unpredictable, emerging without warning.'

He pulled back to look at her properly. 'I think your monster comes out when you drink. Maybe you should go sleep it off.'

She smiled at that. 'You sound just like him, you know. All you need to do now is call me a whore and dismiss me with a shove.'

He scowled down at her. 'Sorry to disappoint you, but that's not really my thing.'

Her eyes moved between his, her smile faltering. 'You must really want my brother's army.'

'Stop.' His tone was quiet but firm.

'Stop what?'

'This shit. We're on the same side.'

She stepped back from him. 'That is assuming Pandarus agrees.'

'I received a letter from him this afternoon. He agreed.'

She blinked. 'He wrote you?'

'Congratulating me on becoming king and apologising for not being able to attend the coronation.' He reached inside his vest and pulled out a piece of parchment. 'Here. Read it for yourself. He says that while he's been flooded with offers of marriage since news of Jayr's death, he feels our match is suitable.'

She stared at the letter. 'Flooded with offers? I do not need to read it to know he is lying.'

Brom stuffed it back inside his vest. 'He's travelling here

for the wedding. You need someone from your family to bear witness.'

'I just love a public consummation. Something about having one's brother present during intimate moments that makes it all the more special.'

He laughed at that, then looked around. The guests had grown bored of watching them stand in the middle of the room, talking in hushed voices, and had returned to their own conversations.

'Listen,' he said. 'I need a queen, but I *want* a wife. Don't hate me before you have cause to.'

'How long a wait will that be, do you suppose?'

He pretended to think on it. 'Weeks. Maybe months. Definitely not tonight.'

She suppressed a smile as the music started up again. 'Fine.'

He enclosed her hand and drew her close once more. 'Do you want to try that dance again?'

Her shoulders softened. 'Let us see if you can lead this time.'

CHAPTER 15

Cora usually woke with a pounding headache after a feast, but the morning after the coronation, she felt surprisingly fresh. She had been halfway to sober by the time Brom escorted her to her quarters, brushing his lips over her cheek before leaving. He could have followed her in. She would not have stopped him, and no one else would have cared. No one was expecting virginal blood hung on the wall following their wedding night. But Brom seemed determined to play the gentleman, and if she were being honest, it was refreshing after three years married to Jayr. Her former husband was not one for invitations. He had preferred to push past her as she stood blocking the doorway, drag her by the wrist to the bed, and shove her onto it. In her drunken state, she had often laughed, something that had infuriated him as he tried to play the dominant husband. Sober was another matter, but sober had been such a rare state in the end it was not an issue.

Slipping on trousers, Cora exited the bedchamber, sending Lief with a message for Pollux to meet her at the behourde. She told Sarey to remain inside; the morning was cold, and there was no need for her to stand by and freeze. She found Pollux waiting with his arms crossed and a defiant scowl on his face. No weapons in sight.

'Where are the swords?' Cora asked.

'I can't train you anymore.'

Her expression did not change. 'Why?' The fact that he had not bowed did not go unnoticed.

'Because my kingdom is on the brink of war.'

Her eyebrows rose. '*Your* kingdom?'

'My time is better spent serving my king. Have your guard show you some tricks if you insist on doing this.'

Lief went to move, and Cora raised a hand. He stopped.

'I think we can forgive Grandor Pollux's lack of manners because his priorities are where they should be—with our new king.' She stepped closer to the man, her gaze unflinching. 'But to be very clear, your blatant disrespect, from your confrontational stance to the arrogant tone spewing from your mouth, will not be overlooked next time. Am I clear?'

For a moment, it looked like Pollux was going to argue with her, but then he stared past her and his entire demeanour changed. Cora turned to see Brom walking towards them. Looking back at Pollux, she said, 'Be sure to bow this time.'

'Thought I'd find you here,' Brom said, kissing her cheek before looking around. 'Where are your weapons?'

Cora stared at Pollux a fraction longer before breaking their gaze. 'I was just telling Grandor Pollux that his time would be better spent elsewhere.' She did not want to taint Brom's opinion of the man when he was dependent on his advisors right now. Not only was Pollux experienced in the role, but the king's army responded well to him, and his pre-existing relationship with King Tuyon would prove beneficial at some point. She put her ego aside —temporarily.

'I was just telling the princess that I'm happy to organise someone else to replace me,' Pollux said.

At least he had used some form of title within the lie. 'Lief can teach me. Grandor Pollux is a little rusty with weapons anyway. It has been some time since he used that sword of his. He is better suited to political conversation nowadays.'

She was not perfect.

Brom looked between the two of them. 'Sounds sensible.'

Pollux bowed to his king, then to Cora, though his expression hardened as he turned to her. 'I'll leave you to it.'

Cora watched him leave before turning to Brom, only to find him observing her closely. 'What?'

'Did I pick up on some tension between you two?'

'Not at all.' Cora knew Brom was the kind of man who would not tolerate bad behaviour towards her. Jayr had not tolerated it either, but only because he took those things as an attack on him. 'Can you fetch the weapons, please?' she asked Lief before turning back to Brom. 'What did you want to see me about?' Better to move the conversation rather than keep lying to him.

Brom crossed his arms, his face turning serious. 'King Pandarus arrives here tomorrow. I wonder if you might direct us on the best way to approach the subject of military support.'

'Just be honest about your expectations from the very first conversation, then stroke his ego while plying him with wine. He can be very generous with the right amount of attention.'

Brom reached up and touched her cheek. The small gesture made her heart leap. She would need to get that under control.

'Your honesty is both refreshing and terrifying.' He withdrew his hand. 'Actually, that pretty much sums you up.'

'Refreshing and terrifying?'

He winked at her. She was beginning to like those winks. They felt like part of a language they were creating just for them. She had seen similar things in other married couples. Tyron and Aldara. Stamitos and Sapphira. They all had small gestures and phrases that seemed to exclude everyone around them. It was a little thrilling and a little unsettling.

Lief returned, and she stepped back from Brom.

The king turned to the bodyguard. 'Make sure you don't leave a mark, or I'll come for you.' His tone was semiplayful.

Lief gave him a lazy nod. 'Yes, Your Majesty.'

He did not trust the man yet. His own life experiences had marked him the same as Cora's had. They were two tainted peas in a tainted pod.

Cora looked up at Brom. 'Before you leave, would you care to spar?'

Those brown eyes warmed. 'With you?'

'Yes, me. Lief will only show you up.' Cora held out a hand, and Lief placed one of the swords in it. 'Come on, mountain rebel. Let us see if the rumours are true.'

'Which rumours are those?'

'The one about you being half reasonable with a sword. The impotent rumour will have to wait until our wedding night.'

Brom burst out laughing. 'I'm sure the large audience will help.' He took a sword from Lief and turned to face her. 'Ready to lose?'

She shook her head and watched him circle her, a tactic no doubt meant to intimidate. 'Is your plan to make me dizzy?'

Brom grinned, and she could not stop her own smile that time. At least only Lief was there to witness it. Brom struck at her, the movement slow and predictable, so she had plenty of time to raise her sword. He was testing her reflexes, gradually building speed as she proved she could keep up. He seemed impressed, and Cora liked that. She ignored the pain that travelled up her arm every time their swords met. Even when he was going easy on her, he was too strong. She tried to be clever, spinning to figuratively slice his middle, but by the time she turned, his sword was pressed lightly to her neck.

'I guess you win,' she said.

Brom lowered his sword, his eyes never leaving her. 'Don't be too hard on yourself. You've only been learning a few days, and you're actually pretty good.'

She transferred her weapon to the other hand in order to stretch out her fingers. 'Shall we go again?'

He nodded and began circling her once more. 'All right. If you insist on humiliating yourself. Prepare to eat sand.'

She flinched at his words, an involuntary response. His expression fell the moment he registered her reaction.

'I didn't mean literally. I'd never…'

He could not even finish the sentence, and that was the moment she realised he knew. Someone had taken it upon themselves to share the story with him. The exciting tale of the day Jayr held her face in the sand until it filled her nose and mouth. The day she could not breathe. The day she realised that he might accidentally kill her. The day she realised that he might *intentionally* kill her.

Brom's pity-filled expression was too much. She tossed her weapon onto the sand between them. There was not a chance in hell she was going to stand around and have him feel sorry for her.

'Cora.' His voice was low and full of regret. 'I'm sorry.'

'Who told you?' Her voice was loud and laced with agitation.

He did not reply.

'Sarey? My mother?'

He shook his head. 'You're allowed to be angry about what happened.'

'I do not recall asking your permission.' She needed to calm down, but humiliation fuelled her. 'You should not believe everything you hear.'

He watched her with a pained expression. 'All right.'

'I mean it. I could handle him just fine. If I thought him a real threat, I would have left for Syrasan and never returned.'

A nod from him.

'*I* was the monster.' She was pacing now. 'I once had a severed bull's head placed in his bed. *I* did that. Did your little spy tell you that?'

'No.'

She stopped. 'Do not look at me with pity.' Her fingers brushed her throat. In her worked-up state, she could almost feel Jayr's hands clamped around her neck, like the night he discovered the bull's head in his bed. When Brom took a step towards her, she moved back. 'Do not come any closer.'

He stopped. 'I'm sorry, for all of it.'

She tried to slow her breathing. 'Never speak of it again.' Turning away from him, she walked towards the castle, Lief's boots shuffling in the sand behind her.

CHAPTER 16

*B*rom did not see Cora until the following day. She had gone for a long ride and then remained in her quarters, declining his invitation to eat together. She stayed there until her brother was due to arrive. Their encounter on the sand had been difficult, uncomfortable, but it had also been proof that she was not frozen all the way through.

He found her in her usual spot at the top of the steps, watching King Pandarus enter through the gates. He was tempted to give her more time, more space if she needed it, but they were to be wed the following day. He did not want their first conversation to be the exchange of vows, so he walked over to join her. She did not even glance in his direction.

'Leave us,' he instructed Lief.

As usual, the bodyguard waited for Cora's direct orders. She cast a tired nod in the guard's direction before turning back to watch the road.

'Keen to see your brother?' Brom asked, unsure how to begin.

'Not particularly.'

He was quickly figuring out that she was not one for small talk. 'It's been a long time between visits.'

Cora looked at him finally. 'We both prefer it that way. He is only here to make a show of handing me over. Any excuse to be the big man. And because you need his army, you will play right along, even though he supports many of the things that you stand against. That is the game you now play.'

He looked out at Pandarus, trotting along on his tall chestnut horse, his purple robe floating behind him. 'You say that with judgement. What would you have me do instead?'

'I say it with resignation. If you wish to stand against King Tuyon on the big things, you must swallow the small things and play the game every king has played before you.' She turned back to watch Pandarus approach, surrounded by thirty-plus guards. 'He will want something in return. Have a think about what you are prepared to give.'

He drew a breath. 'Tell me, will you be negotiating on his behalf or mine?'

She crossed her arms. 'I will help you get your army because it is in the best interest of the Zoelin people, but I will not deceive my family. Do not ask me to lie.'

'That's fair.'

He looked down at his boots. 'Do we need to discuss tomorrow's events?'

'What is there to discuss? I have done it all before. Unless you have decided to include some strange Nydoen tradition I am unfamiliar with.'

'No, nothing to surprise you with. I thought I might ask Droet to bear witness for my part.'

Cora was holding back laughter. 'Your part?'

He felt like they were back onside. 'Sort of the main part, if we're being honest.'

'I know it has been a while, but the last time I consummated a marriage, there were two of us.'

'But you just get to lie there,' he teased.

Her eyes burned brighter with amusement. 'While Pandarus, Droet, and God knows who else watch on. If Droet starts commentating, I will not be able to hold back the laughter.'

'I thought you'd prefer him to Carac.'

'You were right about that.' She looked up at him. 'Might I suggest you refrain from any pleasurable activities between now and then. The quicker the better.'

He tried to keep a straight face. 'No pressure.'

'If you cannot handle pressure, then you might be in the wrong job.' She watched as the horses came to a stop at the bottom of the steps. 'For the record, we are not supposed to discuss it beforehand. You show up, it is incredibly awkward, and then we both completely erase the occasion from our minds.'

'I'm going to need a drink beforehand.'

'But not too much or we will be there all night.' Her smile faded the moment she locked eyes with Pandarus. 'Let the game begin.'

It was the first time the two kings had met. They watched each other with matching distrustful expressions.

'I was rather hesitant to hand my only sister over to a complete stranger,' Pandarus said, 'but it seems she is very loyal to Zoelin and its people.'

They had only been talking for five minutes, and Brom had already decided he did not like the man. It did not help that he had once tried to have Captain Dion beheaded because he was jealous. 'It's important to have some stability amid the change. While I have a lot of supporters around the kingdom, there are still some loyal to my brother. I also happen to be quite fond of your sister.' He looked across at Cora and winked at an angle so only she could see it.

Pandarus took a drink of wine and placed his cup in front of him. 'People love this notion of a hero.'

'Let's hope it's more than a notion,' Brom replied. 'I'm here to implement much-needed change.'

Pandarus chuckled in the most patronising of tones. 'You are new to this. Soon you will realise that the change you seek is a dream you feed them.'

Cora reached for her own drink. 'Brom is not like other kings. You will figure that out soon enough.'

Pandarus looked between them. 'We all end up serving King Tuyon in the end.'

Brom regarded the smug man. 'I serve only my people.'

One corner of Pandarus's mouth lifted. 'Tuyon has taken one of your castles, has he not?'

'And I have a plan to get it back.'

Pandarus scowled across the table at him. 'King Tuyon's army is rumoured to be twenty-thousand strong. Zoelin has what? Five thousand men? Many of whom cannot shoot a bow.'

Brom's finger began tapping on the arm of the chair. Cora reached out and took his hand. It was the first time she had touched him, or done anything remotely intimate. She had disarmed him with a simple touch.

'That is what allies are for, brother.'

Pandarus looked down at their joined hands. 'I guess that explains the rushed wedding. I hope you know my sister has no say over what I do with my army.'

Brom did not deny it. He had promised to Cora to be honest in his dealings, and it was not his negotiation style anyway. 'I really hope Syrasan supports us, but we're prepared to fight either way.'

Pandarus sniffed. 'You know, this reminds me of when we

were forced to fight alone in order to retrieve my brother from the mad king of Corneo. I never forget those who turn their backs on me.'

He was referring to when Prince Tyron had been taken captive some years back. Jayr had not only claimed to be neutral but had been involved in secret dealings with the mad king.

'Jayr is gone. I sit on the throne now, and I'd like to think I treat my allies a little better than that.'

'How convenient,' Pandarus replied.

Cora emptied her cup and gestured for it to be refilled. 'You are being unfair, brother. Brom has already proven he is a better leader. People like him, for a start.'

Pandarus tutted. 'How about some respect for the man who survived your antics for three years? You know, you do not need to be here. I am sure you have lots to organise for the wedding.'

Cora let go of Brom's hand, and up went her cup.

'Respect is earned,' Brom said, 'and I would prefer Cora stay so I don't have to repeat everything to her later.' He wanted to make a point that there would be no secrets between them. He might have used some stronger language if he were not counting on Syrasan's support. His eyes met Cora's briefly, and she placed her cup down and took his hand once more.

'Support us in this fight, brother, and when the time comes—and you know it will—the Zoelin army will protect your borders as if they were their own.'

'The thing is,' Pandarus began, drumming his fingers on the arm of his chair, 'I do not trust you yet.'

'But you can trust me,' Cora said. 'I have made it very clear to my betrothed that I shall not serve this kingdom at the expense of my family and homeland.'

'It is not like you to be so naive,' Pandarus said.

Cora did not even blink. 'Let me put it another way. If King Tuyon gets his way, then Zoelin will continue to trade with Corneo, strengthening relations between the two kingdoms.'

'Companions hardly count as trade,' Pandarus replied. 'That is why I have turned a blind eye to it all these years.'

Brom shifted in his seat as his agitation grew. Cora's small squeeze of his hand made him still.

'Zoelin will essentially be cutting ties with Corneo,' Cora said. 'I thought you would be thrilled.'

Brom spoke up at that. 'Only ethical trading moving forwards.'

'Stand with us,' Cora said. 'That alone may be enough to make King Tuyon rethink his plans.'

Pandarus did not look convinced. 'Or it may be the start of a war.'

'In which case Syrasan will want to be on the right side of history,' Brom said.

Cora lifted one shoulder in a shrug. 'Or you could remain neutral, but we all know cowards make easy targets.'

Pandarus was silent for a long time, his jaw ticking. Finally he leaned forwards. 'Of course we stand with Zoelin. We are allies, are we not? If the need arises, I will send men. My brother Tyron will lead them. His reputation in battle has reached even as far north as Asigow.' He straightened in his chair. 'I imagine Tuyon's betrothal to Princess Beatrix of Galen will prevent our dear uncle from joining the party.'

'More than likely,' Cora replied. 'However, Brom has excellent relations with the captain of Galen's army, as you know.'

Pandarus blinked slowly. 'Well, Captain Dion reports to his king—when it suits him.' He paused. 'This is a rather morbid pre-marriage topic. Weddings are supposed to be happy occasions. Your mother really wanted to come, you know.'

'She is your mother too.'

'Cora was very concerned for her safety,' Brom said. 'She thought it best the queen mother remain at Archdale.'

Cora turned her head to look at him. 'But more concerned for my sanity.'

'She asked that I keep you sober,' Pandarus said.

Cora let out a harsh noise resembling a laugh. 'Can a lady not enjoy a little wine at her own wedding celebration?'

'When have you ever had *a little* wine?'

Brom watched the two of them. There was definite hostility, but beneath it all was a deep sense of family. He said nothing, allowing the banter for as long as Cora seemed comfortable.

When their conversation ended, Pandarus left the room, his guards in tow. Brom and Cora watched the door close behind him, then turned to look at each other.

'I think we make a good team,' Brom said, reaching up and touching her face.

She did not move away. 'It does seem that way.'

'And I think I know how to make you happy.'

Her expression turned to one of concern. 'What happened to a mutually beneficial union?'

'Can't it be mutually beneficial *and* happy?'

She looked disappointed. 'I wish I was the type of woman who said nice things back, fed you hope, or at least convincing lies, but I am far too jaded by this life.' She stepped back from his touch, then headed for the door, leaving his empty hand hanging in the air.

CHAPTER 17

The sun finally broke through the clouds on the morning of the wedding. It was as though God had been holding his breath, waiting to see if Cora would mess it all up before then.

The last time she was married, she had woken late and taken a luxurious bath before spending three hours preparing herself for the ceremony. But the morning of her wedding to Brom, her legs were restless, her fingers twitchy. The walls of her quarters felt restrictive and the ceilings too low. Cora wandered down to the stables, slipped a halter on Ida, and led the mare to the training yard. She sent the groom away and asked not to be disturbed.

'Can you catch me?' she asked Ida, backing away from the mare with a smile.

Ida knew the game. She followed Cora, throwing her head about and pivoting whenever Cora changed direction. They ran to the fence, hooves pounding behind Cora the whole time. Out of breath, she leaned on the fence post, panting.

'All right. You win,' she told Ida, rubbing the horse's face.

A hand was not enough for the mare, who rubbed her entire head against her.

'You nearly pushed me over.' Cora laughed, then ducked and ran off in the other direction.

Ida snorted and turned, the early sun reflecting off her glossy coat. Cora's smile faltered when her gaze landed on one of the scars. She stopped moving, allowing Ida to reach her, then wrapped her arms around the horse's neck. 'Never again,' she whispered. 'That is my promise to both of us on this day.'

Cora led Ida back to the stable before returning inside to prepare for the wedding. The moment she entered the solar, Sarey was upon her.

'Where have you been? The ceremony is in an hour.'

Cora went to the tray on the table and poured some wine. 'We have plenty of time.'

Sarey took the cup from her hand and began unbuttoning her gown. A tub had been brought in and filled, steam rising from it. 'Get in, get in.' She ushered Cora towards it.

The warm water was bliss after running around. She closed her eyes and leaned her head back, but the moment was cut short by Sarey then ushering her *out* of the tub.

'Dress, please.'

'For goodness' sake,' Cora said, climbing out and wrapping the towel around her. 'He is not going to choose someone else from among the guests if I am a few minutes late.' She snatched up the wine as she passed the tray.

'No wine until after,' Sarey said, taking it off her.

Cora let out a heavy breath. 'Is there no one else who can help me prepare?'

Sarey went to fetch the dress. 'Everyone else is afraid of you. You know that.'

An hour later, Cora stood dressed in a red velvet gown, Syrasan's royal colour, as was tradition for the bride. Her face was painted, hair braided, and she wore the gem-encrusted jewels she had been gifted by her father some years back. She looked in the mirror, seeing a beautiful representation of her life and role. Her eyes told a different story.

'Remember to smile,' Sarey reminded her.

Smiling was a life skill taught to women from a young age. A pretty smile ensured that all her father's acquaintances, every potential suitor, thought her a prize worth bidding for.

'You look breathtaking,' Sarey said, stepping back to admire her work.

Cora looked at her in the mirror. 'You must promise to stay with me.'

Sarey's eyebrows rose in surprise. 'Of course I'll stay with you. I wouldn't miss your wedding for anything.'

Cora shook her head. 'I am not talking about the wedding. I am talking about the marriage.'

Sarey's expression softened. 'You don't need me as much as you think. Brom is a wonderful man.'

'Just do not fall in love with some fool and leave me here alone.'

Sarey stepped up to straighten Cora's necklace. 'Men are too afraid to court me, and you would never give your blessing anyway.'

'Not because I do not want you to be happy, but because there is no man worthy of you.'

Sarey met her gaze in the mirror once more. 'That's the nicest thing you've ever said to me. Actually, it might be the *only* nice thing you've ever said to me.'

'Do not make this any more awkward.'

Sarey smiled as she stepped back. 'I think you're ready to get married.'

Brom waited for Cora in the large tent they had erected for the occasion. Carac was flipping a coin beside him, and Pandarus stood on the other side, tapping his foot impatiently as he watched the entrance of the tent.

'Where the hell is she?' Pandarus said.

Carac glanced in the king's direction. 'Perhaps she changed her mind.'

'Must you sound so hopeful?' Brom said.

Pandarus exhaled. 'Finally.'

Brom looked to the entrance, where he found Cora standing with the light spilling in behind her. She really did knock the air from his lungs sometimes.

Carac threw an elbow into his side. 'Stop smiling like a lunatic. It's unsettling.'

He had not even realised he had been smiling, but why would he not? She was a vision in red with her royal sash and lips painted the colour of a sunset. Her hair was braided into a crown atop her head and threaded with flowers. The whole room fell silent at the sight of her.

Pandarus went to collect her, brushing a kiss over her cheek before whispering something into her ear. She blinked, and her eyes seemed to dull. That was the effect Pandarus had on her. Cora's gaze found his, and he offered her an encouraging smile. She began walking towards him, never looking away.

'You look absolutely stunning,' he said when she reached him.

She took in his clothes and boots. 'You do not look so bad yourself. New shoes?'

'Droet insisted.'

'Is there no end to his wisdom?' She turned when an elder approached them.

The man who was to marry them was a friend of Droet's, which was good enough for Brom. Cora had not cared who married them as long as it was legal. The elder gestured for them to kneel, and Brom offered Cora his hand as they lowered themselves down onto the cushions. The guests gathered closer.

'Last chance to change your mind,' Brom whispered.

She cast a disapproving look in his direction. 'Shh. You will miss the part about pledging yourself to the burdens of matrimony.'

Brom suppressed a smile and looked up at the elder.

After a very long speech—half of which Brom did not hear because he was watching Cora, who was pretending to listen attentively—the elder finally wandered off to fetch the pot of blue paste. It smelled like mud. Droet moved forwards for the next part, dipping two fingers into the paste and smearing it down Brom's shoulders, the centre of his chest, and then his cheeks.

'With all my worldly goods, I thee endow,' Brom said. He winked at his almost-wife.

Sarey stepped up to unbutton Cora's gown, exposing her collarbones. Droet dipped his fingers once more and clicked his tongue as he marked the exposed flesh with the paste.

Then came the prayer, followed by the cry of a goat as its throat was cut. He noticed Cora looked past the animal instead of at it. Further proof of heart. A moment later, warm blood was offered up. Brom took the bowl, drank, and then handed it to Cora. She took a small sip before handing it back to him.

'Let her pain be his pain and his pain hers,' the elder finished, taking them out on a high.

Brom snuck a look at Cora and saw her lip clamped between her teeth, amusement burning in her eyes. His reaction also.

The guests applauded and cheered, and Brom kissed his new wife properly for the first time. They were the softest lips he had ever felt, warm and sweet. His eyes sank shut, savouring the sensation until she finally pulled away. He could tell by her expression that she had been as surprised by that kiss as him. She swallowed, eyes moving between his, then reached up and wiped a smudge of paint off his bottom lip. She turned without a word and walked off towards the chairs that had been positioned on the raised floor. Cora took a seat, and Brom sank down beside her, finding no words for his new wife in that moment.

Friends and family came forwards next, offering well wishes and gifts. Pandarus gestured to one of his men, who carried a small trunk over to the newlyweds. It was filled with coins.

'Thank you,' Brom said to Pandarus.

'Thank you, brother,' Cora echoed.

Pandarus accepted the thanks with a nod, looking quite pleased with himself in front of an audience.

Tasia came forwards with a wrapped gift next. It was a quilt in both Zoelin and Syrasan colours.

'It is beautiful,' Cora said sincerely.

Tasia curtsied before moving away.

Sarey offered up a cloak pin, each end shaped in a horse's head.

'I cannot take this,' Cora said. 'It belonged to your mother.'

Sarey offered a small smile. 'And she would have been proud to see her queen wear it. It is not very valuable in terms of coin, but I am convinced it is a lucky charm of sorts.'

Cora placed it on top of the trunk. 'Thank you. Please bring the king's gift.'

Sarey nodded and turned to retrieve a small package

wrapped with hemp and tied with string, handing it to Cora. The queen passed it to Brom without meeting his gaze. 'For you, my love.'

My love.

He knew the endearment was purely for show, but he liked the way it sounded. He took the gift and untied the string before peeling back the cloth. It was three leather-bound books, immaculately stitched. He read the titles, and warmth spread through him. They had belonged to his grandfather. He looked up at Cora. 'Where did you get these?'

She pressed her lips together. 'I saved them from one of your brother's tantrums. I remembered him telling me they had belonged to your grandfather and thought he would regret destroying them. He never mentioned them again, so I repaired them and kept them in my personal library.' She waved a hand. 'They were just taking up space.'

He blinked. '*You* fixed them.'

'I like fixing things, remember?'

He remembered. 'These are… incredible. Thank you.'

She nodded and looked away.

Brom turned and gestured to Carac, who sighed and shook his head before leaving the tent. He returned a moment later with Pup.

'Ah, what is that?' Cora said, sitting a little straighter in her chair.

He was worried how his gift would be received. 'This is Pup, an orphaned wolf we found a few years back.'

Cora's eyes moved over the animal, narrowing on the missing ear and lip. 'What happened to her?'

'She was attacked by a pack last year. No one had the heart to get rid of her. She's hopeless for protection, but she makes a warm sleeping companion on cold nights. I bathed her.'

Cora extended a hand to the animal. 'Hello, Pup.'

The wolf stretched her neck to sniff her, then wandered closer. Cora tentatively stroked her back, sliding her hand all the way up to the missing ear.

'I had this strange idea you might like her,' Brom said, second-guessing himself now.

Cora continued to study the animal. 'Look at your beautiful eyes.'

Pup tilted her head at the sound of Cora's voice.

'If you'd prefer something else, a necklace perhaps—'

'No.' Cora straightened and looked at him properly for the first time since their shared kiss. 'She is perfect. Thank you.'

The feast passed in a blur of polite conversation and introductions. Cora only danced twice, once with Brom and once with Pandarus, before settling herself at the high table where she drank enough wine to intoxicate five people.

'How about some food?' Sarey asked, stepping up to the table.

'How about some silence?' Cora turned in her chair. 'I am about to lay with my husband for the first time, in front of an audience, so if I choose to numb all of my senses, you should be nothing but supportive.'

Sarey showed no signs of pity. 'I think you are numb enough, Your Majesty.' She slid the tray of fruits closer. 'Please eat something.'

Cora reluctantly reached for a slice of pear and popped it into her mouth just as Brom stepped into sight.

'It's time.' His tone suggested he was as nervous about the next part of the evening as she was.

Cora looked past him to where Droet and Pandarus,

along with two other elders, were preparing to leave the feast, then back at her husband. 'We might as well get it over with.'

Brom watched her as she rose from her chair. 'I wish we could skip the theatrics. You know I'm not big on traditions. I would much prefer to enjoy my wife in private.'

'What did I tell you yesterday? We are not supposed to discuss it beforehand. We show up, it is incredibly awkward, and we never speak of it again.' Cora made her way around the table and stepped down, taking the hand offered to her. 'It is not supposed to be fun. We are there to make the marriage legal.' She glanced across at him, reading his discomfort. 'Do not worry, I will not judge you too harshly on this evening's performance.' She hoped he would not notice her unsteady hand as she spoke so confidently on the subject.

'What a relief.'

Sarey followed them out into the corridor. She would help Cora out of her dress and remain in the room to assist afterwards. Lief followed also, but he would wait outside.

'I assume you know what you are doing,' Cora said. 'The logistics.'

Brom glanced sideways at her. 'I have a vague idea of what goes where if that's what you're asking.'

She suppressed a smile, some of the tension leaving her.

'Just tell me if I hurt you. There's no avoiding the awkwardness, but I don't want you feeling any discomfort.'

He spoke the words quietly. They were just for her. He was a completely different breed of man to Jayr.

'I am hardly going to make a fuss and risk delaying the ending.'

That made him smile, and the smile eased whatever tension remained.

They entered Cora's bedchamber in silence. Inside, the

men had positioned themselves around the room so each had a clear view of the bed. Pandarus, for all his faults, stood in the far corner staring down at his boots. Cora focused only on Brom, refusing to acknowledge their audience—and he did the same.

Sarey stepped forwards to help her out of her gown, slipping a nightdress over her head before removing it the rest of the way. Cora stepped out of her drawers and sat on the edge of the bed with her legs pressed tightly together. She was nervous, a foreign emotion that sat uncomfortably in her throat. If she were being honest, it was not the sex, or even the audience—it was Brom. She had felt something during that kiss earlier, something she wanted to dismiss, bury, forget about. Something confusing. It was not the lust she recognised from her previous marriage, not the angry tension, the hateful spark that could turn explosive between the sheets. It was something far more terrifying because it started at her lips and spread like warm honey through her—and she had known by his expression that he felt it too.

Brom gave her an apologetic smile as he approached the bed. He undid his belt but kept his trousers up, searching her face for a moment. 'May I lay you down?'

Cora lowered herself down, hoping he could not see her nerves. She kept waiting for him to look away, but he never did. Then he was above her, propped up on one elbow. He reached one hand down, gently pulling up the hem of her nightdress until it sat just below her hips. Only then did he adjust his trousers, ensuring they were both somewhat modest. Her breaths came a little faster as his bare skin pressed against hers.

He stilled. 'Are you all right?'

'Yes, of course.'

'Are you ready?' he whispered.

Dear God. Would you just hurry up? Jayr would have been done by now.

'The act of love is a wall to be scaled,' Droet said, his voice too loud for the small space. 'Then taken apart stone by stone. Imagine the rubble.' He finished with a soft chuckle as he rocked on his heels.

Brom dipped his head to Cora's neck to hide his smile, and she hid her face also. His body shook gently with laughter, and she relaxed beneath him. When he finally lifted his head, she could see flecks of gold in his eyes in that light. They were beautiful.

Brom brought a hand to rest lightly on her jaw.

The rest was easy.

Warm body, warm breath, warm words.

Finally, he pressed his face into her neck and shuddered against her. 'Did I hurt you?' he whispered so only she could hear.

She shook her head, one palm pressed to his chest, ready to push him away. But she did not push him away. She waited for his breathing to settle, for her own to settle. Then he lifted himself off her and fixed her nightdress before taking care of himself.

'Come,' Pandarus said. 'Let us leave the queen to clean up.'

The strange thing was Cora did not want Brom to leave. She wanted the others to go so the two of them could discuss Droet's comment, laugh about it. A shared sense of humour might be enough to sustain them.

Brom watched her carefully as he fixed his belt. He seemed to be waiting for her to say something, for a cue of some sort. Married people did that sort of thing. When she gave him nothing, he brushed his lips over her cheek before rising from the bed.

'Tell the guests it is done,' said one of the elders to Pandarus.

Droet clapped Brom's shoulder as he passed, heading for the door. 'Hear that? It's done.' He cackled all the way to the door.

'Yes, I heard.' Brom looked down at Cora, eyes creasing at the corners. 'I'll come back later?'

The fact that he phrased the comment as a question threw her. A husband did not ask; he showed up, took what he wanted, and then he left. Brom was no different, even if he wanted her to believe he was. She decided in that moment that the next time he came to her bed, it would be on her terms. She needed to control the things she could. 'Actually, I am quite tired. I think I am going to retire for the evening.'

Brom watched the others file out of the room before looking back at her. 'Are you sure? I can come back.'

She could not tell whether it was a proposition or whether he meant to sleep. 'I will just see you in the morning.' She waited for the disappointment, annoyance, confusion—something—but he only nodded.

'Long day?'

'Yes.'

Another nod. 'Then I'll see you in the morning.'

He followed the others out, and the second the door clicked shut, Cora collapsed back on the bed.

Sarey stood in stunned silence, staring at her. 'Ah—'

'Do not say a word.'

Sarey was silent for the longest time before finally saying, 'I will have some hot water brought up.'

Cora rolled to face the other wall. 'Where is the wolf?'

'Tethered in the courtyard, I believe.'

Cora pulled her knees up to her chest. 'Bring her to me.'

CHAPTER 18

*W*hen Brom woke the following morning, his first thought was Cora. He glanced at the spot on the bed where one would expect to find their wife the morning after a wedding, but the bed sheet remained neatly tucked on that side. Sighing, he rose and decided to go check on her. He needed to make sure she was all right, that he had not hurt her or embarrassed her in some way. He could not figure out if her cold dismissal was a good or bad sign. Perhaps she had felt something during the intimate encounter and gotten cold feet. More likely, she had ticked off her obligations and had no desire to see him again for the rest of their marriage. If they had been alone, he would have taken his time with her. They would have talked first, kissed, maybe for hours. He would have tried to make her laugh. He had never seen her laugh properly before.

When he arrived at her quarters, he found them empty, so he headed to the behourde, only to be intercepted by a stern-faced Pollux in the courtyard.

'Your Majesty,' he said, bowing. 'If you have a moment, I'd like to talk to you about the wedding tour.'

Brom looked past him before nodding. 'What about it?'

'I think you should cancel it.'

'All right. Why?'

The advisor rested his hands on his hips, a rather casual stance in the presence of a king. Lucky for him, Brom was not Jayr.

'There may be some backlash from your recent nuptials. Those loyal to Jayr feel some anger towards you and will likely feel the same towards the queen. After all, she married the man responsible for his death.'

'Those people make up a very small minority, surely.'

'Plus news of the union will reach King Tuyon in the next few days, if it hasn't already. He's no fool. He knows the only reason you would take Cora as your queen is for her... family connections.'

Brom blinked. 'You mean *Queen* Cora?'

'Yes, of course,' Pollux replied without a hint of remorse.

'And it was not a purely political marriage.' Why he felt the need to add that he had no idea. Judging by the look on Pollux's face, he had no idea either. Brom cleared his throat. 'What exactly are you worried about?'

'Your wife links the two kingdoms. She's the glue, so to speak. That makes her a target.'

Brom thought about that for a moment and had to agree. Perhaps the advisor knew what he was doing after all. Brom had been hesitant to keep him on given he had served Jayr for so many years, but Droet was quick to remind him of the advisor's value. Another bridge between old and new. 'I can't very well keep her locked up here forever.'

Pollux shrugged. 'You might have no choice if you wish to keep her alive.' He bowed, then stepped past Brom, walking off in the direction of the castle.

Brom found Cora standing alone in the middle of the behourde, playing with Pup. She was throwing a stick, and the eager wolf kept returning it to her, met with extraordinary praise each time. He could tell she had already trained because she wore trousers with a shirt half tucked into them. Her sleeves were rolled up, and pieces of hair were stuck to her neck.

The smile froze on her face when she caught sight of him.

'Good morning,' she said, smoothing back her hair in an attempt to make herself more presentable.

There was no need for it. With the early light spilling around her, she was the best thing he had ever laid eyes on.

'Good morning.' He wanted to go straight to her, take her face in his hands, and kiss her for an hour or two, but instead he stopped a yard from her and looked around. 'Where's Lief?'

'Not here. I wanted some time alone with this one.' She gestured to Pup. 'You did not tell me how smart she is.'

'I knew you'd figure it out soon enough.'

'You were right, by the way. She is quite the bed companion.'

He nodded. He could not compete with a damaged wolf when it came to his wife. 'Normally we would travel to the nearby villages and continue the celebrations.' He bent to pet Pup when she wandered over. 'But it might be safer to remain inside the castle for now. We can't predict people's reactions.'

'Oh.' Cora looked disappointed. She clicked her fingers, and Pup returned to her. 'My uncle sends his congratulations. I received a letter from him this morning.'

'No army accompanying that message by any chance?'

Cora's mouth lifted in a smile. 'Afraid not.' Her expression turned serious. 'So I am to be locked away here after all.'

'For very different reasons than before.'

She simply nodded.

He cleared his throat. 'I hope last night wasn't too horrid for you.'

'It was fine.'

'Fine,' he repeated. 'Well, I hope to afford you a better experience in the future.'

'Show up alone and you will be halfway there.'

It was his turn to smile.

'I really like getting out and visiting the villages,' she said. 'Seems a shame to let fear get in the way of royal traditions.'

'My concern's for you. Pollux thinks you might be a target.'

'Because of my connections.'

'Yes.'

She thought. 'I will take a sword with me.'

He should have known she would not be afraid. 'It won't block an arrow coming at your neck.'

'I saw Tyron block an arrow with a sword once.'

Brom locked eyes with her. 'He's been doing this a little longer than you. I've heard Syrasan training methods are... more intense.'

Cora raised her chin. 'People will feel distanced if they are not included in the celebration. Those loyal to Jayr need to see that their queen is happy.'

He watched her for a moment. 'And are you happy?'

She hesitated. 'I can play any role. There is not a soul outside of these walls who would have known the true state of my relationship with Jayr. We were adorable in public.'

Brom did not like that response. 'I'd rather people see us genuinely happy.'

Cora tilted her head. 'Give me an example of a royal couple in history, in any kingdom, who were genuinely happy.'

'My grandfather and grandmother,' he said without hesitation.

'They married for love, which eliminates them.'

He laughed and moved closer to her. 'Don't dismiss the possibility of happiness just because you're good at the role.'

She waved him off. 'I was groomed for this role since my gender was revealed at birth. I know nothing else. Not all of us can take off into the mountains and figure out who we are away from it all.'

He let the dig at him pass and leaned on one foot. 'I can't tell if you love it or despise it.'

'We all despise it.'

'But not Jayr.'

'Even him.'

They watched as Pup turned in a circle before plonking down onto the sand.

'All right,' Brom said with a resigned sigh. 'We'll do the tour.'

She looked completely taken aback. 'We will?'

He nodded. 'Tell Lief to meet with Pollux before we leave. I want you safe.'

The most beautiful smile spread across Cora's face. She stepped forwards, pushed up onto her toes, and kissed him. He caught her by the waist, extending the moment. Her skin was hot beneath the fabric. He flattened his hands against it. He expected her to pull away, avert her eyes, or turn her back to him. But she relaxed against him. When she broke the kiss first, she did not pull away. She stared into his eyes, her breath mixing with his, before reaching a tentative hand up to his rough cheek.

'I like that you shave your beard,' she said, swallowing.

He had shaved it to his skin for the wedding. His gaze fell to her lips, and he was torn between taking that mouth of hers again and replying to her comment. 'Then I'll keep it that way.' Her hand fell away, and she slid from his grip. He looked around to clear his mind and waited for his blood to resume circulating. 'I'll have the horses prepared.'

Cora nodded and clicked her fingers. Pup leapt to her feet. 'And I shall see if Pandarus wishes to join us.'

They travelled through Dirith and Rodal, where large crowds had gathered to glimpse their new king and see what Cora looked like at his side. The pair was greeted with music, song, and prayer amid curious stares. People tossed fresh flowers in their path, causing Ida to shy away and Brom to suggest another mount. Cora declined the offer, and they continued to Husea, where they would spend the night.

The village was one of the larger ones in the region, so any royal procession usually finished there. Avens threaded on string hung from rooftops, lutes and drums played, women sang, and children performed shows with puppets. The latter was Cora's favourite part, seeing the dolls and monsters born of their imaginations and listening to dramatic retellings of Zoelin folktales. At the end, the children would present their puppets and let her choose one to take home.

This visit was the same as the others, only this time, Brom dropped down on the grass beside her to watch the puppet show. It was a contrast to Jayr, who had always disappeared to take secret meetings with the elders. Brom leaned on his hands with his feet crossed at the ankle. When someone offered him a chair, he politely declined. Cora noticed that he laughed out loud at the same parts she laughed internally about. Never at the intended humour but at the dark turns in the story that made no sense, a stray puppet going rogue, or a mispronounced word by one of the younger performers that changed the meaning entirely.

Afterwards, the children brought their puppets over. Brom took one of the well-made dolls with a beautifully painted face. Cora chose one of the monsters whose lips had been drawn at a strange angle.

'I might have known you would choose that one,' Brom said.

Cora pretended not to understand.

'My father says King Tuyon wants control of our kingdom,' said one of the older girls as she handed over the puppet. 'Are we going to fight him?'

Brom gave her a reassuring smile. 'Only if we have to.'

A worried look crossed her face. 'But you can't die. We waited so long for you.'

Cora took hold of her hand. 'It is a good thing our king is an excellent warrior.'

'Is that why you married him?'

'Mostly.'

The girl beamed back at her before running off.

Droet limped over as the music started up behind them once more. 'Your Majesty,' he said, bowing shakily before Cora. 'Might I have this dance?'

'Oh.' Cora glanced at Brom. 'Are you sure you are up for dancing, Grandor?'

The old man laughed as he offered her a wrinkled hand with swollen knuckles and twisted fingers. 'I'm quite sturdy on my feet.'

Carac dropped down next Brom. 'Grandfather, our queen won't know this one.'

Cora cast a tired glance in his direction. 'I am a very fast learner.' She slipped her hand into Droet's. 'And I would love to learn from a gentleman such as you.'

'It's a Valter tribe dance,' Carac said. 'It's fast.'

'I am sure I will keep up,' Cora replied, smoothing down her dress.

Droet led her out onto the swept dirt where people had already gathered to watch. He stood opposite her, pointing at the skirt of her dress. 'Hitch it up so you don't trip.'

Cora did as instructed.

People began to clap in time with the music. Cora spotted Brom and Carac among them now. Then Sarey pushed through a gap, her eyebrows rising in surprise. Cora was regretting her decision. She should have politely declined and gone in search of wine. Hitching her skirts a little higher, she mirrored Droet's footwork.

'That's it,' Droet called, grinning madly. 'Just mirror me.'

This is not so bad.

'Now we go fast,' Droet shouted, his steps turning to hops.

Her smile faltered. 'What?' The clapping doubled in tempo. She had no choice but to grip his hand tighter and match it or give Carac the satisfaction of seeing her fail. She glanced in his direction, noting his smug expression. Looking back at Droet, she shouted over the noise, 'Do you mean like this?'

Her feet moved at twice the speed, triggering an eruption of cheers. It was actually a fun dance. When Droet circled her, she followed his lead, turning when he turned and smiling when they almost collided. Droet gestured for others to join them as the music picked up tempo once more. Tasia and Carac joined in, but Pandarus seemed happy to watch and drink.

'Now we move in a circle!' Droet said.

She strained to hear him. 'All right.' A hand took her elbow, and she turned to see Brom. He pulled her into position.

'Like this,' he shouted, showing her the next lot of steps. His feet moved one behind and then one in front, finishing with a kick.

'Oh. I see you are an expert.' She was breathless and half laughing.

He watched her feet for a moment. 'You've got it already.'

'I am competitive by nature,' she shouted back over the noise.

The volume of the music and pace of the dance were making it impossible to move with any grace or composure. It was all hops and turns and trying not to trip over her own feet. It did not matter though because people had stopped watching her, caught up in their own enjoyment. The scene was a blur of faces and colour lit up by orange light from the fire. The music was barely audible over the laughter now.

Then the song came to a sudden stop, one that everyone anticipated except for Cora, who ran straight into Brom. He reached out to steady her, breathless and grinning.

'Sorry,' she said, pressing a hand to her thudding chest. 'Never again.'

'You did great.'

She reached both hands up and took hold of his face as the applause continued around them. 'Liar.'

His smile faded before he brought his mouth to hers. The heat of him was instant. It was not a safe, socially acceptable kiss. It was an opened mouth, trying to draw breath from her lungs sort of kiss, the kind that passed through her like a shiver. But instead of freezing up—her standard response to emotion—she found herself leaning into the sensation, her body softening against his hard torso. Only when the laughter began to die around them did Brom release her from it. He pressed his forehead to hers while they both caught their breath. Cora glanced around, relieved to find no one was paying them much notice amid the excitement.

'I like it here,' she said.

'You like the people or the dancing?'

His warm hands were still wrapped around hers, holding them to his chest. 'I like that there are no walls.'

Brom went to speak, but Lief's voice cut through the noise.

'Archer!'

Cora had barely registered the word when Brom pulled her down into a crouch. An arrow whistled overhead, followed by another, then the scream of a nearby woman as she was struck. Panic exploded. Women snatched up their children and ran for cover while the men took up arms, shouting instructions. A beat later, Lief was on the other side of her, a human shield as she was ushered towards one of the huts.

Cora peered around him, searching for Sarey. 'Where's Sarey?' When Brom did not slow, Cora stopped, but he just dragged her along until her feet began moving again. Another arrow passed in front of them.

'I need shields!' Brom shouted.

Guards arrived with shields, closing the gaps around her and blocking her vision.

'Carac! Find my sister and Sarey,' Brom called.

Cora was shoved through the door of a hut before she heard the warrior's reply. Brom drew his sword, and a moment later, Carac burst through the door with Tasia and Sarey. Brom spun around, weapon raised.

'Easy,' Carac said.

Brom lowered his arm and looked his sister over. 'You hurt?'

Tasia shook her head and leaned against the wall, panting. Sarey went straight to Cora, her hands trembling at her sides.

'Who is shooting at us?'

Cora glanced at her husband. 'I do not know.'

Brom turned to Lief, aiming a finger at his face. 'Do not let them out of this hut.'

He went to leave, but Cora grabbed him by the hand. 'Where are you going? You cannot just walk out into a storm of arrows. It is your responsibility as king to stay alive.'

Brom gripped her jaw with his free hand. 'Remember when you told me there's a monster in all of us?'

She nodded, the look in his eyes unsettling her.

'Mine emerges when people point arrows at innocent people, at children, my family—especially my wife. Don't leave this hut.' He turned and disappeared through the door with Carac at his heel.

CHAPTER 19

*B*rom kept one man alive—the one with the most ink. That man was usually the one giving orders, which meant he could give Brom some answers. Except he refused to speak, even when Brom took him apart piece by piece. He was too well trained, too loyal, or likely too afraid of what would happen if he lived through the interrogation. Out of patience, Brom walked over to the Zoelin traitor and cut his throat.

'Hang him on the gate,' he instructed Carac, who had just stepped into the castle's dungeon. 'Let him be a warning to any man who might be having similar ideas.'

They had travelled back to Drake Castle as soon as it was safe enough to move. They were easy prey out in the open, and Brom knew he would not be able to relax until his wife and sister were safely behind walls once more.

Carac looked around at the morbid scene. 'Your wife's looking for you.'

Brom wiped his dagger and sheathed it. 'Is she all right?'

Carac gestured to a guard to help him with the body.

'Think she's wondering the same thing about you. Anyone would think she cared.'

'Where is she?'

Carac pushed a bloodied finger with the toe of his boot. 'I told her to go get some sleep, that you'd find her when you're done here.'

'Good. Be in the throne room at noon. Tell Pollux to be there too.'

'So he can say "I told you so"?'

'Should have listened to the smug bastard.'

Carac's laughter followed Brom out of the narrow doorway and up the uneven steps.

When Brom opened the door to his bedchamber, he froze. It was not the first time he had returned from somewhere to find a woman sleeping in his bed, but it was the first time he had returned to find Cora sleeping in it. She was curled up on top of the quilt with an arm draped over Pup, who was too comfortable to get up and greet him.

Brom leaned against the doorway, eyes moving over his wife.

His *wife*.

She was wearing the same dress from the evening prior, when she had danced and smiled and forgotten she had sworn to be miserable for the rest of time. He liked the way one hand was tucked under her cheek, making her face appear more pouty than usual. She had removed the hair comb, and her hair spilled around her in a beautiful, dark mess. He rarely had the opportunity to look at her for that long without her shooting a warning glance in his direction, so he remained there for some time before fatigue finally got the better of him.

When he went and sat on the bed, Pup rose, slipping out from Cora's embrace and causing her to stir. Heavy lids blinked open to look at him.

'You look as tired as I feel,' he said.

She pushed herself up into a seated position, blinking at him. Her gaze fell to his bloodied hands, causing Brom to look down at his filthy state. He worried it would be confronting for a woman who had never seen war up close.

'I've not had a chance to wash since returning.' He did not mention the hours spent in the dungeon taking a man apart because she crawled across the bed to him, settling close to him. He searched her face. 'What are you doing in here?'

'Waiting for you.'

'You need something?'

She shrugged. 'Maybe I just wanted to meet the monster.'

He liked her relaxed on the bed next to him. 'The monster retreats quickly when you're around.'

She looked down at Pup instead of at him. 'And I suppose I was wondering if you were still angry at me.'

His brow creased. 'I was never angry at you.'

'It is my fault we were attacked. They were coming for me. Pollux even warned you, and I made you go against his advice.'

He wanted to touch her face but thought better of putting his filthy hands on her. 'This doesn't fall on you. I made the decision in the end.'

'To please *me*. So here I am. Let me have it.'

For a moment he just stared at her, trying to figure out what she meant. Then he remembered who she had been married to. 'Cora—'

'I will not be humiliated in public. So if you want to shout and carry on, all I ask is that you do it in the privacy of these chambers.'

His bloodied hand went to her face, and she did not draw back from it as expected. He touched her as gently as he could. 'I don't want to shout and carry on.'

'Every king needs a scapegoat.'

The corners of his mouth lifted. 'I prefer to own my mistakes. How else will I learn?'

She regarded him with suspicion. 'Is this one of those situations where you pretend not to be mad, then make me pay later?'

His hand fell away. 'That sounds exhausting.'

Cora looked around the room. 'Now I feel lost. I thought we would fight and then make up in bed.'

He had no idea whether to laugh or not. 'Is that the usual order of things around here?'

'Mostly.'

There he was feeling sorry for her again. 'Well, I'm too tired to fight with you.'

Her eyes returned to him. 'The men who attacked us, they were Zoelin, were they not?'

'Yes.'

'Our own people are shooting arrows at us. Do you suppose it is because they are loyal to Jayr or because I was disloyal to him?'

That was what he had wanted to find out. 'Perhaps neither. They might be working for King Tuyon.' He noticed that her sleepy expression was gone, replaced with an inquisitive look that held his full attention. 'What's going on in that mind of yours?'

She slid a few inches closer to him on the bed, and every one of his senses heightened.

'You said you are too tired to fight. What about the making up in bed part?'

Any lingering fatigue vanished in that moment. 'Are you sure it's all right to skip the fighting part?'

She reached for one sleeve of her dress and pushed it down her shoulder, never breaking eye contact with him. 'No relationship is perfect.'

He looked down at the exposed shoulder, then at the

other as she slid the gown down until it sat bunched at her waist. It was the first time he had seen her breasts, and now he could not look away. 'If you're serious, I'm going to need to wash.'

She moved closer still, picking up one of his hands and placing it on her ribs. 'I am not afraid of a little blood.'

It was partly disturbing but mostly arousing. She picked up his other hand and placed it on her breast. His mouth found hers, and she opened for him, sending pleasure through his entire body. She climbed into his lap, knees falling on either side of him. He groaned into her mouth as she pushed against him, hips rocking.

'I want to see what you can do when no one is watching.' She breathed the words into his open, hungry mouth, then stood to remove the gown completely.

The fact that she was wearing nothing underneath the dress was not lost on him. He gave Pup a gentle push off the bed and waited for her to trot out of the room before pulling Cora to him once more. His hands slid to the curves of her hips, his grip gentle.

'I will not break,' she said, her fingers moving expertly over the buttons of his vest. She undid his belt while he explored her body like a curious boy. She slid the vest off him, dragging her fingernails down his back as she did so. A shudder ran through him, and he pressed his lips to her bare shoulder.

'I don't know where to begin with you.' Her skin was warm beneath his lips.

She turned his face up to her. 'Do not fret, husband. You can follow my lead.'

She pushed his chest, and he fell back on the bed with glorious force.

CHAPTER 20

'How soon can you get men here?' Brom asked Pandarus.

The leaders and advisors had gathered in the throne room at noon as planned, and Brom was trying very hard not to look like a man who had just done unspeakable things to the king's sister.

'Within the week. You will be declining Tuyon's proposed terms of trade then?'

'I think we should act now, give him less time to plot my end.'

Pandarus exhaled sharply. 'Trust me, Tuyon already has a plan for every possible outcome. I gather you did not hear back from my dear uncle in Galen?'

'A pleasant letter congratulating us on our nuptials.'

Pollux spoke up at that. 'Neutral is the best outcome we can hope for with Galen.'

'If Cora were not your wife, things might be very different,' Pandarus added, his chest expanding as though he were the hero of this story.

Brom watched him a moment. 'Captain Dion would step down before taking up arms against us.'

Pandarus looked away. 'Yes. Such an *honourable* man.'

The sarcasm was not lost on Brom. 'One of the most honourable men I know.'

Pandarus's jaw worked. 'Well, I will return to Syrasan in the morning and start making arrangements.'

'You should take Queen Cora with you,' Pollux said. 'Much safer for her there.'

Brom straightened in his chair. 'You can't just make that decision for her.'

Pollux leaned on the arm of his chair. 'No, so you must. She's already proven she can't make sound decisions on her own when she insisted on a wedding tour.'

'That's on me.'

Pandarus laughed softly. 'That was all her. Manipulation is an art form—one she is very good at.'

Brom wondered if he had indeed been played. Then he thought back to the previous night. She had come to him, prepared to own the mistake. 'I promised Cora a partnership.'

Pandarus waved off the remark. 'So *un*promise her. She will have her usual tantrum and be over it by tomorrow.'

'Do you want to keep a promise or keep her alive?' Pollux asked. 'And send your sister somewhere safe while you're at it.'

Brom looked over at Carac, who had not said a word. 'What do you think?'

Carac drew a breath. 'I think you have trouble saying no to her. Maybe it's best she have some time with her family. You could send your sister to the mountains with my grandfather.'

Brom tapped the arm of his chair and let out a resigned breath. He was not one to be pressured, but Cora's safety was more important than anything else. 'Let me speak with her.'

Pollux laughed at that. 'You can't speak with our queen, you must *tell* her. She won't like it, but it's the only way.'

Pandarus nodded in agreement while Carac continued to stare at the table.

Brom gave a reluctant nod before standing. 'Excuse me.'

Cora had just mounted Ida and was preparing to leave the stables when Brom entered the mounting yard. One look at him and she knew the meeting had not gone well.

'Good afternoon,' she greeted.

He stopped a safe distance from the mare, whose ears immediately went back in warning. 'Afternoon.' He rested his hands on his hips. 'Where did you run off to this morning? I woke up and you were gone.'

She adjusted her grip on the reins. 'I thought you would prefer to sleep alone.'

'Actually, I'd prefer to sleep with my wife.'

She studied him. 'What happened at the meeting that has you looking as though your dog just died?'

He raised his eyes to her. 'I need to talk to you.' He glanced in Lief's direction and was met with the guard's usual hard expression.

'About?'

'I think you should return to Syrasan for a while.'

She stiffened in the saddle, causing Ida to throw her head up. 'What are you talking about?'

Brom stepped closer. 'I think it's the safest place for you right now.'

She sat with that for a moment. 'Is it?'

'Yes.'

'I see. All you big men sat around the table and decided what was best for me.'

He drew a breath. 'Pollux suggested it, and I have to agree.'

She laughed coldly. 'So much for a partnership.'

'You could have died in that village.'

She rolled her eyes. 'And here we go. You know, I actually bought the lines you fed me last night. You would think I would learn.'

'I meant what I said last night. I'm sorry, but I can't have people shooting arrows at you.'

She felt a familiar anger rising inside of her. 'So I must play the role of vulnerable queen so you can feel like the man in charge.'

Brom crossed his arms. 'They warned me you wouldn't take it well.'

She glared down at him. 'I thought I married a man who could think for himself. Imagine my disappointment.' Cora swung her horse around and rode away from him, gesturing for Lief to follow.

'Cora!' Brom walked after her.

'You have your army now. Leave me alone.'

He jogged to catch up. 'Don't twist this to suit your own narrative.'

'Careful. Ida is prone to kicking.'

He did not move away. 'Where are you going? It's not safe to leave the castle grounds.'

She pulled up her horse and turned in the saddle to look at him properly. 'You said you would never lock me in here.'

'That was before my own people started shooting at you.'

'You made plans behind my back.' She faced forwards and pushed her mare into a trot, forcing Brom to run after her again.

'To protect you.'

'I do not need your protection!'

He laughed at that. 'If you think your average sword skills acquired over a couple of days will suffice, then you're more naïve than I thought.'

If she had a whip, she would have used it on him. 'I have a bodyguard.' She gestured to Lief, who rode on the other side of her, scowling at the king.

'It won't be enough. Cora, stop your horse.'

She did not even slow down.

Brom cursed under his breath and moved to get in front of Ida. The mare's front legs lifted off the ground, and he reached out to steady her. 'Easy.'

Cora grabbed a handful of mane to ensure she stayed on. 'What part of "she does not like men" do you not understand?'

Brom took a step back, hands raised. 'I'm sorry.'

She was breathing hard now. It was not only that he was sending her away, it was that he was sending her away after she had given herself freely to him that morning. 'Is this about earlier?'

His eyebrows came together. 'What?'

'Were you disappointed? Was I too dominant? Perhaps you prefer your women nice and passive in bed, is that it?'

He closed his eyes and shook his head. 'This has nothing to do with this morning. You know very well that neither of us was disappointed.' He drew a slow breath. 'Now I need you to go inside and pack your things, because you're leaving in the morning.'

Cora looked past him to the gate and stilled. Her eyes narrowed on what appeared to be a corpse hanging from the gate twenty yards in front of them. The ground was stained red beneath it. 'What is that?' she asked, the question coming out on a breath.

Brom turned to look. 'It's… He's one of the traitors.'

Cora slid from her horse and walked straight past Brom towards the gate.

'Where are you going?' he called after her.

She did not reply, so he followed. Lief dismounted too, but Brom stopped him in his tracks with a glance. Cora stood a few feet from the gate, her hands limp at her sides as she stared up at the man. There were fingers missing, horrendous cuts along his leg, one ear hacked off. She forced herself to keep looking.

Brom caught up with her, taking hold of her elbow. 'Don't look at it.'

She tore her arm free and spun to face him. 'You did that to him?'

'I was extracting information.' His tone was unapologetic.

She took a small step back. 'So that is where you were last night. It is his blood that touched every intimate part of me.'

He swallowed. 'Yes.'

'You like to torture people?'

He closed his eyes. 'No.'

'You cut off his fingers while he was alive?'

Brom let out a breath, his expression pleading for her to understand. 'I was extracting information.'

'And did it work?'

He looked down at the ground, rubbing his forehead. 'He wouldn't talk.'

She nodded. 'That is some monster you have there,' she said, looking back at the corpse. 'And now you display your handiwork like a war prize.'

'It's not like that. It's a warning to others. I didn't know it would upset you.'

'Is that why you did not mention it last night? Feeding me vague responses instead of admitting the blood on your hands was not from fighting fair on a battlefield, as you once claimed was your preferred method of kill, but from the dirty work you carry out in the dungeon of our home.'

'I'll take it down.'

'No. Do not do that. You are right. It is the *perfect* warning to others.' She brought her hand to her lips, which were numb. 'It is not the sight that is upsetting, it is the insight to the man I married. The difference between you and Jayr is that Jayr owned his darkness. He never pretended to be anything else.'

She turned away from him. 'I will go to Syrasan. You are right. It is *much* safer there.'

'Cora—'

'Stay away from me.'

She did not look back.

CHAPTER 21

*C*ora knew it was a bad idea to go to dinner, because she was angry and disappointed, and that was a dangerous combination for a woman like her. She had let herself believe he was different, lowered her walls and let him in despite knowing better. Of course he would cut off the fingers of men. Of course he would lock her up and send her away on a whim. He was Jayr's brother, his blood—just another king with something to prove.

Now she was seated at the high table, her mind so thick with wine she knew she would never make it back to her quarters unassisted. But still she drank, swatting Sarey's hand away whenever her lady made a move for her cup.

'Touch my drink again and I will have Lief cut off your hand. Am I understood?' She did not mean it. She never meant anything she said in that state.

Brom looked over every time she lifted her cup to her mouth, but he did not comment. Leaning forwards, she glanced at Carac, who was seated on the other side of Brom, picking through a fish with his fork. He stopped eating when he noticed her.

'You need something, Your Majesty?'

Cora went to lean her elbow on the table, but it slipped off the edge. Brom moved to steady her, but she cast a look so fierce in his direction that he retracted his hand. 'Dance with me, Carac.'

He frowned. 'Why?'

'Because it is my last night at Drake Castle, and I want to enjoy myself.'

Carac kept a hold of his fork. 'I'm eating. Dance with your husband.'

She slumped back in her chair. 'Our fierce leader must get used to dancing with other women in my absence.'

Brom laid his fork on his plate and turned to her. 'Is that what you think I'll be doing while you're gone? Dancing?'

Cora made a point of drinking before replying. She set the cup back down on the table harder than she intended. 'I have no idea what you will be doing.'

The king continued to stare at her. 'In case you've forgotten, we're readying for war.'

She brought her face close to his. 'How could I forget when corpses hang like festive decorations around our home?' She withdrew, waiting for that flicker of anger, the one that meant she had pushed him too far. The one that meant she would pay for that comment later.

Instead, she was met with resignation.

'I had the body taken down.'

Or perhaps guilt. That was something new.

'I hope you did not do that on my account. I will be gone in the morning. Then you can hang them inside the castle if you like.' She gestured to a nearby servant to fill her cup. Sarey cleared her throat behind her, but Cora ignored the warning.

'That's not even what you're angry about,' Brom said.

'Do not pretend to know me.'

'You do know it doesn't bother me if you make a fool of yourself and feel like shit tomorrow.'

She let out a rehearsed laugh. 'Given our marriage is for appearances, you really *should* care about appearances.'

He regarded her for a moment. 'So this is what you do? You work your way up to angry and drunk until you get the desired reaction?'

Cora met his gaze as steadily as she could manage in her state. 'Oh, husband. I was angry and drunk before I even left my quarters.' She lifted her cup again, then rose from her chair, holding the table for a moment as the room spun. 'Now if you will excuse me, I am going to find someone else to dance with since Carac is *so* attached to his meal.'

Brom leaned back in his chair, making no attempt to stop her. 'I see the game, though I may need some guidance since it's my first time playing. Tell me, is this the part where I'm supposed to feel jealous? I hope my brother wasn't *that* easy.'

She blinked. 'He was that easy.' She went to step back from the table and he caught her by the wrist. For a second, she felt triumphant.

'I thought people were wrong about you,' he said. 'Imagine my disappointment.'

Her shoulders fell a few inches, her arm going limp as he continued to hold her. The burn in her eyes caught her off guard. She stepped back from him, and he immediately released her arm.

It was one of those moments where she could either choose to stop behaving in that manner or double down on her efforts. She knew the right thing to do was to leave the feast, go back to her room, and sleep off the wine. But years of conditioning, bad choices, anger, hurt, and self-loathing made her reach for her cup and empty it once more. She tossed it onto the table, and they all watched it roll to a stop.

'Sorry, your naivety had me lost for words for a moment.'

She placed a hand on his shoulder. 'In future, you should probably listen to your friends.' She glanced once at Carac before making her way to the dance floor.

When Cora peeled her eyes open, she was certain someone had poured sand into them as she slept. It took a moment for her vision to clear, and then panic rose inside of her as the hall came into focus. She pushed herself up off the floor, wincing as her head throbbed unbearably. Once it eased, she looked around, her gaze landing on a stern-faced Brom sitting in a chair with his arms crossed. Grey light filtered into the room, washing him in an eerie glow.

'Good morning.' His tone matched his expression.

'Where is Sarey?' Cora's mouth felt like it was stuffed with cotton.

'Asleep.'

She brought a hand to her throbbing head. 'Asleep where?'

Brom leaned forwards, elbows resting on his knees. 'In the comfort of her bed, I imagine.'

There was absolutely no way Sarey would leave her on the ground and trudge off to bed. 'Where is Lief?' She looked around, expecting to find him standing against one of the walls, but he was not there.

'I sent him to bed also. He wasn't particularly happy about it, but I assured them both I would take care of you.'

She looked down at the hard wood beneath her. 'You left me on the floor?'

'You left yourself on the floor. You drank until you fell down.'

She pushed herself up to a stand, taking it slow. 'And at what point exactly did you take care of me?'

'I stayed awake to make sure you didn't choke on your own vomit.'

She tilted her head. 'I never vomit. Iron heart, iron stomach.'

He exhaled through his nose. 'Lucky you. You got the matching set.'

She lifted a hand, still trying to comprehend what had happened. 'What sort of man just leaves his wife on the floor?'

His cold eyes never left hers. 'If you choose to drink like that, to *behave* like that, I won't stop you. I also won't coddle you when you make bad choices, because that's how we learn. Sometimes we need to wake up on the floor to recognise there's a problem.'

'I don't have a problem. I have an escape.'

He rose from his chair, dragging a hand down his face. He looked exhausted, which actually made her feel guilty. Crazy, given he had left her on the floor in order to prove a point.

'I don't have the time or headspace to argue with you.'

Shame pelted her stomach. An apology sat on the end of her tongue, but she was too proud to release it. Instead, she said, 'If you are done lecturing me, I would like to go freshen up before my journey.'

They stared at one another for the longest time. Eventually, he waved a hand in her direction.

'Go.'

Her throat closed as he turned away. All that disappointment in his eyes was crushing her. 'Unless you have changed your mind.' She tried to keep the hope out of her voice.

'I haven't.'

'Because you want me *safe*.'

He shook his head. 'Right now, I just want you out of the way.' He walked off, his shoulders rounded in defeat.

She opened her mouth, closed it. Her hands curled into fists at her sides. 'Fine. I am sorry.'

He stopped but did not turn around.

She was a novice when it came to apologising. It took her a moment to work up the courage to continue. 'Is that what you want to hear?'

He resumed walking, leaving her alone in the large hall with her stomach churning and heart thudding in her throat.

CHAPTER 22

'I'll come to Archdale Castle and collect you when this is over,' Brom said.

He was standing so close to Ida he was almost touching the mare. Her ears were forwards for once, which surprised Cora. She gathered the reins and looked down at him. 'All right.' The fight had left her.

His expression softened. 'Listen, about this morning…'

'You do not have to say anything.' Cora felt embarrassed by the whole thing. Parts of the evening prior were slowly coming back to her. The drink. The endless flirting. 'We agreed to honesty. That is what you gave me.'

He shifted his weight. 'I probably would've preferred a little less honesty from you last night.'

How he had the energy for jokes she had no idea. 'I barely remember what I said, but I am confident it was mean.'

They watched as Sarey and Lief mounted their horses, welcoming the distraction.

'I would've preferred you remain at Drake Castle,' Brom said, 'but as much as I hate to admit it, the safest place for you right now is with your family.' He patted Ida's neck before stepping back. 'My men will see you safely to the border. Pandarus will take it from there.'

She glanced in the direction of her brother. 'You mean Lief will take it from there. I assure you Pandarus's sword is purely decorative.'

Brom smiled at the ground, and Cora felt some relief, quickly followed by more guilt. When was she going to grow up?

Pollux approached on foot, looking between them as he came to a stop. 'You need to get moving if you want to make it to the river before nightfall, Your Majesty.'

Brom looked up at Cora. 'Be safe and smart.'

Cora bowed her head. 'And you, husband.' She clicked her fingers, and Pup followed after her.

As the party exited the gate, Cora saw that not only had the corpse been removed but the ground beneath it covered with sand. She turned in the saddle and found Brom watching her from atop the steps, where she normally stood. He raised a hand, and her own went up in response.

'And just like that, all is forgiven,' Sarey said beside her.

Cora faced forwards. 'This is simply a truce.'

'His Majesty holds no grudges.'

Cora adjusted one of her gloves. 'I hold enough grudges for everyone.'

'Well, it might be time to stop.'

The queen did not disagree. Sarey was usually right, though Cora made a point of never telling her so. When she returned to Drake Castle, she would have to make more of an effort. It was not enough to please Brom in the bedchamber—because he was not Jayr.

The heavy hinges groaned behind them as the gates closed.

'Sun has been up for a few hours,' Pandarus said, slowing to ride beside her. 'We will need to pick up our pace for a while.'

Cora glanced at him. 'Fine with me.'

The king pushed his horse into a canter, and the rest of the party followed.

They moved at that pace before slowing to a walk when the horses tired, reaching the river just before sundown.

'We shall spend the night in Veanor,' Pandarus said. They had dismounted to let the horses drink from the river.

Cora was looking across the water, where shadows had settled in. It was unusually cold despite the fact that no snow had fallen in the area for a month. She looked back in the other direction, north, where the Zoelin guards had left them a short while ago. She felt uneasy, exposed. 'We should keep moving.'

'We will stay at Lord Yuri's manor,' Pandarus said, tugging his gloves back on.

It took all of Cora's effort not to groan aloud. 'Must we? Lady Hali irritates me to no end with her incessant talking.'

Pandarus only smiled. 'She is nervous around you. Understandable given how poorly you treat her.'

'I do not treat her poorly. I ignore her completely.' She bent to pet Pup, who was panting at her feet. 'And how is it you manage to be so casual in her presence?'

'Water under the bridge, so to speak.'

'I am sure Lord Yuri does not share your sentiment. No man can dismiss the fact that another once enjoyed his wife.'

Pandarus's horse was returned to him, and he took the reins and mounted. 'We do not exactly discuss it around the dinner table. We eat, sleep, and leave at first light.'

'Your Majesty,' Lief said, offering Ida's reins to her. He was one of the few men who could handle the mare without any trouble.

She took the reins from him. 'Thank you.' Pup leapt to her feet, and the panting ceased as something caught her interest in the trees. Cora looked in that direction. 'What is it, girl? A hare?'

Hooves clicked on the bridge behind them as Pandarus crossed with his guards. Pup began to whine and back away, her head lowered and tail tucked between her legs. The reaction made Lief look in that direction also.

Cora glanced over at Sarey, who was waiting at the mouth of the bridge for her. 'You go ahead—'

She had barely gotten the words out when a searing pain exploded in her left shoulder. The scream that erupted from her made everyone turn and look and prompted Lief to burst into action.

'Protect the queen!' he roared, shielding her with his body.

Cora's eyes went to her shoulder, where she saw an arrow protruding above her collarbone. A cold sensation filled her as she realised she had been shot.

Men shouted, her brother's voice among them. Sarey slid from the saddle but was quickly snatched up by one of the guards and dragged off in the other direction. Lief lifted Cora off the ground and began running towards the bridge. Cora could see Pandarus on the other side, surrounded by a wall of guards. Sarey joined him a moment later. As Lief's boots pounded on the bridge, she remembered her horse.

'Ida!' she shouted, foolishly hoping the mare would follow after them. She strained her head to look and watched in horror as an arrow pierced her rump. 'No!'

Lief drew her closer as more arrows flew from the trees, hissing past them at an impossible speed.

'They hit Ida.'

'I'll go back for her,' Lief said.

Then he stopped. Why had he stopped? Cora looked up at

173

his face and saw it did not look right; his eyes were too wide, his mouth open at a strange angle.

'Take the queen,' he shouted, moving slower this time.

That was when Cora saw the fletching of an arrow protruding from his back. He had been hit. Guards came at a run, but two more arrows struck Lief's back before they reached him. Still, he kept hold of her. Another arrow, then another, then one through the back of the neck. His eyes opened wider still. He tried to draw breath but failed. He began to lean, tip, until he hit the parapet.

'No,' Cora whispered, still tucked in his arms.

Guards continued towards them, but they were too late. Lief flipped over the capstones before Cora could wriggle free. Then they were falling, plummeting towards the angry water below.

'Cora!' Sarey screamed, sounding far away.

Their bodies slammed into the water, turning Cora's mind to pulp. The water was flowing so fast she could barely tell which way was up. Lief was no longer holding her but twisting around her as the water rolled them. She instinctively reached for him with her good arm, kicking her feet to close the gap between them. She got lucky and grabbed hold of the pocket of his trousers, but the water just carried them along, and she wondered how long she could go without drawing breath. She kicked her legs harder, dragging him towards what she hoped was the water's surface. Finally, she emerged with a greedy gasp. Behind her she could hear shouting, but then the water swallowed her once more.

Cora's feet smashed into the rocky bottom, and she was rolled again. She tried to keep hold of Lief, but the water snatched him from her grip. The river finally calmed as it widened, and she emerged once more, gasping and coughing.

'Lief!'

She turned in circles, searching. Where was he? She found him lodged face down on the muddy bank of the river. She swam towards him, thankful that she had insisted on learning how to swim alongside her brothers when they were young. She clawed at whatever she could get a hold of: mud, rock, a strange tree root poking up from below. Her hand was so cold she struggled to keep hold of anything, and the injured arm was useless. Finally, she pulled herself up onto the bank a few yards past Lief. She sucked in greedy breaths as she waded through the shallows towards him, every inhale sending a stabbing pain through her chest like nothing she had experienced before. She stumbled and got up again.

When she reached Lief, she used whatever energy she had left to turn him onto his back. Pain shot through her injured shoulder, but she fell silent when she saw Lief's face. He was barely recognisable. His skin was a strange colour, his eyes open but not looking at her. She staggered back from him, but the moment he began drifting, she went after him, dragging him up the riverbank until she could move him no farther. Collapsing in the shallow water, she held him around the neck as her teeth chattered. The river could not have him. She could not live with the thought of him swollen and drifting, only to be eaten by fish and eels.

Looking upstream, she tried to still her shivering body so she could hear. Her gaze went across the river, where she expected men to emerge from the trees with arrows pointed at her. She did not want to die that way, as easy prey.

A dog whined behind her, and she turned her head to look. It was not a dog but Pup, now running towards her.

'Here! I am down here!' she shouted, her voice barely carrying. Once she heard the horses, she turned back to Lief and pressed her forehead to his.

Cora stared at the yellow wall of the bedchamber, the same one she had stared at for the previous two days. It was *such* a Hali colour—all sunny and optimistic.

'She hasn't said a word since arriving here.'

Hali's voice drifted in through the open door. She had been buzzing around the room the entire time, a persistent fly. Cora wondered who she was talking at now.

'How's the shoulder?'

She could have sworn that was Brom's voice, but that was not possible.

Her gaze drifted from the wall to the doorway, and sure enough, she glimpsed Brom's tall, familiar frame through the gap. He looked in her direction at the same time, as though sensing her eyes on him, and then he was moving towards her.

Cora pushed herself up with her good arm, but her shoulder throbbed anyway. All the emotion she had pushed down since it happened seemed to bubble to the surface in that moment. She swallowed hard to stop from crying.

'I thought you were asleep,' he said as he sat carefully on the edge of the bed.

She looked down at the bandaged shoulder, then at her nightdress. She knew she was a mess, but she could barely think past Lief's body being dragged from the freezing water. They had brought him with them to the manor to be burned, as he would have wanted.

'What are you doing here?' Her voice was hoarse.

He brought a hand to her face. 'I'm so sorry.'

'Why? You did not do it—I hope.' The joke fell flat.

'I heard about Lief.'

Her throat burned, so she did not say anything. She was determined not to cry.

Brom brushed hair back from her face. 'It's all right to grieve him.' His gaze fell to her bandaged shoulder and arm. 'Are you in pain?'

Cora looked up, reading his expression. Anyone would have thought he was the one in agony. 'It is barely a scratch,' she lied.

He searched her eyes. 'Tell me what you need.'

She looked back at the yellow wall, thinking of all the things she needed in that moment but struggling to verbalise them. 'The physician insisted Pup be locked away.'

'I'll find her. What else?'

Cora's throat thickened again as she thought about her next request. 'The men… the archers… they shot Ida. I do not know where she is or if she is alive. Lief was going to go back for her.' She stared harder at the wall.

'I'll send men to look for her.'

Cora's gaze returned to him. 'She will run from them.'

They stared at one another for the longest moment. 'I don't even know what to say.'

'You should not have come. What if those men had attacked you?'

He ran a hand over his shaved head. 'Of course I had to come. I sent you away for your safety, and now look at you. You're lucky to be alive.'

She pulled her knees up, hugging them through the blanket. 'Someone knew to expect us. They knew the perfect time to attack.'

Brom exhaled. 'They waited for my men to leave.'

She rested her chin on her knees, peering up at him. 'You are going to need to be careful who you trust, and those you do trust need to be careful who *they* trust.' She paused, thinking. 'Did your sister make it safely to the mountains?'

'Yes.' He was silent a moment. 'You'll need a new body-guard. Perhaps I'll send Carac.'

'He's your best warrior, and he hates me.'

'He doesn't hate you.'

Cora gave him a weak smile. 'Liar.'

'He just doesn't know you yet.' He fell silent for a moment. 'I can't leave you unprotected. I'll speak with your brother, organise a Syrasan guard for now.'

Cora pulled the blanket up, unable to shake the cold that had gripped her since she hit that icy water.

Brom reached out, swallowing her freezing hand in his warm one. 'You're so cold.' He moved onto the bed properly. 'Lie down.'

'Why?'

He lay down and gently pulled her to him, drawing her close so that she fit in the nooks of his body, creating a cocoon of warmth. His arms seemed to burn through the blanket and fabric covering her. She began to shiver. She willed herself to stop, but it was no use. The warmth of her husband was thawing all of the frozen parts. The sting of tears brought her hand to her mouth. She held her breath, waiting for the sensation to pass, but it was unrelenting.

'You're allowed to feel,' Brom whispered. 'If you hold it in, it'll eat you up eventually.'

She did not deserve this man—of that she was sure. 'Lief was family.' The words caught in her throat.

Brom stroked her hair with his fingers. 'What does family mean to you?'

'It means he saw me at my worst, time and time again, and yet remained loyal to the very end. He would have killed his own king if I had asked him to.' She drew a breath. 'Lief witnessed every ugly part of me, my life, my marriage. And he stayed despite it.'

'I could be your family if you let me,' Brom murmured into her hair.

Cora's eyes sank shut. Her body stilled against his, the warmth finally reaching her bones. 'You will grow to despise me eventually.' She twitched with sleep.

'Why can't I grow to love you?'

That was the last thing she heard before sleep took her.

CHAPTER 23

When Cora woke, she found Pup asleep beside her. Her body ached, and her eyelids felt heavy. She stretched, winced, and then sat up.

'Sarey?' She barely recognised her own voice.

A few moments later, the bedchamber door opened. 'Awake at last,' her lady said, going to the window and pulling open the drapes.

Cora blinked against the harsh light. 'How long did I sleep?'

'Nineteen hours.'

Cora thought she was joking, but her expression suggested otherwise. '*Nineteen hours*? Why on earth did you not wake me?'

Sarey returned to the bed carrying a gown. 'King's orders. He said no one was to disturb you.'

Cora looked down at the section of bed where he had been. 'How long did he stay?'

'He left at first light.'

'He stayed all night?'

Sarey met her gaze. 'You sound surprised.'

'Only because he has far more important things he should be doing.'

Sarey's hands went to her hips. 'His wife, Zoelin's queen, was *shot*. What's more important than that?'

'A minor injury.'

Sarey cast a sceptical look in her direction. 'How are you feeling?'

'Fine.' The throbbing had ceased, so that was something.

'Fine, she says,' Sarey repeated with a shake of her head. 'Are you hungry?'

Cora's stomach turned at the thought of food. 'Just thirsty. Could you have some wine brought up?'

Sarey dropped the dress on the bed. 'What about some broth?'

Cora tentatively swung her legs over the edge of the bed. 'Fine. You can bring it with the wine.'

Sarey made a disapproving face. 'I'll let your mother know you're awake and fetch the physician.'

The queen froze. 'My *mother* is here?'

As if on cue, Eldoris burst through the door, pausing when she caught sight of Cora. 'Awake at last—and looking much improved.'

Cora fought the urge to lie back down and cover her head with the blanket. 'Mother. When did you arrive?' She looked accusingly at Sarey.

'I came as soon as I heard.' Eldoris turned to Sarey. 'Have some broth sent up.'

'With the jar of wine,' Cora added.

Eldoris walked over to the bed with a disapproving look. 'You must take care of yourself as you heal.'

'It is for pain relief.'

'I was just with your physician, and he is under the impression you are much improved.'

'Oh, the shoulder is improved. The wine is for a different pain.'

Sarey cleared her throat before leaving them.

Eldoris tutted. 'Let us get you dressed. Tyron is downstairs with Lord Leksi. They wanted to see you before joining up with their men at the border.'

'Lord Leksi is here? He does not care about my health. He has no doubt come to poke fun at me.'

'Everyone has been very worried about you. Brom asked Tyron to assign a new guard since your other one failed to protect you.'

Lief's swollen face flashed in Cora's mind, and she pressed her leg to the bed for balance. 'He did not *fail*, Mother. He lost his life protecting me.'

Eldoris had the decency to look apologetic. 'Sorry. I know you were fond of him.'

Cora began slowly dressing. 'Has Brom returned to Zoelin?'

'I believe so. He was rather vague. He no doubt has a lot on his mind.'

'No doubt.'

Once dressed, Cora made her way downstairs, where she found Tyron, Leksi, and the kingdom's most incompetent squire, Charis, waiting for her.

'How are you feeling?' Tyron asked, looking down at her shoulder after greeting her.

'Fine.' Her standard answer.

Sarey arrived alongside a servant carrying a tray of food. Cora snatched up the wine, and Leksi helped himself to the apple. He bit into it noisily, then stopped chewing when he noticed everyone watching him.

'Sorry,' he said, swallowing his mouthful. He offered her the apple. 'Did you want some?'

Cora stared at the mauled fruit. 'No, thank you. Did you stop by for a snack, Lord Leksi?'

'No, no.' He took another bite. 'I come bearing gifts.'

'I am fairly certain that whatever it is, I do not want it.'

Leksi chuckled. 'You're going to want this one. It's a new bodyguard, as per your husband's request.'

Cora looked around. 'Do I get to meet him, or does he only appear when there is danger?'

Leksi waved a finger at her. 'I see the river didn't wash away that famous sense of humour.' He stepped up to Charis and clapped him on the back. 'I present Sir Charis.'

Cora's bland expression did not change. She glanced at Tyron to gauge his reaction. He was not laughing. 'Please tell me you are joking.' The boy had shot up a few feet in height since she had last seen him, gained a little muscle, and grown some facial hair, but he still looked like he might trip over his feet if required to run. 'They made you a *knight*?'

Charis's chest expanded. 'Yes, Your Majesty. Just last week.'

'*Last week?*'

Leksi took another bite out of his apple and chewed noisily. 'Tyron mentioned you needed someone trustworthy, someone willing to lay down his life for you.'

'Did he mention competent?'

Leksi feigned offence. 'I trained him myself.'

'He is barely of age'

'He's up to the job. Watch this.' Leksi turned to Charis. 'Catch.' He threw the apple at the knight, hard, hitting him in the face. 'For the love of God...'

'Sorry, my lord,' Charis said, hand going over his nose. 'I wasn't expecting you to throw fruit at me.'

Leksi pinched the bridge of his nose before turning back to Cora. 'His reflexes are usually razor sharp.'

Tyron smiled at the ground. 'Leksi will be coming to

Zoelin with me. Oddly, he doesn't think Charis is ready to fight Asigow warriors.'

Cora's gaze drifted back to the young soldier who was still holding his nose. 'I am inclined to agree with him.' She looked at Leksi. 'So you want to leave him here to keep him out of trouble, have him feel like he is doing something important?'

Leksi cleared his throat and pressed his lips together. 'I see your observational skills are as sharp as ever, Your Majesty.'

They all watched as Charis picked up the apple, brushed off the dirt, and held it out to Leksi.

'Are you kidding me right now?' Leksi said.

The young knight offered it to Pup instead. The wolf took it and lay down at his feet to eat.

'Fine,' Cora said. 'He can stay, but only because Pup likes him—and I prefer the company of children.'

Charis opened his mouth to say something, then closed it again.

'Stamitos is on his way,' Tyron said. 'He boarded a ship at Newford Harbour yesterday. He will stay with you until you are well enough to travel to Archdale.'

'Wonderful. A hopeless knight and my brother with no sword hand.'

'Be kind,' Tyron said, stepping forwards to kiss her cheek once more. 'We have to go.' He looked at Charis. 'Guard her with your life.'

'Yes, my lord.'

Leksi leaned in and whispered, 'If anything happens to her on your watch, I will hang you from the closest tree. Understand?'

Charis swallowed and nodded. 'Yes, my lord.'

'Good.' Leksi gave him a playful punch on the arm, quite

hard, then turned to bow before Cora. 'I wish you a speedy recovery, Your Majesty.'

Cora waited for him to rise. 'Keep my brother alive.'

He nodded. 'I always do.'

Cora was seated in the library with her mother, arguing about how many cups of wine were acceptable before noon, when Hali knocked tentatively on the doorframe.

'Pardon the interruption, Your Majesties, but I've just been informed that Prince Stamitos is here. I thought you might wish to greet him.'

Eldoris was out of her seat before the queen had a chance to reply. Cora rose slowly, ensuring her legs were steady before attempting to walk. It was possible she had overindulged, but how else did one keep their emotions nice and numb after trauma?

Pup leapt up to follow her out.

'I must say, I'm quite surprised that the king gave you a mauled animal for your wedding gift,' Hali said as the queen passed her in the doorway. 'Does no one give jewellery anymore?'

Cora glanced at her tiredly. 'I have enough jewellery.'

Outside, Stamitos had just climbed the steps and was making his way to Eldoris, who stood with her arms outstretched. He was the same charming boy Cora remembered from her youth. She had always felt undeserving of his adoration.

She hung back so her mother could have her moment. Cora knew how much it meant to see him now that he lived in Galen. Their embrace was a sweet sight, with Eldoris closing her eyes and breathing in the scent of her youngest son. He still hugged her like he did when he was a child, without restraint. It was an open expression of love without any thought to who was witnessing it. Cora felt a twinge of envy.

'I swear you get younger every time I see you,' Stamitos said, despite the new patches of grey that streaked their mother's hair.

Eldoris laughed and stepped back from him. 'It is nice to see you looking so well.'

Stamitos looked past her to Cora, and a grin spread across his face. She could always manage a smile for him. He closed the distance between them and took both her hands in his before kissing her cheek. 'There she is. Our war veteran. I was disappointed to hear you still have both arms. I was hoping we might match.' He raised his stump with a grin.

'Well, we all know I am much tougher than you.'

He laughed at that, but then his expression turned serious. 'Sorry to hear about your guard. Quiet man, but I liked him.'

'Thank you.' They had burned his body early that morning, far from the house so they would not have to smell him for days. 'You really did not have to come.'

'Nonsense. It will be just like old times. We can get drunk and play cards until the early hours of the morning, then sleep all day.'

Eldoris wandered over. 'She does not need encouragement. Perhaps you could engage in sensible activities during daylight, get adequate sleep, and use evenings for reading and self-improvement.'

Stamitos leaned closer to Cora. 'Who invited her?'

'I heard that,' Eldoris said, suppressing a smile.

Stamitos hooked an arm around his mother. 'You know I am just playing. You are more than welcome to get drunk with us.'

Cora had stopped listening, the sound of horses drawing her attention to the road. 'Are we expecting more visitors?'

Stamitos looked to the road and narrowed his eyes on the approaching group. 'Zoelin visitors.'

Cora walked in that direction, stopping when she recognised Brom.

'Oh,' Eldoris said. 'Is that the king?'

Cora's breath hitched when she spotted Ida trotting along behind him, and then her feet were moving again, flying in fact. She broke into a run at the bottom of the steps, her throat catching when the mare whinnied in recognition.

The group came to a stop, and Brom dismounted. 'Easy,' he said when she flung her arms around the horse. 'You're injured, remember?'

Cora pressed her face into the mare's neck, breathing hard. She tried to keep it together in front of the king's men. When she was sure she would not cry, she turned to look up at her husband. 'Where was she?'

'In the woods. One of the perks of spending so many years in the mountains is improved tracking skills.' He gestured to the arrow wound on her rump. 'I've cleaned it up as best I can, but you may want to have someone take a proper look at it.'

Cora nodded and swallowed, tempted to wrap her arms around him also. 'Thank you.'

He winked at her. 'Your pain is my pain, remember? That's what the elder said.' He held the rope out to her.

When she took it, her fingers brushed his, and she experienced that lightness in her chest, the one she used to feel in her youth whenever Leksi used to ask her to dance. Of course, she now knew that had only been a young girl's infatuation. This was something else.

'I should go,' he said. 'There are people waiting for me.'

Her gaze snapped up to his. 'Why not rest a while? At least let me make you something to eat.'

His eyes glistened. 'Do you know how to prepare food?'

She had no idea why she had offered that. An unusual desire to give something back. 'I can cook.' A small lie.

He laughed, and her entire body warmed at the sound. She always felt a strange pride when she was the cause of it.

'You can cook for me once we're back at Drake Castle,' he said, taking hold of her face and kissing her with such familiarity, anyone would have thought they had been married for years instead of mere days.

She pressed a hand to his chest, feeling the gentle thud of his heart beneath her palm. 'Be careful. Whatever plans you are making, King Tuyon is likely two steps ahead of you.'

His expression softened. 'I'll be careful.'

'You can trust Tyron. Lord Leksi is arrogant, self-absorbed, and generally exhausting, but he is an excellent fighter and as trustworthy as my brother.'

He nodded. 'Good to know.' His lips flattened into a thin line. 'I'm sorry about everything that happened at the river. I feel partly responsible.'

That was the moment she realised she was in a very different marriage to the one prior. She did not feel triumphant and had no interest in telling him "I told you so". Those were the small victories she had lived for once. 'Blaming you would be convenient, but it is not your fault.'

'This is new territory for me. I knew there'd be some who resented the change, but I never imagined people would turn against me like this.'

'Technically they are turning against me. I do not see anyone shooting arrows at you.'

'It's not personal. You're just a means to my end.'

Her mouth stretched into a smile. 'Well, that makes me feel a lot better.'

He drew a breath and brushed his thumb over her chin. 'I should go.'

She really wished she had a reason to make him stay. 'I think I will remain here at the manor if it is all the same to you.' When he gave her a quizzical look, she said, 'You know I am not one for walls. Plus, only my family knows I am here, so it is probably safer than Archdale right now.'

He thought for a moment, then nodded. 'All right.' He kissed her on the forehead before mounting his horse. 'I'll come for you when it's safe.'

She reached up to stroke Ida's head, only managing a nod.

'If anything should happen to me over the coming weeks, you'll need to remain here in Syrasan with your family. Understand?'

She looked up at him. 'Fine, but I would prefer if nothing happened to you over the coming weeks. I would quite like to see you again.'

His eyes smiled at her. 'I'd quite like to see you again also.' He winked. 'Please behave.'

CHAPTER 24

$\mathcal{A}$ nervous energy possessed Cora over the next few days. Waiting for news from Zoelin was an odd form of torture. It was not a question of whether there would be a war but when and how severe the fallout. Waiting usually drove her to drink, but Stamitos was a healthy distraction. He would accompany her on long rides in the morning and put on sparring displays in the afternoon, partnering with Charis, and occasionally Lord Yuri.

'I am getting too old for this,' a laughing Yuri said one afternoon, dropping his sword on the ground.

The man was painfully decent, and Cora was forced to admit that he and Hali were actually well suited. She liked to talk, and he liked to listen. She liked to cook, and he liked to pretend it was the best thing to ever pass his lips. He liked to read, and she liked to listen to him read aloud. Cora had never seen her pick up a book in the whole time she was there.

After declaring himself "spent", Lord Yuri returned to the house to wash.

Cora stared down at the blunt weapons lying on the ground. Her fingers itched to hold a sword, to feel that burn in her chest and ache in her muscles. But no one at the manor knew of her secret pastime.

They were eating breakfast the following morning when Cora placed her napkin down and looked at Stamitos. 'The physician seems to think I am ready for light physical activity.'

Stamitos glanced at his mother before placing his own napkin on his plate. 'You are already riding horses and taking long walks. What else did you have in mind?'

It was just the three of them around the table, as Sarey was upstairs and Hali was tending to her daughter. Lord Yuri was away for the day. 'Well, I have been learning some new skills of late.'

Out of the corner of her eye, Cora saw her mother's spoon return to her bowl of oats.

'What sort of skills?' Eldoris asked.

'Sword skills mostly.'

Eldoris stared at her. 'Please tell me you are joking.'

Cora kept focused on Stamitos. 'I thought perhaps you could teach me a few things. You know how to fight with a disadvantage. You have no hand. I have no strength.'

Stamitos leaned back in his chair, regarding her with open amusement. 'I had heard rumours you were learning sword skills but laughed them off.'

'I heard no such rumours,' Eldoris said, pushing her bowl away, 'or I most certainly would have followed up on them. Queens do not use weapons, they use words.'

Having barely regained her appetite, Cora pushed her own bowl away. 'In case you have not noticed, Mother, words have not done me much good of late.'

'That is what guards are for.'

Cora crossed her arms and waited for her mother to realise what she just said. Eldoris dropped her gaze to her abandoned bowl.

'I can teach you a few things,' Stamitos said. 'Technique beats strength every time. Fitness is also important. You can be built like a house but tire quickly.'

'How can I get fit without fighting?'

'You could run, swim. Anything that gets your heart pumping is good. The manor's watering hole is deep enough this time a year.'

Eldoris paled. 'Stamitos, please do not encourage her. That watering hole is barely fit for animals to drink from.'

Cora did not think she would be heading back into the water any time soon.

'I should never have let you swim with your brothers as a child,' her mother went on. 'Your father warned me against such boisterous pastimes.'

'You should be happy you did,' Cora replied, 'or I would have drowned in the river a few days back.'

Eldoris fell silent again.

Cora sat straighter in her chair. 'I could add running to my routine.'

'Cora, please—'

'Start small and build up to longer distances,' Stamitos said, not letting his mother finish.

Cora rose from her chair. 'I shall start today.'

Eldoris put her head in her hands.

Stamitos reached across and patted his mother on the back. 'My wife and daughters can all use a bow. Why should a queen not know how to use a sword?'

Cora gave him a grateful smile. 'That is why you are my favourite brother.'

Eldoris looked up. 'Let us pray your husband does not find out.'

Cora pushed her chair in, letting it scrape across the floor. 'Oh, Mother. He already knows.'

*B*rom rode out into the clearing, Carac flanking him. His gaze swept the top of the long wall in front of them, where Asigow soldiers watched their every move. The portcullis rose, revealing King Tuyon seated on a tall chestnut horse. His gaze went past them to the lines of foot soldiers tucked in the trees behind them, and then he shook his head as he dug his heels into his horse and rode out to meet them.

'That's far enough,' Brom called out when the king was a few yards from them.

Tuyon pulled up his horse, then rested his hands on the pommel of his saddle. 'I gather from all this you didn't sign the trade agreements.'

Brom shook his head. 'No. We won't be doing trade with Asigow at this time.'

'And you thought bringing an army to my doorstep would change the outcome?'

The Zoelin king frowned. 'That's actually *my* doorstep, and I had a hunch you wouldn't like my answer.'

Tuyon smirked. 'I heard you married your brother's

widow.'

'That's right.'

'I don't know whether to congratulate you or offer my condolences. That woman is as crazy as your brother.'

Brom shifted in the saddle. 'Congratulate me or move on. I won't listen to you speak poorly of my wife.'

That only made his smirk grow. 'I get it. She is something. There's not a man who's met her who hasn't imagined those pouty lips wrapped around their—'

'Let's talk about when you and your men will be leaving Onuric Castle.'

Tuyon looked around. 'You know, it's very peaceful here.'

'It won't be for long.'

Another smirk. 'I'm surprised you're willing to sacrifice lives just to prove a point.'

Brom wanted to punch that smug face of his. 'I think it's a fairly important point, that we won't be pushed into the buying or selling of people.'

'Such an honourable man.'

Brom knew it was not meant as a compliment, so he said nothing.

'How many Syrasan soldiers did your marriage get you? A few hundred?'

Brom did not even blink. 'I'm going to need you to leave.'

'I was ready to leave, but then you showed up empty-handed.'

'Not empty-handed.'

King Tuyon was not smiling anymore. 'How do you think this is going to end for you? Let's pretend for a moment you got your castle back. Do you think that's the end, that I'll scurry back to Asigow with my tail between my legs?'

Brom stared hard at the man for a moment. 'You can position your tail however you wish, as long as you leave.'

Tuyon laughed. 'I like you. That's why I'm going to return

back inside and give you one final chance to make a smarter decision for your people.' He swung his horse around.

'I've already told you my decision,' Brom shouted at his back. 'Take your men and leave. No one need die today.'

Tuyon pulled up his horse and looked back at him. 'Are you sure about this?'

Brom nodded, his gaze flicking to the men above the wall. His horse moved sideways, picking up on the growing tension.

'Then I guess we're going to have to settle this the old-fashioned way.' Tuyon raised a hand, and every man on that wall loaded their bows and pointed them west. 'If you want me to leave, you're going to have to make me.'

'Hold the line!' Brom shouted, trying to push towards the portcullis. It was no good. For every step forwards they managed, he was pushed back two. Their enemy had spewed from the castle like a plague of locusts. King Tuyon had been prepared, almost as though he had been expecting that exact fight. He seemed to have just enough men to outnumber them, far more than previously reported.

Brom dragged his sword between the ribs of a large warrior before pulling it free just in time to block the axe of the next man. Then came another, roaring, his face splattered with blood. He swung his sword at Brom, who blocked the blow while trying not to trip over the corpses lying at his feet. An arrow struck the man through the neck, and Brom looked in the direction from which it had come. Tyron was reloading his bow. It was his job to pick off some of the stronger fighters, and it was Leksi's job to keep him alive. Brom gave a nod of thanks.

The sound of the portcullis going up made him look in

that direction. Another fifty men ran out to join the fight.

'We can't even get near the gate,' Carac shouted, driving his sword through the stomach of a warrior before pulling it free. 'We've lost almost half our men, and we're farther back than when we started.'

Brom looked around, his breaths coming hard and fast. *Half?* He had no idea how many more men Tuyon had behind those walls. The king was taking down Zoelin soldiers from the comfort of his horse. Unfortunately, the rumours about his fighting skills were not exaggerated.

Brom looked over to where Prince Tyron was now using his sword against men a full head taller than him. 'Fall back!'

'Fall back!' Carac echoed.

Tyron signalled to his men, who had their own system for retreating. Brom glanced at his horse, which lay dead five yards from him, an arrow protruding from its eye. The fighting continued around them, because the Asigow warriors were not about to let them stroll off into the woods. Brom joined the fight once more to enable his men to retreat. An arrow flew past his face, a reminder of how easily it could all go wrong.

'Fall back! Now!' Brom marched along the line of fighting men, every muscle in his body rigid as he slew any Asigow warrior still engaged in combat. Finally, men stopped coming from the castle. The fighting died out, and his men were able to retreat to the trees, taking the injured men with them.

Over his shoulder, Brom saw King Tuyon retreat through the gate, the portcullis lowering behind him.

Brom stepped into the medic tent they had set up to treat the injured. He spotted Tyron seated on a cot with his shirt off and made his way over. 'How bad is it?' He gestured to the bandaged arm.

'Just a few stitches,' Tyron replied, standing and picking up his shirt.

Leksi appeared through the flap of the tent and looked around, eyebrows rising when he spotted Tyron easing the injured arm through the sleeve of his shirt. Wandering over, he said, 'Bit drastic for a scratch.' He turned to Brom. 'I see you made it out in one piece, Your Majesty. That Zoelin physique is working in your favour.'

Brom was still trying to figure Leksi out. The man was part warrior and part jester.

'Didn't feel like dying today,' Tyron replied.

'Me neither.'

Tyron began walking. 'Let us go and get out of the medic's way.'

'I could've stitched you up,' Leksi said. 'Wouldn't have been the first time.'

Tyron patted his friend on the shoulder. 'Not a chance. You enjoy it too much.'

They exited the tent, and Brom looked around at the camp they had set up three miles from Onuric. Carac had taken some men to keep watch.

'Four hundred dead.' Brom felt the weight of that number.

'You will need reinforcements,' Tyron said.

Brom nodded. 'Pollux suggested we test the strength of their army before sending all our men to slaughter.'

Leksi touched the cut above his eye. Dried blood covered one side of his face. 'Test complete. You'll need to fight with every able-bodied man if you stand any chance.'

Tyron's gaze drifted north. 'I was going to say that you have lost the element of surprise now, but I believe Tuyon was prepared for our arrival.'

Brom nodded. 'Likely had eyes on the border and saw

your army cross.'

'The men at the border who attacked Cora.'

Leksi thought for a moment. 'I thought the arrow they took from your sister was Zoelin.'

Brom looked down at the ground. 'There's every chance some of my people are working with King Tuyon.'

'Well, that's awkward,' Leksi said.

Brom rubbed at the fresh growth on his face. 'From now on, we're going to need to limit the people who know our plans, because next time I arrive at that castle, I'd prefer my enemy be at least a little surprised.'

Tyron nodded in agreement. 'You are going to need more men.'

'I can't help but wonder if King Tuyon will wed Princess Beatrix at Onuric Castle,' Leksi said. 'I hear it's slightly less miserable in the warm season.'

'This *is* their warm season,' Tyron said.

Leksi made a face. 'This will not suit a Galen bride. They'd be better off having it at Reave Castle. It's a sea of flowers this time of year.' Seeing Brom's expression, Leksi fell silent.

Tyron shook his head. 'I will leave my men in your charge and return to Archdale, see about getting some reinforcements. You should have some reprieve for the time being, as Tuyon will be waiting for you to arrive at the gate waving your white flag and holding the signed agreement.'

Brom nodded. 'He's going to be sorely disappointed. Can you check in on your sister for me?'

'Honestly, I'm far more worried about Charis,' Leksi said.

Tyron gave him a shove to get him walking. 'We will check on her, Your Majesty.'

'Tell her I'll write when things have settled down.' He watched the men round the corner, then went to wash off his enemy's blood.

CHAPTER 26

'Y ou're improving,' Stamitos said, dropping his sword on the ground and wiping his face with the back of his hand.

Cora rubbed her throbbing shoulder and looked over to where Sarey and Hali stood watching her with their usual worried expressions. Hali's daughter, Adelaide, had lost interest and was chasing a lizard in the paddock behind them. Cora did not mind the company of the girl, but that meant her mother was always loitering nearby.

'How is the shoulder?' Stamitos asked.

Cora's hand fell away. 'Fine.'

Her brother gave her a sceptical look. 'I heard Sarey and Mother talking about you in hushed tones this morning.'

'Sarey is a big traitor who is lucky she still has her tongue,' Cora said loud enough for her lady to hear. 'Mother needs something to focus on while Tyron is away fighting. Unfortunately that something is me.' She looked over to where Charis was playing with Pup. He might have been a big man-child, but she liked that he was bringing the wolf out of her shell.

'How many miles did you run this morning?' Stamitos asked, pulling her attention back to their conversation.

'Around four.'

'I thought we agreed you would work up to four.'

'I did. Yesterday was three. Today was four.'

He laughed. 'I get it. An experience like that does things to your mind.'

Cora did not want to talk about that. Even thinking about it made her hot and short of breath. She glanced in the direction of her hopeless bodyguard, who had yet to pick up on the fact that they were about to leave. Lief had always had superb instincts with no need for constant instructions.

'We're going.' Her tone was pure ice.

Charis wandered over—far too casually.

Cora looked up at the high sun, a relentless presence in Syrasan during the warm season. It had only been a few weeks, but she already missed the cold, crisp Zoelin air.

'Adelaide,' Hali called to her daughter. 'Let's go inside.'

The little girl came running. Instead of taking her mother's hand, she reached for Cora's. Hali pursed her lips but said nothing.

'Why do you wear men's clothes?' Adelaide asked her.

Hali tutted. 'Darling, you cannot say that. It's why do you wear men's clothes, *Your Majesty?*'

Someone was growing a backbone.

'It is difficult to fight and run in gowns,' Cora explained.

Adelaide turned to her mother. 'I like to run. Can I wear trousers?'

'Absolutely not.'

Hali cast a disapproving look in Cora's direction, which made her smile inwardly.

'Mother made tarts for lunch,' Adelaide said, skipping now.

'Actually, I made them for *after* lunch.'

Adelaide frowned up at her mother. 'But queens can eat whatever they want whenever they want.'

Cora's gaze met Hali's. 'What a wise daughter you are raising. I would love a tart for my lunch.'

Hali was about to protest when Pup began to whine. Cora stopped walking, because it was the same noise she had made that day at the river.

'What is the matter with her?' Stamitos asked.

Cora listened, hearing the faint pounding of hooves. 'I hear horses.'

Charis turned to Hali. 'You expecting guests?'

'No.'

Hali went to move, but Cora reached out and grabbed her arm.

'What are you doing?' Hali asked, looking down at her hand.

'She senses danger,' Cora replied.

Hali pulled her arm free. 'Who does?'

Cora nodded towards Pup.

'The wolf?' Hali looked over at Stamitos. 'Ah, I think your sister might have some unresolved trauma.'

Stamitos did not look away from Cora. 'What's going on?'

She met his gaze. 'Can you not feel it?'

'Feel what?'

Her gaze returned to the house. 'Predators.'

'What predators?' Hali said, looking around.

Cora ignored the question and addressed Sarey. 'Collect my mother from the library and hide. Tell the servants to do the same. Do not come out until one of us comes to get you. Understand?'

Sarey stared at her for the longest time, then nodded. She reached for Adelaide's hand. 'Let's go.'

A pale-faced Hali hurried after them.

'If you are right about this, then you need to hide also,' Stamitos said.

Cora headed for the front of the house. 'They are here for me.'

'Who?' Stamitos asked, catching up to her. 'The men from the river?'

'I do not know.' Pup whined louder still, and Cora covered her ears. 'I just know they want me dead.'

'You are beginning to scare me.'

She was beginning to scare herself.

She walked faster, forcing Charis to break into a jog to get in front of her. He drew his sword just as they rounded the corner. The three of them stopped when they spotted eight Zoelin guards standing at the bottom of the steps. The housemaid, Odele, stood before them. One of the men had the tip of his sword pointed at her neck. She was the most annoying maid Cora had ever come across, always barging into rooms and commenting aloud on things that were none of her business, but she did not deserve to die for it.

'Oh shit,' Stamitos said beside her.

Charis looked at Cora. 'What are your orders, Your Majesty?'

She met his gaze. 'There are eight of them and only one of you. I think you should put your weapon away.'

Stamitos drew his sword. 'Two of us.'

'It's my job to protect you, Your Majesty,' Charis said. 'With my life.'

'It will be a very short life if you go in swinging that thing. Swords away, both of you.'

They did as she asked just as the men all turned to look in their direction. Cora marched towards them, showing no signs of fear despite crumbling inside. Pup was no longer with her. She had probably gone to hide with the others. They were down one wolf, which was not ideal.

Cora narrowed her eyes on the man holding the sword to Odele's neck. 'What the hell do you think you are doing? Put your weapon away.'

He looked at his companions before finally withdrawing his sword. Odele fled up the steps as fast as her aged legs could carry her. Cora knew the men were not there in her service.

'Afternoon, Your Majesty.' His tone bordered on patronising. 'There were rumours of men crossing the border. We were sent here to check on you.'

Cora looked between them. 'Only a handful of people know where I am. Who sent you?'

'The king.'

'The king?' She doubted that.

'He was worried.' The man was looking around as he replied, no doubt wondering who else was on the property. Lord Yuri only had a handful of staff, and the groom had travelled with him for the day.

'And what were the king's orders exactly?'

'He wants you to come with us.'

'Where?'

'Back to Drake Castle.'

Brom had promised to collect her himself when it was over. 'Do you have a letter expressing his wishes?'

The guard shook his head. 'No letter.'

Charis's and Stamitos's hands rested on the hilts of their swords, mirroring their unwanted guests.

'I will need written confirmation from Grandor Pollux. He advises me on such things. In the meantime, I am going to need you to surrender your weapons.' She raised her chin.

The guards exchanged glances.

'We can't protect you without weapons,' said one.

She let her gaze burn through the man. 'You dare question your queen.'

None of the men moved, which prompted Charis and Stamitos to draw their swords. The men drew theirs also, the collective sound making Cora flinch. Charis stepped in front of her, stupidly unafraid. He was a Leksi cut-out in that moment, pure male ego as he lurched forwards and smashed the sword out of one man's hand, sending it sliding across the ground. It came to a stop a few paces away. There was a brief moment of stillness before a violent clash of weapons ensued.

There was no turning back at that point. The small group had descended into chaos. Swords flashed and steel screeched, while Charis remained planted firmly in front of her the entire time. Cora's eyes went to the sword on the ground not too far away. Her heart beat faster as she resigned herself to what she was about to do. Then she ran, snatching it off the ground.

'Cora, inside!' Stamitos shouted.

She held the sword with both hands, eyes on the men.

'Now!'

She ignored her brother and marched up to the closest so-called guard, thrusting the sword into his side. No one had expected her to use the weapon, certainly not the man she stabbed, not even Stamitos, who knew she could handle a sword. She stared down at the point where her weapon had entered his body. Panicking, she pulled it free, surprised by the blood on the blade. Had she expected it to come out clean? The man did not even fall down, just covered the wound with his spare hand, his face contorting into some-thing fierce as he took a step towards her. He swung his sword, and she blocked it, exactly as she had done with wooden swords many times. He swung again, but he was weakened by his injury, and the action was sloppy. She could handle one injured man, surely.

She felt the force of the next blow through her entire

body, but then he stepped right, seemingly dizzy. That was her chance. The one her teachers had described many times. A small window of opportunity to finish it. She swung her sword at him, and when he raised his weapon, she changed direction, dragging it across his throat instead. The action was flawless. She expected to feel powerful in that moment, in control, something other than nausea. Her hand flew up to cover her mouth when blood began pouring from the wound, the same way Jayr's had the day he died.

She tried very hard not to be sick.

The sound of arrows hitting flesh made her stagger backwards, doing nothing to ease her nausea. She dropped her weapon, proving herself an amateur. Worse than that, she covered her head and closed her eyes. But the arrows were not coming at her. They struck the Zoelin men around her.

Cora opened her eyes as she was pulled backwards by Charis.

'You all right, Your Majesty?'

It was over.

She stared at him, unable to speak. Tyron and Leksi appeared on horseback, their bows slung over their backs and their swords now drawn.

'Any men inside? Tyron asked.

'I do not think so,' Stamitos replied, panting hard.

'I'll go,' Leksi said. Dismounting, he jogged up the steps.

Cora's gaze returned to the man she had killed, and nausea rose in waves until she had no choice but to turn away and be sick. Sweat beaded on her face. She had no idea what was happening to her. A hand landed on her back, and she straightened with a gasp.

'It is only me,' Tyron said, eyes moving over her. 'Are you hurt?'

Was she? She stepped back from him until her heel hit the

step. She sank down onto it and held up her hands, inspecting them, then looked down at her trousers, which were now sprayed with blood. 'No. I am not hurt.'

CHAPTER 27

*B*rom had just slipped into his tent when Carac stepped in behind him, holding up a letter.

'From Pollux.'

Brom took it from him, nodding his thanks before breaking the seal.

'Surely we're due some good news,' Carac said, collapsing onto the king's cot.

Your Majesty King Brom,

I am hearing rumours of unusual activity in the South. There are fears some of our own may have crossed the border, and I am concerned for the queen's welfare. Please advise if you would like me to send some additional men to Veanor.

Your loyal servant,

Grandor Pollux

Brom cursed aloud and handed the letter to Carac to read, who ran his eyes over it and handed it back.

'But no one knows where she is.'

'Except her family, my advisors, the men who travelled with me to Veanor, and all of the staff at the manor.'

'People you trust.'

'People I *used* to trust. I've no idea who I can trust right now.' Brom went over to where his weapons lay and began strapping them on.

Carac watched him for a moment, then sighed. 'Really? In the middle of a war, you're going to her?'

'I need you to oversee things here until I get back.'

'Let Pollux handle it. It's his job.' Carac rose from the bed, picking up the waterskin and handing it to him. 'Are you listening to me?'

'I can't trust anyone else to handle it.' He straightened and looked directly at his friend. 'I'm only going to ask this once. Tell me you have nothing to do with this, with any of it.'

Carac's face fell. 'Are you serious right now? You think I'd send men after your *wife*?'

'You've made no secret of the fact that you don't like her.'

'I don't have to like her. I'm not married to her.'

Brom felt a pelting of guilt as he took in Carac's expression. 'Sorry.'

'For the record, I'm only going to *let* you ask that once.'

'I'm sorry. I need to know there are at least a handful of people I can trust right now.'

Carac shoulders relaxed a little. 'Next time it's a fight to the death.'

Brom let out a weak laugh, expelling some of the built-up tension. 'I need to go.'

'And I'm sleeping in your oversized tent while you're gone.'

Brom paused at the flap and looked back at him. 'Sleep wherever you want. Just keep everyone alive until I return.'

When Brom arrived at the manor, Lord Yuri informed him that Cora had been taken to Archdale Castle.

'Everyone thought it best she go there until we know more about these rogue attacks,' he said.

'Rogue attacks?'

Yuri appeared confused for a moment. 'The men who came to the manor. I sent my wife and daughter away too. Better to be safe.'

Brom realised at that moment that he was missing a vital part of the story.

'You do not know,' Yuri said, reading his expression. 'I assumed that was why you were here.'

Brom's gut churned. 'Was Cora hurt?'

'No.' He paused. 'She left here in good physical health.'

Good *physical* health. That spoke volumes. 'I'm going to need you to tell me everything. Then I'm going to need a fresh horse.'

Lord Yuri nodded. 'Please, come inside.'

Thirty minutes later, Brom marched from the house to the waiting horse out front. He hoped the anger would subside before he reached the castle, but it only fermented. By the time he arrived at Archdale, he almost drew his sword on the guard who stopped him at the entrance. No one knew who he was, and he hardly looked the part of a king, yet he was ready to behead any man who stood between him and his wife.

Finally he was let through the gate, the guard apologising profusely behind him. He rode right up to the front steps, tossing the reins to the first man who approached him. As he made his way up the steps, he looked up at the red banners hanging from its walls. The warm air smelled of cherries. It was that time of year where grass was beginning to push through the mud, and he imagined the grounds with some greenery. He was picturing Cora strolling across those lawns when a guard stepped in front of him, blocking his path.

'King Brom?'

Brom drew an impatient breath. 'Yes. Where's my wife?'

The man bowed before replying. 'King Pandarus wishes to speak with you.'

He knew there was no point refusing. He was Pandarus's guest within these walls. His eyes went to the windows above, seeing only the sun reflected in the glass. 'Fine. Take me to him.'

The guards led him to the throne room, where King Pandarus, Prince Tyron, and Prince Stamitos were already gathered.

'Here he is,' Pandarus said, looking at him with open disdain. 'You will be pleased to know we have managed to keep your wife alive, despite the best efforts of your own men.'

Brom glanced at Tyron. 'Where is she?'

'We will get to that in a minute,' Pandarus said. 'Sit.' He gestured to a chair, but Brom did not move.

'*Where is she?*' He spoke slowly this time.

Pandarus leaned back, linking his hands in front of him. 'Safe, thanks to Tyron here. If he had not shown up, then who knows what would have happened to her.'

Brom looked at Tyron. 'You have my gratitude. Are there any survivors that I can question?'

Tyron shook his head. 'No.'

Stamitos cleared his throat. 'You should know that Cora killed one of the men.'

Brom closed his eyes. The thought of her trying to fend off men twice her size was too much for him.

'She has not been the same since it happened,' Pandarus said. 'Women are not built for such things. The most dangerous thing she should be handling is a needle and thread, and even then I would have her supervised.'

Brom stared unblinking at him. 'Cora has the right to feel secure.'

'Then provide her with adequate protection. We are fighting a war here.'

Brom crossed his arms. 'She was under your protection at the river. Tell me, how is it you made it over that bridge and she didn't?'

Pandarus's eyes flashed at him. 'Watch yourself. You would do well to remember that it is your own people hunting her. It is best she remain here until I can be assured of her safety.'

Brom knew she preferred to be anywhere but at Archdale.

'She must learn to be a lady again. I have confiscated the men's clothing she arrived in, and I have ensured she has no access to weapons.'

Stamitos shook his head. 'That has not deterred her though.'

Pandarus waved an impatient hand. 'I will shackle her if I have to.'

Brom's gaze cut to him. 'What are you talking about?'

'She continues to run,' Tyron said, rejoining the conversation. 'She has barely stopped since she arrived.'

Brom's brows lowered. 'Run?'

'Ah, that one is on me,' Stamitos said, shifting in his chair. 'I suggested it might improve her fitness. Of course, had I known she would take it this far, I might have kept that information to myself.'

'You take away a person's weapons,' Tyron said, 'and they will fight with whatever they have.'

Brom did not want anyone taking anything else from his wife. 'I want to see her—now.'

Brom found Cora running laps down at the butts. He stood beneath the trees, watching her. She was wearing an expensive silk dress that clung to her wet skin. Her painted face was smeared, completing her slightly unhinged look. Brom let out a breath and looked around, spotting Sarey standing off to one side with a man who was likely her new guard. Pup stood with them, eyes following Cora around the space.

'Perhaps you should take a break,' Sarey called out to her. 'It's been three hours.'

Three hours?

'I am not tired,' Cora said, visibly exhausted. She wiped at her face.

Brom went to her then, walking across the soggy lawn towards her. She almost stumbled when she saw him but then resumed running.

'Cora, stop,' he called.

She did not stop. 'What are you doing here?'

'I came for you.'

'Oh, another pity visit?'

He refused to chase her. 'Stop.' His tone was firmer this time.

She did as she was told, but instead of turning to face him, she dropped to her knees, panting. Brom lowered himself onto the grass beside her, waiting for her breath to slow.

'Now I don't even know what to say,' he began.

She looked up at him, her eyes filled with hurt and accusation. 'Did you send those men to kill me?'

His eyes widened. 'What?'

'No one was supposed to know I was there—but you knew.'

He could hear the pain in her voice. 'I didn't send anyone.'

'I do not even know who to trust anymore.'

'Me neither.'

She blinked back tears and looked away.

'I'm going to find out who did send those men. I promise you that.'

Pup approached them, cautiously, sensing the tension. Cora rubbed her head. 'I killed a man.' The words spilled out of her like a confession. 'I stabbed him. Then I cut his throat.'

His insides tore. 'I should've left more guards.'

'I told you not to.'

'I should've done it anyway.'

She wiped at her face, further smearing the black paint around her eyes. 'And now I think I might be losing my mind.'

Brom rested his wrists on his knees. 'We all lose our minds sometimes.' He watched her. 'Does the running help?'

She nodded. 'I will never be stronger, but I can be faster than all of them.'

'All of them?'

'All the people who want me to fail, to die.'

His chest pinched. It was a while before he could speak again. 'How's the shoulder?'

She looked down at it. 'I have a scar.'

He reached up to touch the area. 'Then I guess that makes you a proper warrior now.'

Cora met his gaze, her face contorting with emotion.

He took a firm hold of her arms. 'Speak to me. Blame me if it helps.'

She took a moment to compose herself. 'I am so angry at you.'

He nodded. 'All right.'

'You told me this was a partnership. You sold me a vision.'

He did not interrupt her.

'You convinced me to trust you, and then you sent me

away—to die.' She gestured to the walls. 'I cannot breathe here. I told you that. Pandarus controls everything, and my mother has made it her life mission to remind me of what a terrible person I am.' She sucked in a breath. 'I know I am a horrible person. Do people think I do not hear the words that come out of my own mouth, that I do not see the effect they have on people?' She covered her face. 'What is wrong with me?'

He wanted to fix her, but he knew it was not that easy. 'Nothing is wrong with you.'

'Then why can I not breathe?'

He pulled her to him, slowly, carefully, until she collapsed against him. He brought his lips to her ear. 'Let me breathe for you.'

She tore free of his grip at that. 'No! This is what you do. You lure me in with comfort and feed me dreams, and then you leave.' She searched his face. 'I am right, am I not? You will go, and I will be left here, suffocating. Who will breathe for me then?' She sat back on her heels. 'Why come at all?'

He wanted to pull her to him again but did not dare. 'Pandarus wants you to remain here.'

'Pandarus took my trousers and sent wine to my room as a consolation prize. I drank it and said nothing. What does that say about me?'

'That you're smart enough to pick your battles.'

A pained expression passed over her face. 'I am tired of fighting.'

'I know.'

She blinked and rose to her feet. He rose also.

'Take me with you,' she said, a plea in her tone.

He wanted to say yes, that she was safest with him and he would protect her better than anyone else, but he could not. 'I'll be returning to the front.'

Cora bit down on her lip. 'If you insist on imprisoning

me, then at least do it at Drake Castle where I can be of some use. Who will rule while you are off fighting?'

'You're not a prisoner, and I don't want you worrying about those things. I need you to trust me.'

She shook her head and stepped back from him. Turning, she marched over to her bodyguard and, before he knew what happening, drew his sword.

'Cora!' Sarey gasped.

The bodyguard had no idea what to do.

Brom moved towards her. 'Cora, what are you doing?'

She turned to face him, gripping the weapon with both hands. 'We are going to fight. If you win, I will remain here at Archdale. If I win, I return to Zoelin with you.'

The young soldier was looking between them with a panicked expression.

'You can't beat me,' Brom said calmly. 'Now give the guard his weapon before you hurt yourself.'

She walked out into the middle of the lawn, turning the sword in her hand. 'If I cannot beat you, then you have nothing to worry about.'

He stared at her. 'That weapon is sharp.'

'Then do not let the blade touch you.' She watched him through her blackened eyes. 'First one to disarm the other wins.'

He glanced again at Sarey, who looked ready to cry. 'Fine. Let's do it.'

Sarey's mouth fell open. 'What do you mean, *fine*?'

A look of concentration came over Cora's face. She shook her arms out in an attempt to loosen them, then paced from side to side in what appeared to be some pre-fight warm-up or ritual. He almost felt bad for what he was about to do.

'All right. I am ready,' she said, bending her knees and watching him carefully. Her fingers worked over the hilt of the sword.

He drew a breath, shook his head, and then lunged forwards, knocking the sword from her hand in one careful swing. It flew through the air, landing on the grass some distance away. Cora stared after it, her hand open in front of her. He thought she might cry, but she pressed her lips together and looked at him. They stared at one another, the only sound Pup's soft whines.

'I guess you win,' she said. Her eyes went to the ground, and then she walked off in the direction of the castle.

'It's not about winning. It's about keeping you safe.'

She did not turn around, or even slow down for that matter. 'You won. We do not need to have a conversation about it.'

He watched her until she was out of sight. When he turned back, the young soldier was standing next to him.

'You know, I normally let her win for a bit. It keeps her spirits up.'

'And who are you?'

'Sir Charis, Your Majesty.' He gave a small bow. 'Bodyguard to Queen Cora.'

Brom glanced at Sarey for confirmation, and she nodded. He looked the boy over once more. 'Thanks for the tip.'

CHAPTER 28

*B*rom fell into the bed they offered him and slept for the rest of the afternoon. He woke to a knock on the door and opened it to find Prince Tyron standing in the corridor.

'I thought you might like to join us for the evening meal,' he said.

Brom looked past him. 'Where's Cora?'

'Reluctantly seated in the hall with the rest of the family.'

Brom rubbed the sleep from his eyes and nodded. 'She hates me right now.'

Tyron's mouth curved into a smile. 'It might seem that way, but you are one of the privileged few who she has let into her inner circle.'

Brom regarded him for a moment. 'Are you in that inner circle?'

'Not today, but ask me again in the morning.' One corner of his mouth lifted. 'You should come to dinner, appease Pandarus, drink his wine, kiss his arse. That is the only way you are getting those additional men.'

Brom nodded and watched Tyron walk off down the corridor.

After a wash, he made his way to the great hall, where tension was so thick in the air that he could barely wade through it. The food had already been served. Boiled eggs, salted fish, and platters of vegetables and fruits, some of which he did not recognise. Zoelin's cold climate made it impossible to grow some things.

It was a family-only gathering, and no one seemed overly pleased by the fact given the lack of eye contact and absence of conversation. Brom greeted everyone before lowering himself into the vacant chair between Pandarus and Cora.

'Are you all right?' he whispered to his wife. When she lifted her gaze to him, he saw that she was drunk. She opened her mouth to reply, but Pandarus spoke up on her behalf.

'I was just explaining to my sister that extreme physical activity is not safe for women of childbearing age. It is no wonder Zoelin has no heir.'

Cora dropped her fork on her plate. 'Tell me, how exactly how does one fall pregnant while living in a different kingdom to her husband?'

'Well, the night is young,' Pandarus said. 'If you slow down on the wine, you might still be awake at the end of the meal.'

Stamitos cleared his throat and turned to Tyron. 'How is Aldara feeling? She must be nearing her time now.'

Tyron swallowed his food before replying. 'She is well. She is convinced it is another girl.'

Pandarus made a disapproving noise. 'Just what this family needs.'

Cora reached for her drink. 'I thought you would be pleased. One less boy in line for your crown.' She emptied her cup and placed it back down on the table, gesturing for a servant to refill it.

'Every healthy child is a blessing,' Eldoris said, moving Cora's cup to the other side of her. 'The world needs women to produce kings.'

Stamitos reached for the bread. 'I love having daughters. It is great arriving home and having so many women pleased to see me. My son well and truly belongs to his mother at the moment. He is forever in her arms or wrapped around one of her legs.'

'That will change,' Tyron replied.

Pandarus stabbed a piece of chicken with his fork. 'Will you listen to yourselves? You sound like a bunch of women.'

Cora stared at her brother. 'Is that what you think we talk about when men are not around?'

'Yes. You excluded. There is not a maternal bone in your body.'

Brom had not even served himself any food yet and he was ready to leave. 'Actually, Cora has very strong maternal instincts.'

Everyone looked in his direction. Cora seemed more surprised by the comment than anyone. Reaching for the eggs, Brom began loading up his plate. The sooner he ate, the sooner he could leave. One by one, the others returned to their food.

'Well, I think it is lovely that you are getting to see a side of my daughter she keeps so well hidden from the rest of us,' Eldoris said, smiling across the table at Brom.

'When will you be returning to Zoelin?' Tyron asked, moving the conversation along.

Brom piled vegetables on his plate. 'At first light.' He glanced at Pandarus. 'It would be helpful if I knew how many men you will be sending.'

Pandarus lay his cutlery down. 'Perhaps it is time to put your ego aside and accept King Tuyon's terms.'

Brom was about to reply when Cora said, 'My husband does not make decisions with his ego. He fights this fight for others, to put an end to the trading of people. That is something every kingdom should be supporting.'

Brom wanted to reach under the table and take her hand, but just because she was speaking up for him did not mean he was forgiven.

'What do you want to be remembered for, brother?' Cora asked. 'Your collection of hunting horses? Send more men, and keep sending them. Have your people remember that instead.'

Pandarus's expression darkened. 'You might be able to get away with these drunken rants in Zoelin, but you are in my home now.'

Brom angled his body towards Pandarus and stared at him for the longest time. Cora reached beneath the table and slipped her hand into his, squeezing. His muscles relaxed.

'Cora is right,' Tyron said. 'Send one hundred men if that is all you can spare, but send them. Everyone is watching.'

Eldoris quietly placed her knife and fork together on her plate. 'Come, Cora. Let us visit the library while the men finish their conversation.'

Cora looked across at her mother. '*Their* conversation?'

'Cora should stay,' Brom said. 'She is queen of Zoelin. The role is not for show.'

Pandarus rubbed his forehead. 'My sister does not need encouraging. Remember, I am the one left with her incessant nagging after you leave.'

Brom threaded his fingers through Cora's, holding tightly. Whatever fight they had earlier that day no longer mattered. He was beginning to realise that his wife was a product of her family life. 'About that,' he began. 'I've decided Cora should return to Drake Castle and rule in my absence.'

Cora stilled beside him. Tyron leaned back in his chair, looking between them.

'And when did you decide this?' Pandarus asked.

'Just now.'

Stamitos reached for the platter of fruits and began picking through what was left. 'Is that wise given some of your people want her dead?'

Eldoris looked around the table. 'Surely you are not serious.'

'Quite serious,' Brom replied.

Pandarus began laughing. *'Rule in your absence?* Left unsupervised, she will drink herself to death before this war is over.'

'Ignore him,' Cora said. 'He is just annoyed that he will have to find someone else to speak down to at mealtimes. Usually it is his wife, but she is having one of her special headaches reserved for family dinners.'

Pandarus slammed his fist on the table. 'Enough!'

Brom shot up from his chair, pulling Cora up with him. He placed himself as a physical wall between them, his gaze fixed on Pandarus. 'I think it's time we retired.'

'And me,' Tyron said, rising also.

Stamitos feigned disappointment. 'But we were just getting to the part where Cora starts throwing things.'

Tyron ignored him. 'Tomorrow we will organise reinforcements.'

'I have not agreed to additional men yet,' Pandarus said, pressing his fingers into the table.

'But you will,' Tyron said, 'because our sister needs our help.' He looked back at Brom. 'Make sure she is safe. Make sure every person with access to her is trustworthy.'

Brom was still holding Cora's hand. 'And how do I do that?'

Tyron nodded towards his sister. 'Ask your wife. Her skills are unrivalled.'

It was a test of self-control. Brom had escorted Cora back to her quarters, and she had dragged him inside, tugging his head down to hers with one hand while peeling her dress off with the other.

'You're drunk,' Brom said, unhooking her hand from his neck.

Sarey finished laying Cora's nightdress on the bed before hurrying from the room. Somehow, Brom managed to wrestle her into it while her mouth explored his arm, which was not helping his resolve.

'I am not *that* drunk,' Cora slurred, swaying a little before balancing herself.

He groaned in frustration before flopping down onto the bed. 'You're killing me.' He gestured for her to come to him.

A smile spread across her face as she crawled across the bed towards him. 'I knew you would change your mind.'

He could not help but laugh. 'I'm not changing my mind.' He pulled her into his arms and settled her head on his chest. 'I'm sleeping with you.'

'Oh?'

Her hand began to wander south and he caught it. 'We are going to *sleep*.'

'Naked?'

He rubbed her back as he chuckled. 'I'm not going to take advantage of you when you can barely stand.'

She turned her face up to look at him. 'You should take

full advantage. Jayr used to say it was the only time I was compliant.'

'Have you not figured out yet that we're very different people?'

'Mmm.' Her eyes sank shut as she placed a hand on his chest. 'Your heartbeat is so even and strong.'

He held her wrist, feeling for her pulse. 'Yours is racing.'

'All that pent-up desire.' He laughed again, which made her open her eyes. 'I like it when you laugh. It feels like it has come from my own mouth.'

'That's because my laughter is your laughter, remember?'

'The elder never mentioned anything about laughter, only pain.'

Brom let out a breath. 'Well, I'm sure it applies to all emotions.'

She was silent a moment. 'What about strength? Can your strength be my strength?'

His expression turned serious. 'What are you talking about? You're the strongest person I know. I was hoping to borrow some from you.'

'You disarmed me in under a second.'

'So?'

'So I will never win against you.'

He brushed hair back from her face. 'We're on the same side, remember? My win *is* your win.'

She was holding back laughter now. 'How far are you going to take this?'

'As far as necessary to make you laugh.' He gathered her closer. 'Why do you hold it in? If you want to laugh, laugh. What are you afraid will happen if you do?'

'I have practised restraint my entire life. My emotions are always rehearsed and usually laced with sarcasm.'

He moved his head closer, brushing his nose over hers. 'Well, you can't hold it in forever.'

Cora sighed contentedly as her eyes closed once more. 'It is such a foolish notion.'

'What is?'

'Sharing pain. If you take another's pain on, it will eat away at your soul until there is no room for anything else.'

He brushed his fingers along her silky throat. 'What did Jayr do to you that would have you say such a thing?'

She was relaxing beneath his touch. 'He just kept taking. Piece by piece, until all that was left is this empty shell you hold right now.' She swallowed, her breath warm against his chest. 'I hate him for it.'

He gathered her closer, cheek resting on her hair, and did not let go until the morning.

CHAPTER 29

$\mathcal{C}$ora woke with that all too familiar headache that came with a main course of wine. But she also woke wrapped in the arms of her husband. She lay completely still for the longest time, marvelling at the way they fit together. Her shoulder fit perfectly into the crook of his arm, and it was as though her head had been made for the gentle slope of his chest. His arms reached all the way around her, and her knee was tucked in that gap beneath his. So much intimacy in a simple embrace.

She should have felt hot, trapped, suffocated. She should have felt panic. Instead she felt calm, her mind quiet, her heart steady. She felt *still*. This was completely new territory for her.

'Morning' came Brom's sleepy voice.

She looked up at him. 'You stayed.'

'Of course I stayed.' He opened his eyes, a lazy smile on his face. 'Please tell me you're sober.'

Her mouth stretched into a smile. 'I am more sober than last night. Does that count?'

His liquid eyes roamed her face. 'You should've just lied.'

She wet her lips, thirsty but not wanting to break eye contact with him for water. 'I am many terrible things but never a liar.'

He ran his thumb over her lips, and she felt it through her entire body. Her head tipped back, willing him to kiss her. He read her perfectly, bringing his mouth to hers. A low, satisfied growl vibrated from him. She felt that everywhere too and deepened the kiss.

'Undress me,' she whispered into his mouth.

'You want *me* to undress you?'

She bit his lip, softly, noticing the change in his breath. 'Yes, I want you to do it.'

He obeyed, tugging up her nightdress with adorable urgency. She arched her back to help him, to tempt him, to draw his eyes down. He ran a warm hand from her stomach all the way up to her throat. Heat pooled inside her.

'Put your mouth on me,' she urged. He bent to kiss the soft flesh between her breasts, and she held on to his head. 'I want you to promise me something.' He tried to lift his head to look at her, but she held it in place. 'I want you to promise me you will not send me away again.'

He gently freed himself from her grip and climbed on top of her, his godlike torso flush against her bare skin. She pressed her thighs together, denying him access. He kissed her neck, and she could see he was smiling.

'Is this how you get what you want?' he whispered against her skin. 'Drive a man to the edge, then make your demands?'

Goosebumps broke out all over her body. 'Is there anything you would deny me in this moment?'

He dropped his forehead to her collarbone, inhaling. 'Sadly, no.'

'I want to remain at Drake Castle.'

He looked up at her, his eyes radiating heat. 'Then that's

where you'll remain. No one's ever going to hurt you again. I'll make our home fit for a queen. *My* queen.' He kissed her again, then brought his mouth to her ear. 'Now please stop torturing me.'

She bit back a smile and opened her legs.

CHAPTER 30

$\mathcal{T}$he silence in the throne room was uncomfortable as Pollux looked from Cora to Charis, then back at Cora.

'Your bodyguard?'

Cora was relaxed in her chair, one arm draped over the side rubbing Pup's head. 'My bodyguard.'

He looked to Brom for confirmation. The king nodded.

'Pup likes him,' Cora said. 'And Ida took to him immediately.'

Pollux glanced down at the wolf, then back at the knight. 'Well, I suppose he proved himself at the manor. We were all very relieved to hear you escaped unscathed.'

Cora watched him carefully. 'Only a handful of people knew I was there, and one of them sent men to kill me.'

He stared back at her, unblinking. 'Is there something you wish to ask me, Your Majesty?'

'Is there something you wish to tell me?'

He angled his head. 'You know, I'm the one who alerted our king to the potential danger.'

Cora glanced at Brom, who nodded, as she continued to

stroke Pup's head. 'You must forgive my distrust, Grandor. I have been through quite the ordeal.'

'I understand, Your Majesty. It is a lot for a woman.'

Something about the way he said *woman* made the comment sound like an insult. Cora looked over at Brom, who was watching his advisor with the same level of interest. 'Of course, we shall find out soon enough. The poor man has to talk eventually.'

Brom's gaze snapped to hers, but she kept her attention on Pollux, whose eyebrows were lowered in confusion.

'What man?' Pollux asked.

'The man they kept alive for questioning.' She saw it then, the smallest flash of something, but it was gone before she could identify it.

'I was under the impression that your brother killed all of them, big hero that he is.'

Her hand returned to the arm of her chair. 'All but one unlucky man. Tyron has him locked away in Archdale's tower. You know how protective he can be.'

Pollux sat forwards, casually resting his hands on the table. 'Well, I wouldn't hold your breath. If they are prepared to kill their own queen, they are clearly loyal to their cause.'

'And what cause is that?' Brom asked.

Pollux rose from his chair. 'Leave it with me to find out. If there's a traitor among us, I'll find him.'

'Or her,' Cora said. 'Now is not the time to be underestimating women.'

Brom stood. 'Keep us updated.'

'Yes, Your Majesty.'

The moment the door closed, Brom turned to Cora. 'Want to tell me what's going on?'

'A feeling.'

'A feeling? Pollux wrote me. Why would he do that if he were part of it?'

She met his gaze. 'That is exactly what I would do. He knew you would never make it there in time. What he did not know is that Tyron and Leksi were already on their way.'

'You're one of the people who told me I should keep him on.'

'That does not mean you should trust him.'

'You said he is loyal.'

'To his kingdom, not to me. We should have him watched.'

Brom sighed. 'I'm supposed to return east, but I can't leave you here if there's any chance of traitors inside these walls. I need you safe and alive at the end of all this.'

He had a way with words that affected her ability to breathe. A few moments passed. They had dived into something, and neither had realised the depth of it. He needed her to live. She needed him to *breathe*.

'I am going to train,' she said, looking down at Pup.

He frowned. 'Now?'

'Yes.' She began walking to the door.

'We rode overnight. You should rest.'

'I will rest when I am dead.' She gave him a playful smile.

'That's not funny.' He caught up to her, slinging an arm around her as if she were some common tavern wench. She liked the weight of it though.

The doors opened in front of them, and she listened for Lief's boots behind her. She glanced over her shoulder when she heard Charis's footsteps instead.

'What's wrong?' Brom asked.

She faced forwards again. 'Nothing.'

'You're not afraid?'

'Fear is a waste of energy. I choose anger every time.'

He chuckled and kissed the top of her head. 'Maybe I'll come train with you.'

She looked up at him. 'Why? Charis makes a perfectly adequate pell.'

He kissed her on the mouth that time. His actions were ridiculous, her reaction more so.

'What are you doing?' she asked.

His eyes moved over her face. 'Kissing my wife.'

'No, you are eroding walls I have spent years building.'

He drew her closer without breaking stride. 'You don't need walls with me.'

'I especially need walls with you.'

His arm tightened playfully around her. 'Go get your trousers on. I'll meet you in the behourde.'

She regarded him with suspicion. 'Why are you so keen to train with me? So you can disarm me in under two seconds, then leave all smug?'

'I didn't leave smug last time. You walked away with your tail between your legs.'

He was right. 'Well, now that I am aware of your dirty tactics, I will be better prepared.'

'Dirty tactics?' His eyes held laughter. 'Shall we make it interesting with a wager?'

That tweaked her interest. 'Go on.'

'Loser cooks for the other this evening.'

She rolled her eyes. 'You seem quite determined to prove I cannot cook.'

'Proper cooking. We build a fire, bring food. Eat together under the stars.'

'While picking insects from our meal?'

They had reached the end of the corridor and turned to face each other.

'Don't you tire of formal dinners in the hall and eating alone in your quarters?' he asked.

'I am surprisingly good company.'

He searched her face for a moment. 'You can choose whatever you like. Your signature Syrasan dish.'

She had never cooked a meal in her life. 'You seem pretty confident I will be the one doing the cooking.'

He shrugged. 'Out of curiosity, what is your specialty?'

'Fish,' she said without missing a beat.

'What type of fish?' he replied just as quickly.

She angled her head. 'The swimming kind.'

'Ah. The ones with fins and a tail?'

'Yes.' She made a point of not looking away.

He leaned on one foot. 'What other ingredients will you need?'

'Parsley, lemon, pepper.' She was not an idiot. She knew what she was eating—just had no idea how to prepare it.

He nodded. 'See you soon.'

Cora circled Brom on the sand, occasionally stepping in one of the patches of remaining ice. There would be no more snowfall until the cold season now. 'Do not go easy on me. There is no victory in being handed victory.'

'Inspiring words, but to be clear, I'm not going to leave you unconscious and bleeding on the ground.'

While he was every bit the warrior and king, there was a playfulness to him that brought much-needed reprieve from all the seriousness. 'All right, big man. Let us see who is cooking the fish tonight.' She took the wooden sword Charis offered her and waited for him to make his way back to Sarey and Pup. Her lady could have remained inside but had chosen to come along. Cora noticed Sarey's change in stance as the bodyguard stopped beside her. Lately, Sarey had taken to watching him whenever she thought no one was looking. Cora was going to need to have words to her lady.

'Ready?' Brom asked. 'First one to drop their sword loses.'

Cora watched him carefully. 'You know, I learned a few new tricks at the manor.'

'I call them old tricks.' He winked at her.

'Her Majesty is a fast learner,' Charis called out. 'Never have to show her anything twice.'

Brom glanced in his direction. 'That so?'

Cora watched his feet for weight bearing, noted the direction of his toes. It was a good way to predict moves. Losing patience, she acted first, delivering a practiced sequence of blows, which he deflected with minimal effort. Her shoulder ached, and her heart sped up. Back and forth they went, power shifting between them. If Brom was surprised by her improvement, he hid it well. She decided to try a move Charis had shown her, ducking beneath his weapon and hooking her foot around his ankle. It was supposed to trip him, but he did not move. Instead, he kicked his other foot over a patch of ice, sending a spray of it over Cora. The cold made her gasp, and she fell onto her backside.

'That's what happens when you fight dirty,' he said with a smug grin.

Cora let go of her sword, scooped up some of the ice in her hand, and threw it straight at his head. He took a step back, spitting. A satisfied smile spread across her face. 'How does it taste, warrior?'

He spat again and wiped his face. 'Like actual shit.' He leaned on his knees for a moment, watching her. 'You're the dirtiest fighter I've ever met. You lose, by the way. First to drop your sword.'

'It was entirely worth it.' She extended one arm. 'Now help a lady up.'

He closed the distance between them, grinning as he took her hand and pulled her up. 'At least you're being a gracious loser today.'

She snaked her hands around his neck, smiling up at him. 'Oh, husband. You really do not know me at all, do you?' With that, she released a handful of ice down the neck of his vest.

He jumped, cursed, and then danced in circles for a moment. Once he had shaken most of it out, he grabbed her around the waist and hoisted her high up into the air. An involuntary squeal escaped her.

'Put me down!'

He flung her over his shoulder. 'But I can't trust you on the ground.' His tone was playful.

She pounded her fists on his back. 'But you trust my feet at this height?'

'Good point.' He swung her around so he was cradling her in his arms. 'Are you going to be nice if I put you down?'

'Probably not.' She was breathless and smiling.

He rubbed his rough face over hers, evoking another squeal.

'You are going to make my skin red!'

He did not stop. 'It is already red from the embarrassment of losing.'

Her head tipped back with laughter—real laughter, the kind you cannot control the pitch or rhythm of. It spilled out of her until she finally went limp in his arms. She felt lighter suddenly. It took her a moment to catch her breath, and when she looked up, she found Brom watching her with a serious expression.

'What?' she asked, her smile fading.

He shook his head. 'Do you have any idea how long I've waited to see that?'

Cora looked over to where Sarey was watching them with pure adoration. 'Put me down.'

He kept hold of her. 'No. I want to see you laugh again.'

Her eyes searched his. 'Why?'

'Because it was the most arresting thing I've ever witnessed.'

She was breathing hard, her face just inches from his. It was attraction in its purest form. Normally she felt it below the hips, but this was everywhere, coursing through her limbs and threatening to burst through her fingertips. 'Please put me down.'

He placed her gently on the ground and stepped back. 'You better go get some rest. You've got a big meal to cook tonight.'

She really tried not to smile.

'Swimming fish, lemon, parsley,' he said. 'Am I forgetting anything?'

'Pepper.'

He nodded. 'Pepper.'

She turned away from him, clicking her fingers so Pup came running. 'Better start building that fire, warrior.'

CHAPTER 31

*G*rey light washed over the castle grounds, swallowing the rising smoke from the fire. The cool air was made bearable by the flames. Cora stood five feet away, knife in hand, staring down at the dead fish laid out on the tree stump. It looked very much alive in its uncooked state, with its bulging eyes locked on hers.

'Everything all right?' Brom called out from his spot on the blanket. He was waiting for her to admit she had no idea what she was doing.

'Fine.' A small lie. Instead of sleeping that afternoon, she had gone to the kitchen and asked the castle's head cook to teach her how to cook fish. He had offered to prepare it for her, but that had felt like cheating. In the end, he had removed the scales for her and left the rest intact. All that was left to do now was stab it through the stomach the same way she had stabbed the man at the manor, slice it open the same way she had sliced the man's throat open, and remove its insides.

She crouched, took hold of the cold, slippery thing, and drove the small knife into its stomach. She wiggled the knife all the way to the tail, exactly as she had been shown. When she opened it up, she brought the back of her hand to her mouth.

'How's it going?' Brom called to her as he poked at the fire with a stick.

She forced her hand back down. 'Really well.' Holding her breath, she removed the insides, abandoning any bits that did not come away easily. She pushed them carefully to one side before positioning the knife behind the fin. Or was it in front of the fin? She tried to think while maintaining eye contact with the fish.

Brom appeared at her side.

'You've never done this before, have you?'

She thought about lying. She had made it that far. But even the smallest lie felt enormous when it came to him. She placed the knife down and rose. 'No.'

'Why didn't you just tell me?'

She looked around for the wine and realised none had been brought out. *Perfect.*

'What are you looking for?'

'Nothing.' She turned her face up to him. 'Are you now going to pretend you know what to do next?'

He kissed her and bent down, picking up the knife. She watched as he moved it this way and that, his actions quick and efficient. Once the fish was in neat pieces, the head discarded, he washed them in the pail of water and dropped them into the waiting pot. He looked over at the other ingredients.

'You can help me with the next part.'

She crouched beside him and passed him the butter, salted broth, lemons, peppercorns, and the carrots she had sliced earlier, which were various unconventional shapes. Brom added everything to the pot and placed the lid on. Cora watched as he carried it to the fire and settled it in the hot coals before going to sit on the blanket. He gestured for her to join him.

'So this is what you were doing up in the mountains all those years,' she said as she settled next to him. 'You were living your best peasant life.'

He placed an arm behind her. 'My grandfather taught me to fish. He believed every man should have basic life skills, regardless of status. He taught me everything from hunting to carpentry.'

She watched the joy on his face as the memories washed over him. 'Who taught you how to fight? Your father?'

The joy vanished. 'No. I had various teachers. My father was busy ruling, and any spare time he had went to Jayr.'

'Because he was next in line for the crown?'

He nodded. 'Probably. They were always close. I was more like my grandfather, an outcast.' He paused. 'He was a lot like Droet, actually, minus the crazy.'

Cora smiled. 'So you went to live among people like you, people your grandfather trusted.' She paused. 'Because you were afraid of losing that part of yourself?'

He thought for a moment. 'When people in power draw a line in the sand, you have to decide which side of the line to stand on. The more relations broke down with the Nydoen people, the more I realised I was on the wrong side.'

'So you took off. Went to rule your own kingdom of sorts.'

'Wasn't quite like that.'

She watched him a moment. 'Then how was it?'

He thought before replying. 'In hindsight, I think I wanted to hide. I was never supposed to rule anybody. I was supposed to support my brother through his reign, the way Tyron supports Pandarus, despite having very different views of the world.' Something resembling regret passed over his face.

A sad realisation hit Cora at that moment. 'You never wanted the crown. That is why you hesitated, why you gave Jayr so many chances to do the right thing.'

He watched the flames. 'I am a warrior at heart, not a ruler. I wanted him to be a better king so I could live my outcast life in peace. But from the moment I arrived in those mountains, everyone expected things from me. Some were easy. I could fight if needed, take children from men who had no right to them. I could play the hero before slinking back into the mountains.'

'But they wanted more.'

Another nod. 'They deserved more. I'm here only for them. I understand I have a job to do, but I'm still getting used to the fact that it won't end. After all of this, there will be something else, and then something else. The burden of responsibility won't grow any lighter.'

Cora wanted to touch him. 'You can absolutely do this, you know. You might not want to, but you are up to the task. There is no better king, no one more qualified than the boy who learned how to be a man from his grandfather all those years ago. I have complete faith in you—as does most of the kingdom.'

When he looked at her, she saw the flames reflected in his eyes.

'Is that why you said yes to me?' he asked.

'Well, it is one of the reasons. You did offer me a crown.'

He laughed lightly as he reached up to brush his thumb over her lips. 'Always so painfully honest.'

She picked up a piece of bread, tore it in half, and offered one side to him. He opened his mouth, and she popped it in. 'I am envious of your relationship with your grandfather. Good mentors are vital in those early years.'

'Who was your mentor?'

'My mother.' Her tone was flat. 'She taught me valuable

life skills also, like how to secure a powerful husband and keep him happy.'

He regarded her in the fading light. 'Did any of the lessons stick?'

Her gaze slid to him. 'Married twice so far.'

'So far?' he asked with a laugh.

She shrugged. 'I have a cousin waiting in the wings in case you die.'

He shook his head. 'That's reassuring.' They watched the fire for a moment, and then Brom turned to her again. 'Do you think your father would've approved of Jayr?'

'Absolutely not.' She held her hands out, warming them in front of the flames. 'He said no the first time Jayr asked.'

'Then Pandarus handed you over after his death?'

She was not sure how much to tell him, whether he would understand, but decided there was little that could surprise him at that point. 'Actually, I handed myself over. The match was my idea.'

Brom was silent a moment. 'You knew the type of man he was?'

'Yes.'

'And you wanted to marry him?'

'He was a terrible person. I was a terrible person. There was no better match at that time.'

Brom took her cold hands in his warm ones and rubbed them as he processed that. 'The thing is, terrible people don't marry terrible people. Terrible people marry good people and go about destroying them. Bad people usually don't realise they're bad people.'

She looked up at him. 'My entire family cannot be wrong about me.'

His expression turned serious. 'Do you know what I think?'

'I am sure you will tell me.'

'I think at various points in your life, you made some poor choices. Instead of self-correcting, you chose self-loathing. You made up stories about yourself and repeated them over and over until they were all you knew.'

Cora pulled her hands free of his, no longer cold.

'You told yourself that you're selfish and destructive,' he continued. 'Then told everyone else the same thing.'

'I am selfish and destructive.' She wanted to look away but did not.

'Everyone is at times, but that's not your whole story. You're also smart, loyal to those deserving of it, and have a disturbing ability to see people for who they are.'

She faced the fire again, not enjoying feeling transparent. 'You know, there are much easier ways to get under my skirts.'

'And you're funny.'

'Next time lead with that.'

He leaned back on his hands. 'This is nice. For a moment I almost forgot we're at war.'

It was. It was really nice for someone who did not do *nice*. At some point in their conversation, she had forgotten about the absence of wine. 'Would you like to dance?'

Instead of reacting with surprise or confusion, he said, 'What type of dance? Something fun from my homeland? Or something pretentious from yours?'

'Something pretentious.' She stood and offered her hand to him like he would her. He took it but used his legs to get up, knowing he was too heavy for her to take the full weight of him.

'Do I know this dance?' he asked.

She shook her head and raised her arms, bringing her hands to his so they were palm to palm. 'I will teach you. First we circle each other.'

Pup had been sleeping on the other side of the fire, and now she sat up to watch them, always fearful of missing out.

'Like this?' Brom asked, exaggerating each step and turning his nose up in the air.

'*Now* you look like a king.' She bit back a smile when he did a playful turn before bringing his hand to hers once more.

'You have to admit Zoelin dances are much more fun.'

'Fun, yes. Flirtatious, no.'

His eyebrows rose. 'Is this how men flirt where you're from?'

'It is one way. Let me guess—in the mountains, men slaughter chickens and leave them at the woman's doorstep.'

He laughed. 'I once gathered flowers for a woman, and she fed them to her pig.'

Cora moved slowly, enabling him to keep up. 'I cannot imagine a woman turning you down without good reason. Did you sleep with her sister or something?'

'So cynical.' He gave her a coy smile. 'Actually, she wanted us to get married. I couldn't commit, not with everything happening.'

'So you gave her flowers and broke her heart?'

'She's since married and has two children.'

Cora watched his face for hints of jealousy. Nothing. 'Did you love her?'

'I don't think so. I didn't have space for it then.' He watched her a moment. 'What about you? Was there anybody before Jayr?'

Leksi immediately came to mind. She shook her head. 'Only a young girl's infatuation that went on far too long.'

He nodded like he understood. Their imaginary song came to an end, and Cora gathered her skirts and curtsied before him. He replied with a bow, and then they both stood there looking at each other.

'We better check on the fish,' she said.

They did it together, carefully lifting the lid. Smoky aromas took over the air, making Cora's stomach rumble. Brom poked at the fish with a fork.

'It's ready.'

Cora held out the bowls while he ladled the soupy fish into them. It was one of the most normal things she had ever done. No one was around to help them, to serve them, to appease them. It was just the two of them beneath a million stars. Brom handed her a piece of bread and a fork, and they ate on the ground with orange light flickering over them.

'I've said it before, but I'll say it again,' Brom said. 'We make a good team.'

Cora smiled to herself as she reached for another piece of bread.

'Wait,' Brom said, putting his bowl down and pulling the pot closer to them. 'Dip it in here. This is the best part.' He tore off a chunk of bread and soaked up some of the liquid.

Her mother would have had heart failure at seeing her eating straight from the pot in that way. She dipped it, then popped the soggy bread into her mouth before emitting a soft groan. 'Why does it taste so good?'

He swallowed his mouthful before replying. 'Something about the little burnt bits makes it taste better.'

She stilled to watch him eat. He put the bread down when he noticed her.

'Why so serious?' he asked.

She wished she could just enjoy the moment, but she was always thinking ahead to tomorrow, to next week. 'I do not want you to die, not even for a good reason.'

He took the bowl from her hands and pulled her to him, resting her head in his lap so she could see the stars. 'Look at that. It's like the clouds lifted just for us.' His fingers stroked her hair.

She was looking at him. 'You cannot win. You must know that. Even with the additional men my brother sends you.'

He continued to stroke her hair. 'The number of men does not decide the outcome.'

'It influences the outcome rather heavily though.'

He leaned back on his hands and looked up. 'Sounds like you want me to live. That's extra motivation right there.'

Cora focused on the stars then. 'If you die, this will have been for nothing.'

He looked down at her. 'The marriage?'

'All of it. Jayr's death, the marriage, the waste of life. I will be the most bitter, drunk widow the world has ever seen.'

The image was supposed to repel him, but he just watched her as though she were the most fascinating thing in the world. 'Or you'll grow more resilient, more compassionate.'

'That is what good people do. I self-destruct, remember?'

'Time for a new story, wife.'

He winked at her, and she swallowed down all the emotion that tiny gesture evoked. She reached for his hand, threading her fingers through his. Not only did it feel natural in that moment but necessary.

'The first day I saw you walk through that gate, I knew everything I'd heard about you was wrong,' he said. 'You held that boy like he was your own flesh and blood.'

'Someone had to.' She fell silent. 'I could barely believe what Jayr was doing with those children. I have never felt so helpless and useless in my life.'

'So you wrote to me. You betrayed Jayr.'

'Yes.' Her eyes met his. 'And when he bought more children, I wrote you again, but he intercepted the letter.'

Brom's expression turned serious. 'What did he do?'

'He behaved like Jayr.' She did not go into the details, and he did not ask. He had seen the bruises.

'And you continued to be the people's queen.'

Her eyebrows came together. 'You always see the good in me, trust blindly. It is paralysing.'

'It's not blind. I see you very clearly.'

Her free hand came up to cover his. 'Do what you have to. Battle, win, lose. Just come home at the end of it all.'

He pulled her up so she was seated on his lap and buried his face in her neck. 'If for some reason I don't make it back, know it wasn't for nothing.'

She closed her eyes, savouring his warm breath on her skin. 'Just come back.'

CHAPTER 32

*B*rom woke to pounding on the door of his bedchambers. Cora, who was asleep in his arms, jumped at the noise and sat up.

'Wait here,' he said, kissing her head before sliding from the bed and snatching his trousers off the floor. When he opened the door, he found one of the few trustworthy men who had joined him from the mountains standing there. 'What's going on?' He went to pull the door closed behind him, but Cora caught it. She was wrapped in the bed sheet, completely distracting both men as she leaned in the doorway.

'I've got news about Grandor Pollux, Your Majesty.'

'Go on.'

'He met with someone from your army yesterday afternoon. We took the man aside and questioned him. Eventually got out of him that your advisor plans to travel east to Onuric Castle.'

'For what purpose?'

The soldier hesitated. 'The man died before we could extract any further information.'

A soldier from his own army who would rather die than share information with his king? That was not good. Exactly how far did the deceit go? 'Pollux only met with the one man?'

'Yes, Your Majesty.'

Brom looked back at Cora, whose expression gave nothing away. 'Tell me what you're thinking.'

Her gaze slid to his. 'Pollux is the traitor.'

'Perhaps he's heading to the camp to question someone over the attacks.'

She shook her head. 'You do not believe that. You know there is only one reason that soldier refused to talk. He was protecting Pollux. This is bigger than we realised.'

'You think he's working with King Tuyon?'

'Probably this entire time.' She pushed a lock of hair back from her face. 'I underestimated him.'

'This doesn't fall on you.'

'I am coming with you to Onuric Castle.' She said it like she was announcing she would be taking a bath or going for a walk.

Brom turned back to the soldier. 'Send word to Prince Tyron that I'll meet him on the road, and then send word to Carac and tell him to take Pollux into custody for questioning.'

'Pollux will beat the messenger,' Cora pointed out.

'Then he can answer to me when I get there.' He looked back at the soldier. 'Have the groom ready my horse, and ready the reinforcements for immediate departure.'

'Prepare both of our horses,' Cora said from behind him. 'I will be travelling with the king.'

Brom drew a breath before facing her. 'Absolutely not.'

'Have you not figured out yet that there are no safe havens? How do you know he is not luring you away from the castle to get clear access to me?'

'I can't take you into a war zone.'

'The safest place for me is with you, even if that place is a war zone.'

He wanted to tell her no, but she was right. Leaving her alone at Drake Castle was risky, and no one would protect her like he would.

Turning back to the soldier, he said, 'Ready the queen's horse.'

Brom and Cora met Tyron and his men in Wetus that evening. When they arrived, Brom was handed a letter from Carac asking why he had not been told that Pollux was going to Onuric to meet with King Tuyon. No one had been told, because no one knew. There was only one reason Pollux would attempt such a lie—he had no intention of returning.

That night Brom lay awake watching Cora in the dark. She was nestled safely in the crook of his arm, her sleepy breaths hitting his bare skin. Charis's snores reached them from outside, but that was not the reason Brom could not sleep. It was every other noise. Everyone was suspicious, every shadow a threat. When Cora woke early, she did not say anything. They just lay together in silence, watching the light change.

They mounted their horses early and made their way to the camp, where a stern-faced Carac greeted them. After filling him in, they sent a messenger, requesting King Tuyon meet them at the clearing. A group of archers from the king's army volunteered to wait amid the trees on either side of them in case things took a turn for the worse. Brom had already organised some of Tyron's men for the task, but he agreed to the last-minute change as he wanted his own men to feel valued and useful.

Once again, Cora insisted on going to confront Pollux, despite strong objections from everyone. Tyron had one last go of talking her out of it before they left.

'Save your energy' came her reply.

Leksi warned Charis that if a weapon touched the queen, it better have gone through him first.

'Stop fussing,' Cora said. 'They only targeted me to disrupt Syrasan's involvement, but we are all quite involved at this point. If Pollux is indeed the traitor, he knows Tyron will not be withdrawing his men anytime soon.'

Brom marvelled at that mind of hers.

Mounting their horses once more, they made their way out into the clearing, eyes on the trees ahead of them. Cora glanced at Brom as horses emerged thirty yards in front of them. And there was Pollux, riding alongside Tuyon like a loyal dog.

'Here we go,' she said.

They had not come alone. Armed men waited behind them. Leksi glanced at Tyron, his hand brushing his sword before resting on his leg. Carac's gaze swept the trees, where their own men were concealed. He was the type of warrior who was always prepared for the worst possible outcome.

Tuyon and Pollux rode out alone, stopping ten feet away and dismounting, their actions slow and deliberate.

'I'll go alone,' Brom said.

Cora slid from the saddle, ignoring the look he gave her. 'Not alone.' She slipped her hand into his, and his instinctively closed around it. He realised in that moment she was more afraid of being alone and feeling useless than of dying. She was a warrior. His grip on her tightened as they made their way towards the waiting men. They were met with Tuyon's neutral expression and Pollux's sharp gaze.

Behind them, he heard weapons being drawn. No one was taking chances that day. The tension in the air made

Brom wish Cora was safely back at camp, yet he could not help but admire how tall and sure-footed she stood at his side.

'Tell me you didn't bring your wife for protection,' Pollux said, a smile playing on his lips.

'I brought myself,' Cora replied.

Tuyon's gaze fell to their joined hands. 'Pollux tried to tell me the relationship was not a faux. I have to admit, I didn't believe him.' He looked at Cora. 'Didn't think you had it in you, Your Majesty.'

She tilted her head. 'Back at you. While the two of you are adorable together, I fear you have been led astray by a traitor.'

Pollux sniffed. 'Someone had to step up.'

'You think this is a step up?' Brom asked. 'Sorry to disappoint, but it's only a sharp decline from here for you.' He heard a bow creak behind him and glanced over his shoulder to where Tyron had an arrow trained on Pollux. He looked back at the advisor. 'You better start talking before the prince shoots you. I hear he's been waiting years for the chance.'

Pollux grunted in response.

'I really wanted us to be friends,' Tuyon said, getting the conversation started. 'I wanted us to do business.'

Brom blinked. 'We have very different approaches to business.'

'I was patient, waited for you to get your head together, but it seems you're not up to the task. You don't have what it takes to lead.'

'Funny,' Cora said, 'we were just saying the same thing about you.'

'Better put your wife back on her leash,' Pollux said, no longer smiling.

Cora glared at him. 'Perhaps he could borrow yours, if Tuyon does not mind letting you off for a while.'

Pollux shifted his weight from one foot to another. 'How many lives do you have?'

'More than you, I promise you that.'

Brom narrowed his eyes on Pollux, not liking the spite directed at Cora. 'What did he offer you in exchange for turning your back on your kingdom?'

'I act *for* my kingdom' came his reply.

'You stand with our enemy.'

'For the good of Zoelin.'

Brom shook his head. 'No.' Cora was watching Pollux through the entire interaction. He could practically hear her mind ticking over.

'Regent,' she said all of a sudden. 'He has offered to make you regent.' She smiled. 'I am right, am I not?'

Pollux said nothing.

Cora looked up at Brom. 'King Tuyon has no interest in remaining in Zoelin, or ruling it for that matter. He only wants control of the trade. Pollux is a superb puppet.'

'I'm no one's puppet,' Pollux replied, his tone louder than necessary for the distance between them.

A bow creaked behind them once more.

Tuyon laughed quietly. 'Smart woman you have there. You know, I might have married her myself if she were capable of carrying a child.'

Brom's hand instinctively went to the hilt of his sword, but a small squeeze of the hand stopped him. He drew a calming breath and focused on Pollux once more. 'You'll never be regent, because my people won't accept your common, traitorous blood in any position of real power.'

The corner of Pollux's mouth twitched. 'You sure about that?'

'I'm confident the East will be in safe hands,' Tuyon said. 'All is well that ends well.'

Brom's blood was running hot now. 'This ends in death,

with this traitor's body hanging on the gate of Onuric Castle for the crows to pick at.'

Pollux exhaled sharply through his nose, a sort of laugh. 'You really don't get it, do you? Your enemy is bigger than us. Your enemy arrived with you.'

Brom's lungs slowed.

'You know the archers you so helpfully placed amid the trees?'

It was no surprise he was aware of them, as it was a common tactical move. 'What about them?'

'They won't be much help to you.'

'And why's that?' Brom's grip tightened on Cora as she looked in the direction of the archers.

'Because they are loyal to Pollux,' Cora said, pre-empting the response. 'The arrows are not trained on them—they are trained on us.'

Everything seemed to move in slow motion then. Brom pulled Cora behind him, shielding her from weapons, from words, and drawing his sword. In the same moment, Tyron, Carac, and Leksi swung their bows in the direction of the trees. Brom's eyes locked with Pollux's as all of his senses worked together. The man's stance was so casual, so relaxed, that Brom knew Cora had guessed right.

'I admire your ambition,' Tuyon said, looking around, 'but there's no room for heroes here.'

Pollux drew his sword and took a step towards them. His foot had barely touched the ground before Tyron's bow swung in his direction. Pollux must have sensed it before he saw it, because he darted right, and the arrow pierced his arm instead of his heart. A moment later, arrows rained from the sky.

'Cover!' Brom called out, wrapping his body around Cora as he dragged her back towards the horses.

Charis reached them in under a second, swinging his

shield over Cora with a determined expression. Syrasan archers took aim at the trees but hesitated, because they did not understand what was happening.

'Loose!' Leksi shouted, pointing to the trees.

Arrows passed overhead.

'Get her out of here!' Brom shouted at Charis.

It was a good thing Zoelin soldiers were not known for their strong archery skills. Most of them fell short, and the rest missed entirely.

Cora's eyes widened as Charis tugged her out of Brom's arms. 'No—'

'Go!'

Luckily, the Syrasan archers did not miss. Brom watched Cora until she reached the trees, then turned, searching for Tuyon and Pollux, but they were gone, swallowed up by the soldiers who were charging towards them.

'Incoming!' Brom shouted, gesturing for his own men to join the fight. He prayed that whatever was left of his army was loyal to him.

Swinging his sword, he braced for battle.

CHAPTER 33

Cora stood against the wall of the tent with her arms crossed and fingers pressing into her flesh. She had insisted on remaining in the tent while the physician removed an arrow from Brom's leg.

'It's nothing,' Brom lied.

Her eyes met his. 'I have been shot with an arrow, remember? You are lucky to be alive.' Her gaze fell to the leg once more as the physician finished washing the wound and began to bandage it. 'We would never have met him out in the open if we had known our own soldiers would shoot at us.'

Brom's eyes sank shut. 'And the bastard got away.'

Cora glanced at the entrance of the tent, where Charis and Carac were waiting outside. Their injuries were superficial. Tyron and Leksi were dealing with the dead. 'I never thought him a coward.'

Brom said nothing.

'I would normally suggest you stay off it for a few days,' the physician said, gathering the soiled instruments in a piece of cloth, 'but I don't suppose you'll listen.'

Brom stood, testing the leg. 'Good as new.'

Another lie.

Cora let go of her arms because she was starting to get pins and needles. She struggled to get a handle on her emotions. Anger clashed with fear, extinguishing all hope. Brom would not survive another encounter with the northern king, and that realisation was killing her with every passing moment. 'I should have taken a weapon with me.'

Brom sank down onto the cot, assessing her for a moment. Turning to the physician, he said, 'Leave us, please.'

The physician bowed, collected his bag, and exited the tent.

Once they were alone, Brom gestured for her to come to him, but she was afraid of coming undone if she moved. Fear anchored her. Her feelings for the man were no longer neat and contained. They had morphed into something dangerous.

She remained where she was. 'How many of our men followed Pollux into the castle?' Her words caught in her throat.

His outstretched arm fell to his side. 'Around two hundred.'

'Two hundred.' She swallowed. 'And how many additional soldiers did my brother bring with him?'

Brom wiped at the dried blood on his lips. 'Three hundred and twenty.'

She looked away, not speaking for the longest time. 'I think it is time to be sensible.'

'What does that mean?'

Her gaze returned to him. 'Give him what he wants before we are left with nothing.'

He shook his head. 'No.'

It was the only response she had expected. 'You cannot win this fight, and you know it.'

'It's not about winning. I have a job to do, a responsibility, a mess to clean up.'

'Jayr's mess.'

'Which is now *my* mess.'

Cora's shoulders fell a few inches. 'If you insist on dying here, then you better get used to the idea of me dead beside you.'

He blinked the image away and looked down. 'Stop it. You wouldn't last five seconds in battle.'

'And you will not last much longer than that.'

He shook his head. 'It was a mistake to bring you here.'

'Do not say that.'

'I should've left you at Archdale. There are far worse fates than a dysfunctional family.'

Her eyes burned. 'Well, you did not leave me there because you know the best version of me is the one standing at your side, not hiding away.'

He gripped the edge of the cot, tapping one finger furiously against it. 'You can't stay here.' His words were just above a whisper.

'If you stay, I stay. That is how it is with us now.'

'What are you talking about? I never agreed to that.'

'You promised you would never send me away again.'

He rose but did not go to her. 'You're twisting my words. I never agreed to let you remain at the *front line*.'

'It is my choice.'

He shook his head furiously this time. 'No. You don't get to choose this.'

She closed the distance between them, taking hold of his face and forcing him to look at her. 'If you have sentenced yourself to death, then you have sentenced us both.' When he shook his head again, she squeezed his face hard, trying to still it. 'Stop telling me *no*.'

'No.' He removed her hands from his face.

Panic pounded her insides. 'I will not return to Drake Castle without you.'

He wore the most broken expression. 'You're not going to Drake Castle. You're going back to Syrasan.'

She stepped back from him as though he had pushed her, eyes searching his. 'You cannot send me back there. You promised.'

He was silent.

'You promised.' She knew he had heard her the first time. 'Did you lie? Are you a liar?'

He ran a hand down his face. 'The circumstances change things.'

She shook her head, rejecting his confession. 'You said no lies between us. *You* said that, and I trusted you.'

'And I meant it, but I couldn't predict this.' He pointed east. 'This is messy, violent war. I'd be crazy to let you stay. Some promises need to be broken because you will die here if I don't. You said it yourself, we can't win. Do you think Tuyon is going to just let us leave?'

'He might if you give him what he wants!'

He tilted his head in a plea. 'That's not the man you married.'

She stepped forwards and shoved his chest with both hands, the force of it making him step back into the cot. 'You are a liar just like your brother.' She hissed the words at him, eyes welling with tears.

His face was impassive. 'I won't apologise for keeping you alive.'

'What is the point of being alive if you're dead at the end of all this?' She was panting, struggling to get enough air. 'You are choosing defeat. You are sentencing yourself, my *brother*, and every man fighting alongside you to death.'

Brom blinked. 'I'm sending your brother with you. You'll need him when this is over.'

Her face collapsed. 'That is suicide. *You* need him.'

He stared at the ground between them.

'No.' She tried to bring strength to her voice. When he took a step towards the exit, she flung herself in his way. 'I am not leaving you here. When there is no one left to fight at your side, there will be me—'

He took a firm hold of her arms, the heels of her feet lifting slightly. 'Don't you get it? I can't watch you die.'

'And I cannot leave here knowing your fate.' A sob tore from her throat. 'I love you.' As did those words, words she had never spoken aloud to anyone. 'I love you. I am a survivor, but I will not survive your death.' His grip eased, her feet returning to the ground. He appeared defeated, and that gave her hope. 'Your death is my death,' she whispered.

He reached a hand into her hair, then, bending down, kissed her forehead, her eye, and her cheek, her tears pouring freely. When his mouth found hers, she inhaled sharply, finally getting the air she needed. The kiss was firm, desperate. Only when her tears had stopped falling did he pull away to look at her. 'I can't save my kingdom, but I can save you.'

Her eyes moved between his, wanting more words, better ones. She licked her lips, tasting blood. Probably his, possibly her own. She did not know or care. Their blood was the same.

She opened her mouth to speak, to beg, to fight, but nothing came. He was too close. When she went to step back, her foot rolled. He reached out to steady her, and she slapped his hand away with surprising force. The pain in her chest was unbearable. It was as if he had stabbed her straight through the heart, twisting the knife for good measure.

'If you do this, if you send me away, you will never see me again.'

He went to reach for her, but she shoved his arm away, a

raw, painful noise escaping her. 'Your days of touching me are over.'

He linked his hands atop his head. 'Don't say that.'

'You are as good as dead.'

'The war is not lost yet.'

'More lies.' Her voice cracked as she stared coldly back at him. 'If by some miracle you survive this, I will never give you the chance to do this to me again.' She took a few more steps, not trusting her back to him. Only when she reached the flap of the tent did she turn and push through it.

CHAPTER 34

*I*da's hooves made a hollow sound on the bridge as they crossed the Lotheng River. It was like an echo of her own emptiness. Cora stopped the mare at the highest point, staring down at the fast water below. She could see Lief's wide eyes as he fell.

'We should keep moving,' Tyron said.

Cora jumped at the sound of his voice, pulled from the memory. She looked from him to Charis, who was watching the trees like he was expecting Pollux himself to emerge and slaughter them all, then to Sarey, who was wearing her "worried mother" expression. She pushed Ida into a walk and clicked her fingers, gesturing for Pup to follow. 'No one cares if I live or die now. No one is coming for me.' Certainly not Brom after her departure speech.

Tyron waited for her to catch up to him. 'Once you are settled at Archdale, I am returning to Zoelin to fight.'

She glanced sideways at him, expecting nothing less of the man who lived his life by some code of honour many others had moved on from. 'What will your wife say about that?'

'She understands the fight.'

Cora watched Pup for a moment. 'I do not want to go to Archdale.'

Tyron sighed. 'If not there, then where?'

'Veanor. To the manor.'

He regarded her with suspicion. 'I thought you could not stand Hali.'

She shrugged. 'She is less irritating than Mother.'

Tyron smiled to himself as he checked their surroundings. 'I am sure Lord Yuri and Lady Hali will be thrilled to have you.'

'You are such a liar.'

Another smile. 'Lord Yuri likes you.'

'The man is too kind for his own good.'

'You say that like it is a flaw.'

She closed her eyes as they stepped down from the bridge. 'It *is* a flaw.'

Tyron was silent a moment. 'He sent you away because he loves you. You cannot be angry at him for that.'

'Watch me.'

Tyron called one of the guards over, instructing him to ride ahead to the manor and advise the lord and lady of the house of their impending arrival. He turned back to Cora. 'I will do everything in my power to keep Brom alive.'

She swallowed. 'And yet it will not be enough.'

CHAPTER 35

*I*t took Cora's mother four days to learn of her whereabouts, then one more to travel to the manor. She showed up, uninvited, fussing, on the same day a letter arrived from Tyron. More than a thousand fresh Asigow warriors had arrived at Onuric Castle. They were not preparing for war but for an annihilation. The remaining Zoelin and Syrasan forces did not stand a chance against an army that size. Everyone knew it, just no one said it aloud.

Cora lay down on the bed the day she received that letter —and she could not find the strength to get up again.

'Tyron is the equivalent of three armed soldiers,' Eldoris said in the chair beside her, working away on a tapestry for her new grandchild. Aldara had chosen to remain at their home near Wripis for the birth. Another family member who avoided Archdale Castle at all costs.

Cora blinked at her mother from her nest of blankets on the bed. 'What are you talking about?'

Eldoris looked up from her needlework. 'I am simply saying that we should not be focused on the numbers. We have some clear advantages, like strong archers and highly trained swordsmen.'

Cora wanted to cover her head. 'Even if every Syrasan soldier was equivalent to three of our enemy's, your math falls over.'

Eldoris's expression fell. 'Must you be so pessimistic?'

'I am being *realistic*.'

Eldoris dropped the tapestry onto her lap. 'Perhaps you could try prayer instead of wine. The drink is making you unbearable.'

Cora had appreciated the quiet of the manor for the first few days, but now her thoughts were competing with her mother's voice. The problem with drink as a crutch was that it prevented her from running, training, and tolerating the company of other people. 'Where is Sarey?'

'With your guard. Are you aware that the two of them have been spending a lot of time together?'

She was aware, just had not gotten around to having the long overdue conversation.

The sound of Hali's footsteps approaching made Cora tense up. She was always trying to do something helpful, but the fact of the matter was that no one could help her.

'Your Majesty,' Hali called from the doorway. Her voice was always a few pitches too high for the mood of the room.

Cora stared at her, not saying anything.

'I wondered if you might like to take a walk.'

'Did Sarey send you?'

Hali looked suitably guilty. 'We just thought being such a lovely day...'

Cora's eyes sank shut. 'Leave, please.'

More footsteps approached, and when she opened her eyes this time, she saw Sarey marching towards her. Charis hung back in the doorway with Hali. Sarey tore the blankets off her.

'What in God's name are you doing?' Cora shouted, her head pounding.

'I can't bear it any longer.'

Cora pulled at the blankets like a child. 'Let go at once, or I will have Charis take your fingers off.' She knew Charis would do no such thing.

Sarey yanked the blankets free, causing Eldoris to shoot up from her chair in shock. Her lady turned to address the queen mother. 'May I have a few moments alone with her, please?'

'No,' Cora said, pulling her knees up.

Eldoris looked between them, then bent to pick her tapestry off the floor before quietly leaving the room.

The second they were alone, Sarey turned back to Cora, head shaking. 'Stop playing the victim. It doesn't suit you. Now get up.'

Cora glared up at her. 'Charis, arrest her.'

The bodyguard shifted but did not move from his spot.

Cora sat up then, a hand going to her head as it pounded until she thought she would be sick from it. 'Do it!'

'Really, Your Majesty,' Hali said, tutting.

Sarey bent to Cora's eye level. 'I can live without fingers, but I cannot watch such a remarkable woman self-destruct.'

Hali entered the room and fetched one of the gowns hanging behind the door. 'It's a lovely day for a walk.'

Cora swung her legs over the edge of the bed, eyes narrowed on her host. 'Is that what you would do if your husband was about to be killed? Take a nice long walk to feel better?'

Hali stilled beside the bed, looking nervous. 'I hear he is an excellent fighter.'

Cora pressed her hands to her eyes. 'Charis, once you are done taking off Sarey's fingers, please gag Hali.'

Charis cleared his throat. 'But we're Lady Hali's guests.'

'A decision I am beginning to regret.'

Sarey took the gown from Hali and tossed it on the bed. 'Get dressed.' She then picked up the jar of wine from the bedside table and handed it to Hali. 'No one's to bring her anything to drink except water or tea.'

Cora's hands fell away from her eyes. 'Touch that wine and I will cut off your hands myself.'

A wide-eyed Hali froze, staring down at the jar of wine. 'I could make you some myrtle tea. It's quite pleasant.'

'She is not in charge here!' Cora shouted, pointing at Sarey.

Sarey walked over to the dresser and snatched the small hand mirror off it. Returning to the bed, she fell to her knees in front of Cora and held it up. 'Look at yourself.' She thrust it closer. 'Look! You're not in charge either.'

Cora had no choice but to look. She swallowed as she took in the sight of her dishevelled hair falling down one side of her face. Black paint was smudged from her eyes all the way to her hairline. Red wine stained the cracks in her lips, even her teeth. She looked down, her hand going to her chest.

'Keep looking,' Sarey said, 'because you are drinking yourself to death. Is that how you want to leave this world?'

Cora forced her gaze up again. The broken woman reflected back at her was difficult to look at. After a minute, she dropped her head into her hands. 'At least he will not be here to see it.'

Sarey finally lowered the mirror and sat back on her heels.

'At least you are here to hold my hand,' Cora added. 'Tyron will be forced to retreat eventually. Who will hold Brom's hand as he bleeds out in the mud, when all his men, his friends, lie dead around him?'

Sarey shook her head. 'I don't know, but this isn't helping

him.'

'He refused my help.'

'As you refuse mine?'

Cora stared at her, saying nothing.

Sarey must have been encouraged by her silence because she took a firm hold of Cora's arms. 'When the people you love need you, you don't give up on them at the first hurdle.'

Cora searched her lady's eyes. 'Tell me what to do.'

'You are queen of Zoelin.' Sarey tightened her grip. 'You must figure it out as only a queen can. But you can't do that under the fog of wine while drowning in self-pity. Get up. Get your head clear.'

It was one of those crossroads Cora had come to so many times in her life. Historically, she had always chosen defiance. It had felt like a win when the alternative was admitting error. Altering her behaviour had always been viewed as a walk of shame. But she realised in that moment it was more than that. It was an act of humility, a value she admired in others but had never possessed.

Tears rolled down her cheeks as she stood. Without saying a word, she walked out of the room, past her mother who had been listening at the door, across the landing, down the stairs, through the house to the back door, and outside. She went to the closest tree, moving behind it so no one would see her. Holding the trunk for balance, she pushed two fingers down her throat and vomited onto the ground. She rested her forehead against the tree until everything stopped spinning. When she straightened, she found Sarey, Charis, and Hali standing a few feet away wearing concerned expressions. Cora wiped her mouth with the back of her hand. The good thing about those low moments was there was only one direction a person could go from there.

'Lady Hali,' Cora said, clasping her hands in front of her, 'I wonder if you might bring me that tea now.'

CHAPTER 36

*H*eavy rainfall was unusual for that time of year, but down it came. Brom stood beneath a canvas shelter, water pooling at his feet. He was throwing his dagger up into the air and catching the blade between two fingers, then up again, catching it by the handle. He had been standing there an hour, maybe more, ever since he had visited a barely conscious Carac in the medic tent. One tiny error on the battlefield and he had almost lost his closest friend. Brom's leg had prevented him from getting there any faster. Plus he was tired. Everyone was tired. It was not just the fighting but the fatigue that came from constantly looking over one's shoulder.

Someone appeared in Brom's peripheral vision, and the dagger fell into the mud.

'Sorry,' Tyron said.

Brom glanced at Tyron as he bent to pick up the dagger, finding him unshaven, his tunic soaked through.

Tyron crossed his arms and looked out at the rain. 'I heard about Carac. How bad is it?'

'Bad.' He flicked mud off his dagger.

'How many Zoelin dead?'

'Another two hundred this morning. You?'

'Eighty.' Tyron rubbed his forehead. 'They continue to outnumber us three to one, and those odds will not improve with time.'

Brom sheathed the dagger and looked across at the prince. 'Even with the next lot of reinforcements, we stand no chance of getting near Onuric Castle.'

'Afraid not.'

'Should've cut Pollux's throat when I had the chance.'

'And I should have shot him in the face at close range years ago, but you know, peace and all that.'

Water dripped from the seams overhead, landing between them. They watched as a group of soldiers passed by, mud sucking at their boots.

'I don't know what to do now,' Brom said. 'I feel like I'm waiting to die.'

Tyron picked up a stick and scraped at the mess on his boots. 'It is bigger than one agreement, one castle, one piece of land. You back down now and you will find yourself in the same position as your brother.'

'And if I don't back down, people will continue to die until there's no one left to kill.'

Tyron tossed the stick away. 'Pandarus will not send any more men, not for a lost cause.'

'Can't say I blame him.'

Brom watched a wagon roll by, corpses piled high in the back. It pulled up to let Leksi pass in front. The lord came at a jog with his head angled against the rain. Joining them beneath the shelter, he shook himself off before speaking.

'I have good news and bad news.'

Brom exhaled. 'Start with the bad.'

'King Tuyon is gone.'

'Gone where?'

'Back to Asigow. Apparently he left Onuric before this morning's attack.'

Brom cursed. 'It means he thinks the fight is as good as over.'

'What is the good news?' Tyron asked.

'He left Pollux as regent of the East.'

More cursing from Brom.

'And how is that good news?' Tyron asked.

Leksi shrugged. 'He's not nearly as intimidating as Tuyon. I could take him in combat.'

'You would have to get near him first.'

Leksi looked to the king. 'When do the reinforcements arrive?'

Brom wanted to punch something. 'It'll be at least another five days, and it's only an additional two hundred.'

'That's not enough to blockade,' Leksi said.

Tyron spoke up at that. 'Even if we could blockade the castle, Tuyon would just send more men.'

'Ah,' Leksi said. 'The perks of a large army.'

Brom closed his eyes for a moment. He really needed to sleep. 'Our next move must be unexpected and devastating. Give them no time to regroup, no opportunity for Tuyon to send more men.'

'I think we are past the element of surprise,' Tyron said. 'I can guarantee you the men who followed Pollux to Onuric do not make up the entirety of his network. There will still be spies among your own men.'

'Then we share no information until the moment we pick up our weapons to leave,' Brom said.

Leksi nodded as he thought. 'We could send our archers in first, nice and discreet. Pick off the watchers and wall guards, give us a chance to get near the place.'

'Pollux will be alert with more men arriving at the camp,' Tyron said. 'And they will know when they do.'

Brom looked between them. 'Unless they never arrive.'

Leksi cleared his throat 'Except that we sort of need them.'

'We set them up at a separate camp.'

'A secret camp,' Leksi said, understanding. 'Genius if we can manage to keep it a secret.'

Tyron nodded in agreement. 'Better still, I could withdraw my men.'

'Ah, how is that better?' Leksi asked.

Brom felt some of his energy returning. 'And then you take them to the new camp until we make our move. A diminishing army will have Pollux rubbing his hands together. He'll get cocky, complacent.'

All three of them looked out as the rain stopped.

'Well, that's a good omen,' Leksi said. 'I shall tell our men we're leaving.' He gave a small bow to the king before striding off.

When Tyron went to follow after him, Brom asked, 'Have you heard back from your sister?'

The prince looked almost apologetic. 'No, but she is not big on writing letters at the best of times.'

Brom offered a weak smile. 'Sounds about right.' He straightened. 'We'll make our move when the reinforcements arrive.'

'Any letters for me?' Cora asked as she stepped inside the kitchen, Pup trailing at her feet.

Hali was kneading dough on the bench, a dusting of flour covering her hands. 'No, nothing.' Her eyes narrowed on Pup. 'Do you recall our recent conversation about no animals in the kitchen?'

'Yes.' Cora leaned casually on the bench. 'Not even from Tyron?'

Hali continued to watch the wolf as she worked the dough into a ball. 'Nothing from Zoelin at all, Your Majesty.' She lifted the dough and placed it into the waiting bowl before covering it with a cloth. 'Perhaps *you* could write. I'm sure your husband would like to hear from you.'

'I doubt that. We did not exactly separate on good terms.'

'And yet you wait for his letters.' She regarded Cora a moment. 'What happened?'

Cora would have normally made some snarky remark before slinking from the room. She never conversed with Companions. She refused to acknowledge their existence most of the time. But she was forming a new understanding of the world, a deeper understanding. For years she had been so lost in her own woes, she had forgotten about all the other women trying to survive their circumstances. It did not mean she liked Hali, only that she was prepared to have a polite conversation across the dusty bench top. 'I told him if he sent me away, we were done. He said something. I said something.'

'Sounds like a normal quarrel. Every couple argues. The only difference is that your subject matter is a bit more serious. Funnily enough, they usually all boil down to the same common themes.'

Cora regarded her for a moment. 'Tell me, do you physically hurt your husband when you argue?'

Hali stilled, her eyes widening slightly. 'Ah, no. I'm more of a whiner.'

'Well, I push, shout, claw, and fling words designed to break a man. You and I are not the same.'

Hali picked up the jar of preserved peaches and tried to take the lid off. It did not budge. Giving up, she placed it back down on the bench. 'You know, my father always said it's perfectly healthy for couples to fight as long as they know how to fight fair.'

Cora rolled her eyes and picked up the jar, opening it in one easy twist. She placed it in front of Hali. 'Well, your father sounds incredibly boring.'

Hali pressed her lips together in disapproval. 'You're getting stronger, you know.'

'Not strong enough to be of any use.'

'What do you mean?'

'I will never be as strong as a man. My skills will only be of use if one of the maids turns on me one day, which is quite probable given how poorly I treat them.'

Hali exhaled. 'There's your mistake. You're trying to fight like a *man*. If there's one thing I learned as a Companion, it's that we're two very different species. Women must play to their strengths.'

Cora drew circles in the flour. 'I cannot flirt my way out of this one, if that is what you are suggesting.'

'Ouch. Flirting is one instrument in a lady's toolbox. You need to select the best tool for the job.'

Cora frowned at her from across the bench. 'I was not trying to manipulate him, I was trying to support him. If that required me taking up arms, so be it.'

Hali laughed. 'King Brom *loves* you. He's not going to let you die. What sane man would?'

'He rendered me useless.'

Hali began spooning the peaches into a bowl. 'All he did was send you somewhere safe. You're rendering yourself useless.' The spoon froze mid-air as Hali realised she had overstepped. 'What I meant is—'

'Do not back down now. You are finally becoming tolerable.'

Hali frowned. 'Oh. Well, that's good… I think.'

Cora tapped a finger on the bench as she thought. 'You know, I think you might be right.'

'I am?'

'Yes. I am not a prisoner here. Brom wanted me out of Zoelin, so I left Zoelin.'

'Right.' Hali looked unsure suddenly.

'But there is a whole world outside of Zoelin and a hundred ways to fight a war.'

Hali's hand went over her face. 'Dear God. What have I done?'

'I just thought of a way to help using something else in my toolbox.'

Hali's hand fell away. 'Is it by any chance an instrument the queen mother would approve of?'

A smile spread across Cora's face. 'Absolutely not.' She paused. 'I think it is time I paid my uncle a little family visit.'

*C*ora's hands rested lightly on the taffrail as men shouted around her, ropes flinging in all directions. She had arrived at Newford Harbour in Galen after spending the night at sea.

'There's Prince Stamitos,' Sarey said beside her, nodding in the direction of the dock. 'Who's that with him?'

'The infamous Captain Dion is my guess,' Charis said. He bent to pet Pup, who was whining at Cora's feet. She had not enjoyed the sea voyage one bit.

'*The* Captain Dion who was rescued from the jaws of death by his lover?'

'That is the one,' Cora replied.

Once the ship was secured, the three of them descended the gangplank towards the waiting men. Stamitos kissed his sister before stepping back to look at her properly.

'I am not going to lie. I am very nervous about the vague details of your visit.'

'Can a woman not visit her family without cause for suspicion?'

Stamitos gave her a knowing look. 'What did Mother say of you coming here?'

'She thinks I have completely lost my mind. She told me if I put one foot on that ship, she would never speak to me again. So here I am.' Stamitos tutted, and Cora turned to his companion. 'Captain Dion, I presume?'

He bowed. 'Just Dion, please. Welcome to Galen, Your Majesty.'

She looked him over. 'My husband speaks very highly of you.'

'Does your brother not also speak highly of me?' He looked pointedly at Stamitos.

The prince shook his head. 'You do not need two of us singing your praises, surely.'

The corners of Dion's mouth lifted. 'I speak very highly of your husband also. We're all very saddened by what's happening in Zoelin right now.'

Cora got a good feeling from the man. Plus Pup also seemed relaxed in his presence, which was a good sign.

'So, what's your agenda here?' Dion asked.

He was straight to the point, and Cora liked him even more for it. 'Well, I have come for your army.'

Dion and Stamitos exchanged a look.

'You understand your uncle's hands are tied,' Dion said. 'His daughter is betrothed to King Tuyon.'

'Yes, I heard. Such a romantic story. My cousin will make a wonderful brood mare.'

'It's no love story, but not many royal matches are.' Dion appeared uncomfortable. 'Yours excluded, of course.'

'Of course.'

Stamitos let out a breath. 'What exactly is your plan, sister?'

Cora's eyes remained on Dion. 'Would you fight along-side my husband if it were up to you?'

The captain hesitated. 'I'm loyal to my king.'

'That was not the question.'

He looked around before replying. 'Yes. If it were up to me, I would join the fight against King Tuyon. Sometimes these powerful men need reminding of their limits.'

Cora nodded. 'And how soon could you depart north?'

'I've no orders—'

'*If* ordered by your king,' she added.

Dion squinted against the low eastern sun. 'Within hours of receiving orders, Your Majesty.'

Cora looked over her shoulder at Sarey and Charis before her gaze settled on Stamitos. 'Let us go to Reave Castle, shall we?'

When the wagon pulled up, Cora was surprised to find the captain's wife, Astra, waiting at the top of the castle steps. She stood with her hands clasped in front of her, wearing a short-sleeve cotton dress that was casual by Companion standards. Her hair was braided to one side, her lips painted pink. The women eyed each other as Cora climbed the steps, all that history between them. They had been forced to coexist at Archdale for years. Enemies of sorts, and yet the similarities between them were undeniable.

'Welcome to Reave Castle, Your Majesty,' Astra said with not even a hint of hostility. She had always been good at that, while Cora had never bothered to keep the disdain from her voice.

Cora looked her up and down when she came to a stop in front of her. Sarey and Charis stood off to one side. 'I suppose I should not be surprised to see you hanging around my uncle's castle. Always the Companion.'

Astra looked past her to where Dion and Stamitos had

just arrived on horseback. 'Let us speak quickly and frankly before they reach us.'

'I am always frank.'

'You need my help.'

'With what?'

'Swaying your uncle's mind.'

Footsteps began ascending. 'You do not even know why I am here.'

Astra tilted her head. 'Of course I know.'

The muffled conversation of the men was getting clearer. 'I do not need or want your help.'

'I am trained in the art of persuasion.'

'I might be self-taught, but the man is blood, which gives me a distinct advantage.'

'*Not* sharing blood gives me a different sort of advantage.'

A smile played on Cora's lips as the men arrived. Both women turned to face them, and Stamitos looked suspiciously between them.

'A rather civil reunion,' Stamitos said. 'I gather you remember Astra.'

'I do not remember every woman who passes through Pandarus's bed, but I do remember this one.' She was allowed one small dig, surely. 'Astra has kindly offered to accompany me for the visit.'

Stamitos extended his arm. 'We shall all go.'

'No,' Cora said, threading her arm through Astra's. 'I think we can take it from here.'

Dion was watching his wife closely, no doubt looking for cues. 'You're sure? A military perspective might be helpful.'

'No offence, Captain,' Cora said, 'but your military perspective has proved fruitless thus far.' She offered a smile. 'I think it is time for a fresh approach.'

~

The women sat at the small table in King Linus's private solar, waiting for him to join them.

'Wine?' Astra asked, reaching for the jar between them.

'No.' Cora looked away from it, hoping to reduce the temptation. 'No, thank you.'

Astra leaned back in her chair, regarding the queen with a quizzical expression. 'Good for you. It will get easier, you know.'

'What are you going on about?'

'You know.' Astra picked up the jug of water and filled the queen's cup. 'Giving up is a mental war, and we all know you will win that fight. What made you stop?'

Cora met Astra's gaze. She considered playing dumb or shutting the conversation down, but her old ways were no longer serving her. 'There is nothing more exhausting than self-loathing. I simply tired of waking up hating myself.'

Astra nodded. 'We have all been there.'

The door opened and King Linus walked in, apologising for the delay. Cora rose, waving off the apology.

'A king is always being pulled in five directions at once.'

Linus kissed his niece before sinking down into the spare chair. He looked between them. 'I almost forgot that the two of you were acquainted. I imagine you became quite close over the years.'

Neither of the women replied.

'As much as I love seeing my niece,' Linus said, eyeing Cora, 'I really hope you did not travel all this way to ask for something I cannot give.'

Apparently they were done with small talk, which suited Cora just fine. 'You must know that you are on the wrong side of history.'

Linus poured some wine for himself. 'Actually, I am on no side at all.'

'You know that no action speaks volumes, dear uncle.'

He leaned back, letting out an enormous sigh. 'Beatrix, your beloved cousin, is to marry King Tuyon next month. What would you have me do?'

Cora could think of five hundred things she would have him do in that moment, but she needed to be smart in her approach. 'If it is a powerful man you want for your daughter, then King Tuyon is a smart choice. He is the type of man to force the hand of another, a king prepared to kill in cold blood if they do not comply.'

Linus's mouth flattened into a thin line. 'Many kings fit that description, as you well know.'

She decided to be direct. 'I would like to make a suggestion.'

'And what is that?' He sounded far from interested in her reply.

'That you set some terms before handing over your youngest daughter to the man. The union is supposed to benefit you both, after all.'

'And would these terms have anything to do with what is happening in Zoelin right now?'

She jutted her chin out. 'Yes.'

'You would have me invite war to my own doorstep?'

'If Asigow defeats Zoelin, war will be at your doorstep whether you like it or not. We are the buffer between Asigow and Galen, remember?'

'Until the wedding. Then my daughter will be the buffer.'

'That is an enormous responsibility for one so young and inexperienced,' Astra said. 'While Princess Beatrix will make a splendid wife, and no doubt go on to produce many healthy sons for her husband, she has no political pull.'

'She does not need political pull. She has royal Galen blood flowing through her veins.'

Astra shook her head. 'That is not enough to keep anyone safe. Once King Tuyon wins this war, his sense of entitle-

ment will grow. The union will only serve as further rein-forcement that he can have whatever he wants.'

Linus was silent a moment. 'What more could he possibly want?'

'Everything,' the two women said in unison.

Cora glanced at Astra before continuing. 'His confidence is growing. His power is growing. Soon he will be unstop-pable and it will be too late to act.'

Linus crossed his arms over his chest, appearing sceptical. 'My daughter will be queen of Asigow.'

Cora wondered how he could be so naive. She leaned forwards, heat pooling in her eyes. 'Your daughter will be powerless. If she tries to stop Tuyon or gets in the way of what he wants, he will crush her spirit and break her mind until all that remains is the shell of a woman who faintly resembles your daughter. Trust me, I know. I am that woman.'

There it was. Her confession. The facade stripped away, revealing the damaged woman Jayr left behind. It was an uncomfortable moment for her uncle, she could see that, but it was worse for her.

She straightened in her chair, drawing breath. 'Zoelin has a law that prevents a queen being harmed, and yet I barely survived the last three years married to Jayr. Asigow has no such law. It is a king's right to bring his wife into line. Can you imagine?'

There was a long uncomfortable silence.

'Your Majesty,' Astra began, 'what Queen Cora is saying is perhaps you should set clear moral boundaries *before* you hand your daughter to him. We would all hate to see your lovely daughter used as a weapon against you later on.'

'My moral boundaries are perfectly clear.'

'Really?' Cora asked. 'Tell me, are you opposed to the trades being forced upon our kingdom?'

Linus scratched at his wiry beard. 'You know I am.'

'And yet you do nothing.'

Linus's jaw ticked. 'You speak your mind too freely. I bet your poor mother is in pieces back home. Does your husband even know you are here?'

'Probably not. He is a little busy fighting a war right now.'

Linus blinked slowly. 'And I am sorry for it, but even if I could help, it is too late now anyway. My sources tell me the war is all but lost. King Tuyon has returned to Asigow in preparation for the wedding.'

Cora sat with that information for a moment. She had a strong urge to cover her uncle's mouth with her hand and scream at him to take it back. 'It is not too late. After the wedding is too late. When my husband lies dead, that is too late.' She felt her throat close. 'Please. Send Tuyon a letter. Tell him that you are sending your army north. Tell him to withdraw his troops immediately or you will have no choice but to act.'

Linus scratched at his beard once more, the action growing harder. 'I cannot do that.'

Astra reached out and covered his hand with hers. 'You are king of Galen. You hold all the power here. The Syrasan army is at the front as we speak. Everyone knows what they stand for.'

Cora placed her hands on the table. 'It is the best way to protect your daughter in the long term. Let him see you unafraid.'

Linus looked back at Astra. 'You told me Beatrix was my best chance of aligning with Asigow.'

'Of your two daughters, she is. But she is only a chance. A gamble. You must make King Tuyon *earn* her hand for the match to be of value to you.'

Cora reminded herself to breathe. 'My husband is the king the Zoelin people deserve and a trustworthy ally. Your own captain is prepared to ride out and fight by his side at a moment's notice. That is what strong leaders do.'

Astra squeezed his hand encouragingly. 'I have known you are a hero at your core since the day you pardoned my husband and stood by him. Your people still talk of that day. In fact, there is a song written of your merciful act. If you were to change the course of history, the legend of King Linus would be written about for years to come.'

Oh, she was good. Cora watched as Astra let go of his hand and leaned back in her chair with an adoring expression. She would bet her entire fortune there was no such song, and yet if her uncle wanted to hear it, Astra was the right person to produce one on the spot.

Linus's expression softened into resignation. 'Two thousand men—and not one more.'

Two thousand was a thousand more than Cora had been hoping for. She rose, her heart pounding as fresh hope soared through her. 'I will travel with your army.'

'Into a war zone?' Linus asked.

Astra rose from the table. 'You mean to return to Syrasan, surely.'

Cora shook her head. 'No. I will be returning to Zoelin. The fight has changed, and I am very much a part of it now.'

CHAPTER 38

The Galen heat was stifling. The breeze blew from the south, warm and carrying the scent of grapes and berries. Galens loved the warm season, finding the cloud cover and frosty air of the cold season too much for their fragile veins. Cora had acclimatised to Zoelin temperatures now, where, even in the warm season, the peaks of the mountains were dusted with snow. There was a purity to the atmosphere, something honest about it.

'I cannot breathe this air,' Cora complained to Sarey. 'It actually sickens me.'

They had spent the night at Reave Castle while Captain Dion went ahead to Swanton Fort to prepare his men. Cora had barely slept, despite being fatigued from their time at sea.

'I find the air rather pleasant,' Sarey replied. She was on her knees next to Cora, fighting with the button of the queen's trousers. 'Breathe in, would you?'

'*Breathe in*? What are you talking about?' Cora said, pushing her hands away and taking over the task. She fiddled for a moment, but Sarey was right, the button was a good inch from the intended hole. 'Perfect. I am bloated from my time at sea.' She sucked in her stomach and forced the button through, but she knew it would be uncomfortable over a long journey.

'Do people bloat at sea?' Sarey asked. 'Is that a thing?'

'Evidently.'

Her lady sat back on her heels, staring at Cora with a strange expression.

'Why are you looking at me like that?'

'Because you didn't bleed this month.'

Cora tore the button off and handed it to Sarey. 'That explains the bloating. Bad timing as always.'

Sarey shook her head. 'You're not due, you're *late*.'

'I am never late.'

'Exactly.'

Cora straightened as she realised what Sarey was implying. 'I am not with child, if that is what you are suggesting.'

'How do you know?'

'Because of history and facts.'

Sarey rose and went to fetch a needle and thread. 'Well, now we have new facts. Maybe your body was waiting for a better man to come along.' She knelt to reattach the button.

Cora stared at the ground. 'Say nothing to anyone. It is likely just stress or God playing a cruel joke.'

Her lady was silent a moment. 'Perhaps you should rethink going to Zoelin. You might be carrying the heir to the throne.'

'Perhaps you should concentrate on sewing the button in the right spot this time.'

Sarey smiled to herself and did not say another word.

It was already light when Cora emerged from her bedchamber. She stepped out wearing a fitted shirt tucked into high-waisted trousers, which had been let out an inch. She had even convinced her uncle to give her a sword. It was made from steel, not wood, its edges sharp. The weight of it on her hips made Cora feel slightly off balance but strong. She wore laced boots, her hair braided tightly and tucked at the nape of her neck.

Charis almost fell off his chair when he caught sight of her.

'Are we training?' he asked her, confused.

'No' was all she said as she passed him.

King Linus was waiting outside, ready to see her off. Every muscle in his face tightened when he saw her.

'It is completely unacceptable for a queen to go about wearing men's clothing,' he said as he followed her down the steps to the waiting horses. 'Now is not the time for rebellious acts.'

'Rebellious acts? Really, Uncle. If I was trying to be rebellious, do you really think I would opt for trousers? Gowns are splendid for gatherings but not practical for war.' When she reached her horse, she took the reins from the groom. He went to help her mount, but she held up a hand to stop him. Cora turned to her uncle and kissed him on the cheek. 'Your help will not be forgotten.'

'I just pray I do not live to regret giving it.'

Cora slipped her foot into the stirrup and mounted the quiet gelding. 'I promise you will have no regrets.'

Linus stepped back, looking far from convinced. 'Off you go, then. Captain Dion waits for you at Swanton Fort.'

The two thousand armed soldiers standing in formation was the best thing Cora had ever seen. The foot soldiers were divided into neat units of eighty men, each armed with a bow, sword, and shield. In front was the cavalry, four hundred men atop sturdy horses bred for battle.

'Good morning, Your Majesty,' Captain Dion said as he marched through the archway towards her.

Cora bowed her head in greeting. 'It seems you are ready to depart.'

He stopped just short of her horse, looking back at his men. 'We've been ready to go since King Jayr's death.'

Her gaze swept along the soldiers to the fort behind them, its green flags floating in the breeze. All that was left to do was go to Onuric and crush their enemy. They would take back the castle and ensure Pollux paid for his crimes. Tuyon would think twice about testing them in the future.

'Let's move out,' Captain Dion shouted. He went to mount his horse.

Cora's gaze drifted north, and she allowed herself a smile.

They made it to the border by noon. Cora stopped before the river to watch the men cross. The sound of boots scuffing the road was oddly calming. She kept waiting for them to stop, to hesitate, to change their mind, but they marched on while water rumbled and thrashed underfoot.

'You sure about this?' Sarey asked, looking more than a little worried. 'Brom specifically instructed you to leave Zoelin.'

'And I left.' Cora glanced across at her, noting how close her lady's horse was to Charis's. 'He said nothing of returning.' She turned back to watch the last of the men cross, then looked down at Pup. 'Our turn.'

Pup whined.

Cora forced herself to look down at the water, letting the memory fill her, choke her, welcoming it instead of fighting it. That way she would never forget the man who died protecting her. She had stared death in the face that day. It was no small thing.

They did not stop marching until they reached Rodale, a village five miles south-east of Drake Castle. The castle would have been a more sensible place to set up camp, but Cora could not risk it. She had no idea who she could trust anymore.

Only Brom. Always Brom.

Cora smiled when she spotted Ida enclosed in a small yard at the edge of the village. Untouched grain sat in a pail by the fence. She never ate when she was anxious, nor did she accept food from strangers.

'Ida!' Cora called. There was no way she was riding into a war zone on any other horse. She had organised everything prior to departing Veanor, praying her plan would work.

The horse swung her head in Cora's direction, ears pricked. She emitted a whinny that shifted the leaves on the nearby trees. The queen smiled as the mare trotted over to the fence, stamping the ground and turning left, then right. She pressed her head to Ida's when she reached her, eyes closing as they breathed in each other's scent, fear, and pain. That was how it had always been between them. After Jayr had taken a whip to her, Cora had slept in her stall for three days. She had thought of every possible way she could take revenge on her husband over that time, her mind going to places so dark she feared she might not find her way back. She had eventually—or perhaps Sarey had pulled her out of it. Lief had slept on the other side of the stall door like a loyal dog.

Cora ran her fingers along the scar on Ida's chest. 'A lot of people are going to die.'

The mare was listening to her voice.

'We need to make sure Brom is not one of them. I want him to live. I *need* him to live.'

Ida snorted and rubbed her large head against Cora's arm.

'She missed you,' Sarey said, walking up beside her. 'You're not tempted to take the nice calm gelding instead?'

Cora suppressed a smile. 'Tempting, but no.' She turned to face her friend. 'I want you to remain here.'

Sarey's forehead creased. 'What do you mean?'

'What I mean is soon I will be leaving, travelling overnight to reach the camp by morning. You will stay behind.'

'No.'

'No? You are telling your queen no?'

Sarey sighed. 'I go where you go.'

'I cannot be worried about you too.'

Sarey looked over at Charis, who was waiting out of earshot. 'I want to come.'

'Do not fret. I am leaving Charis with you.'

Sarey's gaze snapped back to meet hers. 'What? He's your *bodyguard*. You can't leave your bodyguard behind.'

'The man has no fear or experience. That is a dangerous combination.'

'But he'll protect you with his life. Surely you know that by now.'

Cora nodded. 'I do know that. I also know you will be quite devastated should anything happen to him.'

Sarey opened her mouth, then closed it again. 'But you're *pregnant*.'

'We moved a button an inch. Let us not get ahead of ourselves.'

'You should stay here with us.'

'I cannot.'

'Why?'

'Because this is my fight, my kingdom, my heart shattered

into a million pieces if it all goes wrong. I must bear witness to this moment, whatever the outcome.'

Sarey searched her queen's eyes. 'Promise me you won't do anything foolish. You lead the army there, let the men do the fighting, and return with your husband.' Her gaze fell to the weapon. 'And keep that thing in its sheath.'

'I am quite aware of my limitations.'

Sarey pressed her lips together and took both of Cora's hands. 'I love you, you know. Yes, you're my queen, and I serve you as such, but you're also my sister.'

Cora's throat thickened, and she instinctively withdrew her hands. 'Which is exactly why you and Charis are staying here.'

Sarey reached out to straighten Cora's cloak pin, the one she had given as a wedding gift. 'Why are you not shouting at me and having Charis drawn and quartered for even looking in my direction?'

It was possible she had grown up. She could thank Brom for that. He had a way of pushing her to be better—not for him but for herself. He had pieced her back together like one of the vases lining the mantel in her solar. 'You deserve to be loved by someone kinder than me.' She glanced at Charis. 'What he lacks in brains, he makes up for in heart.'

Sarey's eyebrows rose. 'Oh. Well, that's nice. At least part of it.'

Cora turned back to Ida, eyes going to the arrow scar on her rump. Her hand instinctively went to her own scar on her shoulder.

'If Pollux succeeds,' Sarey said, 'it'll mark the beginning of the end for us.'

'Pollux does not get to win, he gets to die. Afterwards, I will hang his body on the gate of Onuric Castle myself. History will remember him as a traitor.' She reached out and stroked Ida's head.

'And you will be remembered as the queen who led two thousand Galen soldiers onto the battlefield. The Ice Queen, the widow with the marked face, the witch who rose from freezing waters to change the course of history.'

A smile played on Cora's lips. 'So glad I did not marry the Galen cousin.'

CHAPTER 39

The archers moved through the pines like ghosts. Large men slipping between tall trunks, bows in hand and feet rolling silently across forest debris. It was an hour before sunrise, and the guards atop the walls of Onuric Castle were leaning against the embrasures, bows slung lazily over one shoulder. Others stood in pairs in front of the curtain wall, their gazes occasionally drifting to the trees. Brom stilled every time their eyes brushed over him. Tyron and his men were already in position. The prince had selected his strongest archers for the assignment. It was the best chance they had at getting near the gate—but it was only a chance.

Brom gestured to his men, and they all settled into a crouch to wait. He peered through the darkness, searching for Tyron, finding him five yards away, flattened against a trunk. He was watching a guard atop the wall down his arrow. His experience was evident in his steady hands and even breath, in the way he directed his men with the smallest gestures of his head. Leksi was close by, his bow also poised and ready.

Breathe.

A moment later, twenty-five arrows flew free, striking their targets. Men cried out, some falling from the wall and plummeting to the ground below. Footsteps ensued, soldiers spilling from the turrets to investigate. Another nod from Tyron and more arrows were released. Men were falling almost as soon as they appeared, multiple arrows striking them at once.

A minute later, the portcullis rose and men ran through it, clutching bows and spears. Brom knew their arrows might miss but their spears would not. Every kingdom had its strengths. They needed to kill as many of the men as possible before they reached the trees.

Here they come.

Even Brom's men could not miss at that close range. He signalled, and they rose around him and began shooting. Brom released his first arrow. It pierced the closest warrior through the chest, and he immediately reached back for another one, loaded it, and shot at him again. While their enemy was disadvantaged with no armour to protect them, these were not men who could be taken down by a single arrow. Their ancestors had fought bare-chested in the snow for centuries, claiming the dangerous temperatures drove better outcomes. Nowadays they wore vests made of leather and fur, but not thick enough to stop an arrow.

He focused. One arrow after another. Next man, next arrow. Next kill. That was all he could do, the only plan they had. But there were not enough arrows for the number of men. Soon the warriors reached the trees, crashing through the terrain with all the grace of a charging ox. Their swords were drawn now, slashing at the shrubbery. This was the moment that Zoelin soldiers came to life. It was their sword skills that set them apart.

Brom secured his bow on his back and drew his weapon.

He could just make out his enemy in the poor light. The sound of steel slamming into steel marked the beginning of the next stage. It was disorienting at first, but once he joined the fight, his body moved automatically, precise and forceful. As soon as a man fell, another took his place. They needed to keep moving forwards in order to make it to the portcullis. But when he allowed himself a glance in that direction, all he saw were more men spilling out. He had hoped they would have more time before word spread of their arrival. He did not let the thought trip him though.

'Eyes behind!' Leksi shouted at the same time Brom heard a stick snap behind him.

He pulled his sword free and swung around. Weapons met. He could make out the distinct Asigow markings on the man's arm. His attacker had come from behind—and he was not alone. Two more men emerged from the shadows.

Brom staggered back as he tried to protect himself against one of the new arrivals. He did not dare fall because that would be the end for him. Planting his feet, he fought back. Out of the corner of his eye, his saw a blade coming from the other side, but it never reached him. Leksi blocked it. A moment later, the three Asigow men lay dead at their feet.

Brom gave Leksi a nod of thanks before turning to take in the rest of the scene. Not only were they no closer to the castle, but they no longer had the option of retreating. They were surrounded and outnumbered. All he could do was rejoin the fight and continue for as long as he could keep hold of his sword.

Setting his jaw, Brom stepped into the bloodbath.

～

Dion sent some men ahead to the camp. They were half a mile out when they returned at a gallop, their horses skidding to a halt in front of the captain.

'They're mid-battle, sir. Heavy losses. The camp is empty except for the wounded.'

Cora pulled Ida up next to the captain, blinking away her fatigue as she processed the news. She knew the situation was dire if the only people left at the camp were those too injured to fight. She waited for the captain to respond. It was an enormous ask to send soldiers who had marched overnight straight into battle. But Brom was out there, and he needed help.

Please, God, let him be alive.

Dion looked east to where the sun had just kissed the top of the mountain, then back at his men. They were still in formation, relatively alert despite their fatigue. It was Cora who had insisted they keep moving overnight, as though sensing their urgency.

'Prepare the men for battle,' Dion instructed. 'If we wait any longer, I fear our efforts will have been for nothing. I'll go in first with the cavalry.'

Cora released the breath she had been holding. 'I am coming with you.'

'Absolutely not. You can wait in the medic tent with the injured.' He swung his horse around, ending their conversation. 'Cavalry to the front! Let's move.' He pointed to two nearby foot soldiers. 'Escort the queen to the camp. She's not to leave there.'

Cora watched as the horses moved out at a canter, disappearing around the bend in the road. She wanted to follow. She wanted to gallop out onto that battlefield with her weapon drawn and pretend she stood a chance against their enemy. Perhaps she would have if Sarey had not put foolish ideas in her head about babies and heirs.

Swallowing down her agitation, she followed the guards to the camp.

~

They were going to die.

All of them. Brom, Tyron, Leksi, and every man fighting with them. They were tired, their numbers dwindling. They were losing. Asigow warriors kept arriving, each fresher than the one before them. Every time they killed one, two more replaced them. Brom was bleeding from his arm, ankle, shoulder, eye. He could taste it too; the inside of his cheek had burst when a shield collided with his face.

His fingers were loosening around his sword, his shoulder aching. All he could do was keep going, keep fighting, and try not to die too quickly.

He snuck a glance over at Tyron and Leksi. They stood back to back, sweat pouring down their faces, their teeth stained red and fancy armour sprayed with blood. Maybe belonging to their enemy—or maybe their own.

Brom tripped on a corpse just as a spear passed by. He almost laughed at the realisation that if he had not stumbled, the spear would have gone through his face. Lifting his sword, he managed to block the blade coming at him. It felt like it would never end. Each warrior was more determined to kill him than the last. Death would bring relief. It might even earn the forgiveness of his sister, but not his wife who had begged him to live. She had not wanted much for herself, really. A handful of people around her she could trust, an assortment of broken things to fix, her family safe. And him to love. What had it cost her to admit it? What had it cost him to not say it back?

Slam.

A shield smashed into him. He managed to stay upright,

but God, he was tired now. His reflexes were getting slower, and every blow knocked another piece of him loose.

'Fall back!' Tyron shouted suddenly.

Brom glanced in his direction. Surely the prince knew there was nowhere to fall back to. Yet Tyron was transfixed on something in the distance. The sound of horses approaching made Brom's opponent glance over his shoulder. The king used the distraction to his full advantage, driving his weapon through the man's middle and thrusting upwards. Only then did he give himself permission to look. He expected to see mounted Asigow warriors coming to finish the job—but the riders were not Asigow. The men had green uniforms and polished chest plates, the kind you could see your reflection in. They wore helmets and carried bows and swords, cutting down those standing in their way.

They were Galen.

Brom felt only confusion for a moment as they charged towards him, killing men left and right. He braced, expecting to be struck down, beheaded, or opened up in front of his men. He did not drop his sword, but he did not raise it either. If they were there to kill him, he could do nothing to stop them. Wind whipped his face as the horses tore past him, meeting his enemy head-on. Brom turned, panting and sweating, his mouth so dry he doubted his ability to swallow. When he looked over at Tyron, he found the prince bent over, trying to catch his breath. He had fought hard.

'Well, that was unexpected,' Leksi said, turning in circles.

Brom ran a hand down his face. 'I have no idea what's happening right now.'

Leksi chuckled. 'Bet that wife of yours knows.'

Before Brom could ask what he meant, a horse pulled up between them. It was Captain Dion.

'I'm dead, aren't I?' Brom asked.

'Not yet,' Dion said. 'There are another sixteen hundred soldiers on their way.'

Brom shook his head, unable to comprehend those numbers. 'How?' He could only manage the one word.

'You can thank your wife. This is all her.'

'Told you,' Leksi said as he stepped past to deal with a warrior who had wandered a little close for comfort.

Brom swapped his sword to his other hand, stretching out his cramping fingers. 'Cora wrote King Linus?'

Dion shook his head. 'She sailed to Galen and achieved more in a few minutes than I have in months.'

'Cora's in Galen?'

Dion shook his head. 'No. Your wife's *here.*'

Brom blinked. 'In Zoelin?'

'Waiting at the camp. Quite reluctantly, I might add.'

Brom looked in that direction while men continued to fight around them. He was torn between anger that she had disobeyed him and pure joy at having her so close.

'You should go to her.' Dion nodded towards the wound on his arm. 'You can't fight with that anyway. Go get yourself patched up.'

Brom shook his head. First he would take back Onuric, and then he would go reprimand his wife—before burying his face in her. 'Not yet. I'm not finished here.'

Passing his sword back to his other hand, he headed for the castle's gate.

CHAPTER 40

The smell of blood seeped through the trees, along with the sound of weapons clashing and men roaring. Cora had never heard anything so haunting in her life. Dismounting, she tethered Ida to a tree next to the medic tent and looked around at the abandoned camp. The groans of men drifted through the flap, adding to the eerie scene. Drawing a breath, she pushed her way inside and looked around at the rows of cots packed close together. Larger gaps were filled with more men laid out on blankets on the ground. So much suffering. And the smell. Her hand twitched at her side, wanting to cover her nose and mouth. Not a physician in sight. They were likely closer to the battlefield, preparing for the next round of men.

She stepped between the bodies, feeling helpless. She had no idea how to help them, yet she wanted to.

'Cora?'

She whipped her head around, searching for the source of her name. She looked from face to face until she spotted Carac, pale and still, his eyes blinking up at her. Cora went to him, kneeling in the narrow space between two cots. The man in the next bed was likely dead; his eyes were open, but they did not follow her. She tried to focus on Carac, who was not faring much better.

'Here to kill me in my sleep?' he asked, one corner of his mouth lifting.

She nodded. 'You woke and ruined my plan.'

Some life flashed briefly in his eyes. 'What the hell are you doing here?'

'I brought some help.'

He gave the slightest nod. 'Good. We really need it.'

She was quiet a moment. 'What happened to you?'

'Sword wound.'

Her eyes went to his stomach, where blood seeped through bandages. 'How bad is it?'

'The medic had to stuff bits back in.'

She looked down at her lap, the image too much. 'Well, you have made it this far. You might as well aim for a full recovery now.'

His eyes closed in a silent laugh. 'Don't pretend you want me to live.'

'Brom needs friends. He needs family. You are both. You are the brother he deserves.'

Carac watched her. 'I warned him not to fall in love. I told him you're selfish and spoiled.'

She saw that his lips were parched. 'Well, you were spot on.'

He laughed, then winced.

Cora's gaze went to a nearby jug of water. She picked it up, smelled it, and then poured some into a dirty cup for him. She had to lift his head so he could drink.

'You've changed,' he said, out of breath from his efforts.

Cora shrugged. 'Do not get too excited. It might be temporary.'

'Do you love him?'

She swallowed. 'You said I was incapable of love.'

'I did.'

She watched him a moment. 'You know, having a civil conversation with you on your deathbed is an enormous inconvenience. Now if you die, I shall be forced to care.'

His eyes smiled at her. 'How many men did you bring with you?'

'Two thousand.'

He was struggling to focus on her. 'You played the uncle card.'

'Yes.'

'I wish I could fight with them.'

Her brow creased. 'Me too.'

The sound of a horse approaching made Cora stand. She looked down at Carac, unsure about leaving him. He nodded towards the exit. 'Go on. You don't want your reunion in this place.'

Cora reached out and touched his arm. 'Do not die. By order of the queen.' She gave him a weak smile before making her way outside.

Her guards stood to attention when she stepped out. Pup leapt to her feet, following at her heel. Cora turned in circles, searching for the horse amid the trees. She finally spotted it between the narrow trunks of the pines. But it did not stop at the camp, or even slow down for that matter. She sucked in a breath as she recognised Pollux. He did not look in her direction, and a moment later, he was gone from sight.

Where was he going? The battle was the other way.

The answer came to her like a cold wave of water.

The bastard was fleeing.

She looked up at the mountain that sat between Onuric Castle and the Asigow border. Once he crossed, there would be nothing they could do. He would never pay for his crimes. Lief would still be dead, and Pollux would be alive.

Cora looked over to where Ida was tethered. She had a few seconds at best to decide if she was mad enough to pursue him. Encouraged by the fact that Tyron had shot an arrow through Pollux's sword arm during their last encounter, she broke into a run towards the mare. She untied the reins in a few swift tugs and swung herself up into the saddle.

The two guards immediately ran after her.

'You can't leave, Your Majesty!' shouted one of the men. 'Captain's orders.'

She dug her heels into Ida's side, and the mare lurched forwards. The men on foot stood no chance of catching her. 'If he crosses the border, we shall never see him again!'

The guards stopped running, throwing their arms up in defeat.

Cora glanced down at Pup, who was running alongside the horse. 'I have been very patient, but now I need your help. Find him. Do you understand me? Where is he?'

Pup's good ear twitched, listening to Cora's voice, then pricked forwards again as her stride lengthened. The wolf was her only chance of finding him in time.

They wound through dense trees until they came to the base of the mountain, where Pup ran in circles for a minute, sniffing the ground and whining. Disappointment hit. They had lost him. Pup stopped altogether, panting. Cora looked around, frustrated, and that was when she spotted a narrow path snaking along the side of the mountain. It was her best shot, so she took it.

The queen was no tracker by any stretch of the imagination, but she could definitely make out hoof prints in the mud. They seemed fresh, but what did she know?

The path took them higher and higher, Ida's breathing laboured as she climbed the sharp incline. They were about halfway up when Cora caught sight of Onuric Castle. The persistent fog had finally lifted, offering a clear view of the fight below. The battle spread almost a mile long, like a scene from a nightmare.

A low growl pulled Cora's attention. She looked down at Pup, whose grey fur was now a putrid brown. Her good ear was pricked forwards, the hair on her back standing up. Cora looked back at the path and dug her heels into Ida's sides. The mare moved at a steady canter, but each time they turned a bend, there was nothing there, so she pushed Ida harder. They tore around the next corner, then the next until she finally caught sight of a horse. She flattened herself against the mare's neck as they sped up again. At the next bend, Ida was forced to pull up fast to avoid colliding with Pollux's horse.

He was facing her, and there was no hiding the surprise on his face when he saw who it was.

She should have been afraid, but she felt only anger. 'Where the hell do you think you are going?' She pointed north. 'If you think King Tuyon is going to welcome you across the border after you abandoned your post and his men, then you have no idea the type of man you are in bed with.'

The path was so narrow at that point that Pup was forced to stand in front of the horse. At least she was not hiding as expected.

Pollux looked down at the fighting below them. 'Tell me, what witchery did you perform to get King Linus to agree to this?'

'The type of witchery where you die at the end.'

His eyes went to the sword at her hip. 'I hate being wrong, but it seems I underestimated you.'

'Do not be too hard on yourself. Most men do.'

'You're far more conniving and unstable than I realised.'

She laughed, sending a puff of steam into the air. 'From the mouth of a traitor.'

His eyes darkened. 'Why did you follow? You could've lived.'

'There is no way I am letting you cross that border. You must pay for your crimes.'

A smile played on his lips. 'You think *you* can stop me leaving?'

All she knew was that she had to try.

Cora drew her sword, because she had no idea what else to do. She would probably die if it came to blows, but she pointed the weapon at him anyway. He looked down at it with disinterest.

'You were supposed to die that day,' he said.

Her eyes never left his. 'I have had a few of those days. You are going to need to be more specific.'

'The day Jayr died.'

Her sword hand dropped a few inches.

'When have you ever attended a social event and not drunk the wine?' He rubbed his cheek, smiling. 'You're a drunk, for God's sake.'

Cora's arm fell to her side. 'You?'

'Me.'

'You poisoned your king?' The words seemed to stick in her throat. 'You were the closest thing he had to a friend.'

'He was digging our kingdom into a hole so deep we'd never have been able to claw our way out.'

Her mind raced to play catch-up, trying to think back to that day. She had buried it deep in her mind. '"Long live King Brom." That was what his killer said before he died.'

Pollux tutted like he was disappointed. 'What would you have me do? Stand up and take credit for it? Brom was going to do it eventually. The timing was perfect.'

She saw him in an entirely new light in that moment.

King Tuyon had not lured him into being his pawn. Pollux had orchestrated the entire thing.

'But a witch is not so easily killed,' he continued. 'How many lives do you suppose you have left?'

Her glare held heat. 'Get off your horse, big man. Let us see.'

Pollux laughed. 'The thing with you is I can never tell if you're being threatening or suggestive.'

'Yes, I know you have *great* difficulty reading signals from women, so let me be very clear. I am being threatening.'

He nodded, still smirking. 'The problem is, if I kill you, I think that husband of yours will make it his life's mission to hunt me down. So I think I'll just be on my way.' With that, he offered a mocking salute and swung his horse around. But the horse did not get far, because Pup stood in the middle of the muddy track, slightly crouched and teeth bared. The horse's front hooves lifted off the ground for a moment, almost causing Pollux to topple from the saddle.

There she was. The wolf of before, the one who took on an entire pack to protect her village. Cora felt her own confidence grow as she watched the hair on Pup's back bristle.

'Get off your horse, *traitor*.' She slipped from the saddle. 'I will take you to my husband dead or alive. Either is fine by me.'

Pollux struggled to keep his horse calm as Pup crept closer. 'Is this really how you want to die? On the side of a mountain in the mud?'

'I prefer that to poison at a feast, you coward.'

All humour left his face. He slid from his horse, eyes never leaving hers, then drew his sword. 'You're insane. You know that, don't you?'

'Yes.' She stopped walking. 'You could always take yourself back down the mountain and throw yourself at the mercy of your king.'

His sword twisted in his hand. 'I think I'll just kill you and leave.'

Pup darted around the horse and went to stand in front of Cora. Pollux's mount sidestepped away from the wolf, then took off up the path.

It was Cora's turn to smile. 'How long will it take to reach the border on foot?'

He glanced after the horse. 'I'm Zoelin. I was born to trek these mountains on foot.'

She shook her head. 'You gave up the right to call yourself Zoelin the day you sold yourself to King Tuyon for a bit of power that does not belong to you.'

Raising her sword, she lunged at him.

Brom spat blood and ran his tongue over his teeth, finding them still in place. His opponent raised his sword to strike again, but the king was ready this time—and he was quicker. He slashed the man's chest before shoving him with the heel of his boot, sending him crashing backwards. He was just three yards from the portcullis, and he knew that every able-bodied Asigow man was already fighting. They were so close.

'Brom!' Dion called.

He glanced in the captain's direction. He was on foot now, his bewildered horse stranded in the mud ten yards back. Brom's eyes shifted to the man standing with Dion, whose uniform was far too clean for the setting. Brom weaved between the fighting men in their direction.

'What's wrong?' he asked when he reached them.

'Cora went after Pollux—'

'What the hell are you talking about?'

'On horseback. I think I might know where she is.' Dion

threw his head in the direction of the mountain. 'Is that your wife?'

Brom squinted, searching until he spotted movement on the mountain. What he saw made his hand go slack around his weapon. About halfway up was his wife—unmistakably Cora. He would recognise her anywhere, because watching her was one of his favourite pastimes.

He narrowed his eyes on the man with her. It could not be Pollux, because he was inside the castle, awaiting his chance to fight Brom.

But Pollux was not inside the walls of Onuric. He was standing on that mountain with Cora.

Panic took hold of him.

'You can take my horse,' Dion said.

Brom would have taken it without permission. He fought his way to the animal and tried to mount, but his boot was so thick with mud that his foot slipped from the stirrup. Cursing, he swung his leg over the horse's rump and landed hard in the saddle. The horse threw its head up, not pleased by his new rider.

'Ha!' Brom turned in the direction of the mountain, sending a spray of mud up into the air.

Every strike of Pollux's sword rattled Cora's bones. He had held back at first, years of conditioning likely working against him.

'You cannot mark a queen.'

But at some point, he had figured out that the only way to beat her was to fight her like she was a man. That was when the fight changed. She was no longer attacking, she was just trying to defend herself and failing, slipping, leaning, until eventually he knocked her sideways into the mud, her weapon stuck beneath her. She braced for pain, for death. But she had forgotten about her secret weapon—Pup.

The wolf leapt at Pollux, jaw snapping, latching onto his arm before his weapon had a chance to reach her. It was just enough time for Cora to roll, lift her sword, and slash his leg. Pollux roared through gritted teeth, then slammed a fist into Pup's side to free his arm. The sound of air leaving the wolf's lungs as she hit the path made Cora feel sick. The queen got to her feet, a roar tearing from her as she went straight for Pollux's throat. But he blocked her, and the next blow, and the next. The ease with which he defended himself made her want to fall down and beg him to just die already. But Cora would not give him the satisfaction of her begging for anything.

The next time their swords met, he brought his face close to hers. 'All right. You've had your fun. Now I have to go.' With that, he pushed her.

Time seemed to slow down in that moment. Cora's back rounded, her arms flinging forwards with the force of the push, as though there were an invisible fist pressed to her chest. She instinctively reached a foot behind her, seeking ground, knowing the only way to remain alive was to stay upright.

But there was no ground. He had pushed her off the path.

In a moment, she would fall down the face of a cliff, arriving at the bottom a pummelled corpse.

But just as she began to tilt, Pollux reached out and grabbed her by the throat, his hand like a vice on her neck. For a moment, she thought he might save her, return her feet to the path, but instead of pulling her in, he extended his arm so her toes scrambled in the mud, unable to grip anything at that harsh angle. She swung her sword, more of an instinct than a plan, but he knocked the weapon from her hand. She heard it tumble, bouncing off the rocks below.

Pup had finally made it to her feet, and she came at Pollux again, but he was ready this time. He turned his weapon on her, and she pulled up just short of the tip, snarling.

Cora clawed wildly at Pollux's arm, trying to relieve some of the pressure, but his fingers only tightened until she could draw no breath at all.

'Did you think I would just let you fall to your death?' he asked, head tilted to one side and eyes narrowed. 'No. I'm going to watch you die, slowly, and then I'm going to cut off your head and leave it here for your husband to find.'

Her legs continued to move, her boots sliding. A tear betrayed her, rolling down her reddened cheek. The lack of air was making her lose control of her body, her emotions, her mind. That was a sort of death in itself.

As her vision blurred, she pressed her eyes shut and faced the darkness.

CHAPTER 41

*B*rom pulled his horse up the moment he spotted them. Pollux was holding Cora over the edge of the mountain. Her face was red and stained with tears. The struggle had left her, or rather the man had choked it out of her. Pup was crouched and snarling at the tip of a blade.

Brom leapt off the gelding, drawing his sword as he broke into a run towards them.

'One step closer and I drop her,' Pollux hissed, his dark eyes narrowing on the king.

Brom stopped, knowing Cora would never survive such a fall. 'If you hurt her, I will tear you limb from limb and let the wolf feast on you.'

Cora's eyes opened at the sound of his voice, the whites of them so red he expected her to cry blood at any moment. She began writhing, desperate for air, but he needed her to be still so Pollux would not drop her. The man was visibly thrown by Brom's arrival but hid it well enough. His eyes moved between the king and the wolf.

'Put her down on the path,' Brom said, his spare hand

outstretched in hope of evoking some calm. Cora's eyes kept sinking shut, and he was about to lose his mind.

'So you can kill me? I don't think that's wise.'

Cora was holding Pollux's arm with one hand while the other went to her chest, tugging at her cloak. What was she doing?

Dying. She was dying.

'If you put her down on the path, I'll let you walk.'

'And spend the rest of my life looking over my shoulder?'

Brom's breathing was laboured as he looked between Pollux and his wife. Then it stopped altogether when he saw what was in her hand. Her cloak pin. She was gripping it between her fingers, her bloodshot eyes fixed on the traitor.

'I won't come after you,' he said, eyes returning to Pollux. 'I swear it before God.'

Pollux's grip on Cora's neck eased just enough so she sucked in a breath. It should have been a simple exchange from that point—her life for his. Pollux should have placed her back on the path, put his weapon away, and run. Brom would have kept his word if it meant she lived. Cora must have known it too, because she raised her hand and thrust the needle of her cloak pin into his arm as hard as she could.

'No!' Brom shouted, maybe out loud or maybe in his head. The sword fell from his hand, and his feet were moving in her direction before the roar even left Pollux's mouth, before his fingers loosened and Cora began to fall.

Typical. She would rather die than see a traitor, Lief's *killer*, walk free.

She was making the decision for him.

The air left Brom's lungs at the same time Cora finally inhaled. He continued towards her, knowing he would not reach her in time. He was supposed to finish the job, to kill Pollux. That was how one honoured such a sacrifice. That was what she wanted him to do.

But he did not do that.

Instead, he leapt off the edge of the mountain after her.

Cora's eyes were wide and bright with fear as she fell. His hip hit the slope first and he began to slide, arms outstretched for her. But the distance was too great, and she slammed into a rock before he could grab her. She had barely had time to draw breath before it was knocked out of her once more. As he continued to slide, he reached out, trying to grab hold of any part of her. Finally, he got a handful of shirt. His fingers held tight to that piece of fabric as they continued down the mountain. He tried to anchor them with his other hand, clawing at mud and roots in hope of stopping their descent. Finally, he caught hold of the sharp edge of a rock. They came to a sudden halt, Brom panting and Cora groaning beneath him. Her shirt had ridden up her side, revealing scored flesh.

'I've got you.' Brom glanced down at the five-hundred-foot drop below.

Cora coughed, her hands going to her throat as tears poured freely down her face. Each cough was followed by a sharp intake of breath.

'Breathe. That's it.' He felt his fingers slip a quarter of an inch on the rock. 'I'm going to get you out of here.'

Above them, Pup was howling and pacing. Cora brought a shaky hand to the cut along her hairline, then looked up at him. 'You jumped.' Her voice was barely recognisable.

He grimaced as his fingers slipped a little more. 'I did. And now I need you to do something for me.' Her shirt slipped higher, and she dropped a few inches with a gasp. Brom held tightly to the rock. 'I've got you,' he repeated. 'But I need you to try and climb up to me.'

She nodded, coughed again, then slowly and carefully began to move. Her fingers pressed into the dirt and rock until she was vertical.

'Good.' Brom still had the full weight of her. 'Now I need you to climb.'

More coughing. 'I do not think I can.'

'I need you to try.'

She blinked against the blood running into her eye as she reached up, trying to grab hold of anything she could, but everything kept snapping or coming away in her hand. 'I cannot do it.'

'You can.' His tone was firmer this time. 'Climb up.' His hand was tiring, and he was not sure how much longer he could hold on.

Cora's face creased with concentration, her body shaking. The toe of her boot found a nook that enabled her to push herself up.

'That's it.' The moment she was holding her own weight, he let go of her shirt and grabbed hold of her wrist, pulling her the rest of the way up to him. Her arms went around him, and she buried her face in his neck. She cried and coughed as he held her tightly. 'Shh. It's all right.'

Pup's whimpering ceased above them, and Brom looked up. Leksi's head popped into view, his eyebrows rising in surprise.

'I'm having some difficulty reading this situation,' Leksi said. 'Do you want to be rescued or left alone for a few minutes?'

Relief pulsed through Brom. 'Definitely rescued.'

Leksi disappeared and returned a moment later holding two bridles. He fiddled with the straps, joining them together, then attached one end to his horse before lowering the other end to them.

'I need you to hold on tightly so I can reach the strap,' Brom said.

Cora nodded, wrapping her legs around his middle. 'It is a good thing I wore trousers.'

'Too soon,' he said, grabbing hold of the bridle. He let go of the rock, his bloodied hand going to Cora's back, drawing her closer. 'I've got you.'

∼

When Cora was finally dragged up onto that path, she was met with a wolf to the face. 'I am all right,' she croaked out, burying her face in the muddy fur. 'I knew you were not broken.'

Brom pulled Cora to her feet, eyes moving over her as she looked north. Disappointment crushed her. Pollux was long gone, as was the horse Brom had arrived on. They would never catch him now.

Her sword lay in the mud a few feet away. She walked over to it, her legs like a newborn calf's beneath her, and returned it to its sheath. 'He was supposed to pay for what he did.' The words set off more coughing.

Brom wiped his bloodied hand on his trousers. 'It was you or him. I chose you. I'd choose you again.'

'Might be a little premature for the dramatic speeches,' Leksi said, nodding up the path.

Cora and Brom turned just as Tyron rounded the bend on horseback. Brom's horse trailed behind, a body slung over the saddle with six arrows protruding from its back. Cora's heart stilled.

It was Pollux.

Cora took in Tyron's serious expression. He was not a man who took pleasure in killing, but this was a wrong put right, a weight he had carried for years. It was a weight Cora would have carried for the rest of her life.

Pulling up, Tyron dismounted and glanced back at the traitor, the tyrant, the man who had once done unspeakable things to his wife. It was a fitting end.

Cora walked past him to the body. She took hold of Pollux's lifeless arm and studied the wound she made with her cloak pin. The gift was long gone.

'Looking for this?' Tyron asked, holding up the mud-covered pin.

She let out a breath and went to him. 'Thank you. For both.' She ran her thumb over it before slipping it into her pocket.

'You might want to wash that before using it,' Leksi said.

'Funny.' Cora lifted her gaze to him. 'I used to say the same thing about the women you bedded.'

'Ouch.'

Tyron studied her for a moment. 'You all right?'

Her ribs ached, her throat was raw, and her head pounded. She nodded. 'Yes.' She would lick her wounds in private later.

Brom extended an arm to Tyron, and when the prince took hold of it, he pulled him into an embrace. 'I've got no idea how to repay such a debt.'

'Pandarus will think of something, I am sure.'

Brom's tired eyes smiled at the prince as he stepped back, then wrapped an arm around Cora, kissing the top of her filthy hair. She held his hand and rested her head against his shoulder. They were bleeding, filthy, forever changed by the events of that day, but they were also united by them.

Their kingdom, their enemy, their wounds, their pain.

The four of them turned and looked out at the battlefield below. The fighting had stopped. The only movement was the soldiers wandering about collecting the dead and tending the wounded. Beyond that sat Onuric Castle, a slightly less depressing sight now that the orange flags had been torn from its walls, blue banners raised in their place. They had done the impossible, defeated an enemy everyone said they could never beat.

Cora looked up at Brom. 'We will burn the dead together.'

He searched her face for a moment, then brushed a finger along her bruised throat. 'It's not easy seeing so many dead, all laid out in neat rows. The sight and smell will haunt you.'

Her fingers moved between his. 'Your haunting is my haunting.'

Leksi leaned closer to Tyron. 'Seems I was wrong about there being no man alive who can survive your sister.'

Tyron's mouth turned up in a smile. 'Quite wrong.'

Ignoring them, Cora looked over her shoulder to where Ida was standing five yards away, wearing only a saddle. 'It is all right, girl. It is over.'

The mare snorted and made no move towards her.

'What do you want to do with the body?' Tyron asked.

Brom looked down at his wife. 'I guess we'll burn it.'

'No,' Cora said. 'We will hang him on the gate. Let the men see what becomes of traitors.'

Leksi looked at Tyron. 'A little dark, but fair, I suppose, given the numerous attempts on her life and the awkward cliff moment at the end there.'

'Your help was much appreciated,' Brom said before turning to Tyron again. 'You're lucky to have him fighting at your side.'

Leksi rolled his eyes. 'Always the handsome sidekick.'

'No one called you handsome,' Cora said.

'Not out loud.'

The queen stepped back from the edge. 'Let us get off this mountain.'

'Excellent suggestion,' Tyron replied.

Leksi handed Ida's bridle back to Cora. 'I'll let you do the honours. She bites, you know.'

'She is an excellent judge of character,' Cora replied, taking the bridle. She slipped out from beneath Brom's arm and made her way over to Ida.

The king followed, helping Cora onto her horse before stepping back and raising his hands. 'I never touched her.'

She watched him, hating the distance between them suddenly. She had never experienced anything like it before. Weirdly, it no longer scared her. 'Ride behind me.'

Brom looked down at the mare. 'But she hates men.'

'But not you. Ida knows you are different. She has known it since the first day she met you at the stables. She just needed time.'

They stared at one another for a moment, and then he stepped forwards, letting Ida sniff his hand before slipping his foot into the saddle and gently lowering himself behind Cora.

The mare kept still despite the new weight.

'Don't worry,' Leksi said, passing them. 'I have some clean trousers you can borrow.'

Cora shook her head as she nudged Ida forwards.

'I should reprimand you for going after Pollux,' Brom said, 'but I'm too impressed you survived as long as you did. You fought well.'

'He was injured,' Leksi called over his shoulder.

Cora looked heavenwards. 'He knows that.'

'And she had a wolf.'

'Yes, thank you, Lord Leksi.' Cora blinked against the glare. 'He is right, of course. Pup was reborn back there. The fight has not left her. She just took a little longer to fix.'

The wolf looked up at the mention of her name.

'But you still fought like a warrior,' Brom said into her ear. 'Wolf or no wolf, you drew your sword despite the odds. I will never doubt that lion heart of yours again.'

She tipped her head back to rest it on his shoulder.

'So Pup is reborn,' Brom went on. 'What about you, my queen? Are you fixed too?'

The day had proven that miracles were possible. Bringing

a hand to her stomach, she thought about the button Sarey had moved an inch to the right, then the trauma she had endured in the hours since. Her hand fell away. 'We will find out soon enough.'

She should have dismissed the idea entirely. That was the sensible thing to do—the Cora thing to do. But against all logic, she was hopeful for one more miracle.

'No one's ever going to lay a hand on you again,' Brom said. 'I swear it.'

'I know you speak the truth because no one is ever going to separate us again—not even you. I am untouchable at your side.'

He was quiet a moment. 'That doesn't mean I won't question some of your decisions.'

Angling her head, she looked up at him. 'You do not have to worry about me. I am the Ice Queen, the witch who emerged from frozen waters to change the course of history.' She winked at him.

His gaze fell to her weapon. 'Plus you have a sword now.'

'Made of Galen steel.'

He chuckled. 'Impressive.'

'Behave and I might let you have a turn.'

'Your sword is my sword.'

Suppressing a smile, she straightened and glanced over her shoulder at Pollux. 'We protect each other. That is how it is now.'

Brom's warm arms tightened around her, and her head tipped back to rest in the curve of his neck. They continued down the mountain in silence.

EPILOGUE

The water thrashed beneath the bridge. It was the beginning of the warm season, which meant all the melted snow and ice fuelled the river. Cora closed her eyes for a moment, remembering the man who had given his life for her. Had it really been a year?

'You want to stop for a while?' Brom asked.

She opened her eyes and looked across at her husband. He rode with a loose rein, one hand resting on his thigh instead of his sword. That was what peace looked like on him. Her gaze flicked to Tasia and Carac, who were already on Syrasan soil, waiting for them. 'No. We should keep moving.'

Brom's gaze fell to their son, who was fast asleep against her chest. 'Want me to take him for a while?'

She looked down at the sleeping boy and kissed the top of his fluffy head. 'Seems a shame to wake him.'

Brom watched her for a moment. 'You'll have to share him eventually.'

She smiled at him, then looked back down at their son.

Their miracle.

A few hours later, their party arrived at the manor in Veanor. It was pretty that time of year with its lush green lawns and clear blue sky. Hali had been rather keen to host the gathering and oversee the food.

Many of the guests were waiting out front when they arrived.

'Welcome, Your Majesties,' Hali said, curtsying before them.

Lord Yuri bowed next to her. 'Nice to see you both again.'

A year ago, Cora might have just strolled past them—but that was a year ago. 'Lady Hali,' she replied with a polite nod.

Hali pushed herself up on her toes, trying to get a look at the sleeping infant. 'This must be Prince Lief. I've been dying to meet him.'

Cora removed him from the wrap and handed the sleepy baby down to her.

'You give him to Hali,' Brom said, a coy smile on his face.

'Well, you know how persistent she can be.'

Hali sucked in a breath as she took him. 'Oh, he's divine.' Lief's bright green eyes blinked up at her. 'Well, look at that. What a startling little darling you are. Do you want to come meet the other children?' She was already walking away with him.

'It will be a fight to get him back now,' Yuri said, looking after his wife.

Brom walked around Ida and helped Cora from the saddle. She did not need help, but he did it anyway. Once she was on the ground, he threaded his fingers through hers and turned back to Yuri.

'Thank you for hosting us for the next few days.'

'It is truly an honour. Hali loves visitors, as you well know.' He gestured behind him to where Leksi, Petra, Dion, and Astra were waiting. 'I will let you greet the others.'

'Be nice,' Brom whispered in Cora's ear.

She looked up at him. 'When am I not nice?'

Brom led her forwards. 'You told Carac only an hour ago that if he didn't stop singing, you'd have his tongue removed.'

'He sang the same song, off-key, for the entire journey. Everyone wanted him to shut up, but it always falls to me to say something.'

Brom laughed and kissed the top of her head.

'There she is,' Leksi said, bowing before them. 'The queen, the legend, the myth—and wearing a dress. I'm honoured by the effort.' He glanced over to where Hali was standing, surrounded by curious children. 'We were just saying we hope the little one has the king's ears. Children can be cruel.'

Petra dug an elbow into her husband's side. 'We were saying no such thing, Your Majesty. My husband is attempting humour.'

Cora nodded a greeting at Petra. 'One would think he would give up after all this time. He must be exhausting to live with.'

Petra pressed her lips together to stop from smiling. 'We get by. Congratulations on the safe arrival of Prince Lief.' She tugged on Leksi's arm. 'Let us go meet him.'

Brom clapped Leksi on the back as they wandered past. He then stepped up to shake hands with Captain Dion. Cora loved that he had found brothers in this world.

'Prince Stamitos and his wife send their regards,' Dion said.

Brom nodded, then turned to look at Astra. 'I've waited a long time to meet this wife of yours.'

'Your Majesty,' Astra said, curtsying. When she rose, she folded her hands neatly in front of her. Always the Companion. 'My husband has told me so much about you, I feel as if I know you already. Plus the entire kingdom has spoken of nothing but the battle for Onuric Castle since it happened.'

Brom nodded. 'Your husband was quite the hero that day.'

'As was your wife,' Astra replied, eyes going to Cora. 'You are looking as beautiful as ever. Motherhood agrees with you.'

Cora regarded her. 'I was never one for sleep anyway.'

The front door to the house opened, and Tyron and Aldara walked out, baby Luanda perched on her hip. Mako and Zelia ran ahead of them.

'Slowly,' Tyron called out to no avail.

The children stopped in front of the king and queen, bowing and curtsying before rushing forwards to hug their aunt. Cora squeezed them back. Brom ruffled Mako's hair and picked Zelia up, emitting an exaggerated groan as he did so.

'What are they feeding you? We only saw you a few months ago and you're taller again.'

Zelia giggled. 'Beetles and slugs.'

Cora laughed. 'Has your mother been cooking?'

'I heard that,' Aldara said as they joined the group. She kissed Cora's cheek before pulling her in for a hug.

'Does Lief have ink yet?' Mako asked.

Brom looked down at him. 'His older cousins must go first, so you better roll up your sleeve.'

Mako's eyes grew large, and he turned to Tyron. 'Can I, Father?'

Tyron patted his shoulder. 'You have to earn the honour.'

'But I have been learning to fight and everything—and doing chores.'

Aldara laughed at that. 'What do you think?' She looked up at Brom. 'Does shovelling manure earn him ink?'

'It's a good start.'

Hali joined them, crouching down so the children could see their cousin. The baby glanced between the new faces and a smile broke on his face.

'He remembers us,' Zelia said.

Cora looked around at all the grinning faces. It was quite ridiculous. Even more ridiculous that she was among them. When Lief opened his mouth to yawn, everyone laughed and fussed. Fair reaction. He was ridiculously cute when he yawned. Even Pup wandered over to see what all the fuss was about.

'Where are the bride and groom?' Cora asked, looking around. They had left Drake Castle a week earlier to prepare for the wedding.

'Here they come,' Aldara said, nodding towards the road.

Cora turned to see them riding up. Sarey slipped from the saddle the moment she spotted Cora, rushing forwards to greet her. Charis whistled to Pup, who took off at a run in his direction.

'Excuse me,' Cora said, going to meet Sarey.

Her former lady curtsied before throwing her arms around the queen. Cora laughed. 'It has only been a week.' She pulled back to look at her friend. 'Your happiness is a little unsettling.'

'We have finally figured out where we are going to live.' She threaded her arm through Cora's as they walked back to the group.

'Please tell me it is not some filthy hut by the sea?'

'No. Though I do like the sea.'

'You know, it is not too late to change your mind. We could still have the feast.'

Sarey looked over to where Charis was crouched down, getting licked to death by Pup. 'And let some other woman swoop in?'

Cora regarded the drool-soaked bodyguard. 'I do not know about *swoop*. That makes her sound willing.'

'Be nice.'

'You are the second person to say that to me in a matter of minutes.'

'Well, we all know you don't play well with others.' Sarey stopped. 'Now where is that delicious baby of yours?' She let out a disappointed sigh when she saw Hali with him. 'I see I was too slow.'

Cora's gaze passed over the group crowding her son. Her chest felt light, then pinched when she realised who was missing. 'Did my mother receive the invitation?'

Sarey turned to her. 'Prince Tyron delivered it in person.' Reading Cora's expression, she added, 'The wedding is not until tomorrow. There is still time.'

Cora had not seen her mother since the day she set sail to Galen. She was heavily pregnant by the time Brom convinced her to write and share the news. Her pride had prevented her from writing sooner; she did not want to be the first to reach out. A few weeks later, she had received a polite letter of congratulations back. That had been the moment she realised the damage done was too great this time.

Cora cleared her throat. 'She is likely busy managing Pandarus's life now that she has relinquished control of mine.'

As much as she wanted to pretend she was fine with the new arrangement, she was not. She wanted her mother to meet her son and fuss over him like she did all her other grandchildren.

'You could visit her after the wedding,' Sarey suggested.

Cora looked in the direction of the house. 'Come. I want to see your wedding gown.'

Brom leaned against the outside wall of the house. Tasia stood beside him, watching the dancing that followed the wedding ceremony. Brom was only watching Cora. Not much had changed there. She was wearing a blue silk dress that opened at the back for the wedding, revealing ink along one shoulder. He had done it himself, complete with a wolf which covered the scar left by the arrow. Lief was in her arms, like always, while their nurse lingered nearby looking lost.

So much for not being maternal.

Back home, he would often find her pacing with their son, singing songs and smiling at every face he made. He would often slip quietly into the room and watch her, enjoying those moments before she noticed him, before her smile faltered and she was all business once more.

'You don't have to stop just because I'm here. I see you— always have,' he would say.

Years of conditioning could not be easily undone. She was a work in progress, but lucky for them, they had all the time in the world.

'I want to return to Onuric Castle,' Tasia announced beside him.

Brom looked at her, eyebrows raised. 'I thought you hated it there.'

'I hated being a *prisoner* there.'

He took in her strong posture and serious expression. 'I happen to like having you at Drake Castle.'

She met his gaze. 'And I have enjoyed being with you, but I have no purpose. I feel like the sad princess waiting to be married off.'

'I already told you, you can marry whomever you please.'

'Perhaps I do not wish to marry at all.'

He had never considered that. 'What will you do at Onuric that you cannot do at Drake Castle?'

'I would be in charge, in control of something, even if that something is a depressing castle that receives no visitors.'

Brom pushed off the wall. 'Then you should return there

if you think it'll make you happy.' He waited for her to look at him. 'But not as some lady of the house—as regent of the East.'

Her eyes searched his. 'What?'

'I need someone I can trust, and our people in that region need to feel protected.'

'But a woman cannot be regent if the king is alive.'

'Says who?'

'Every other man.'

He shrugged. 'One of the perks of being king is that you can change outdated laws. There's no better fit for the role.'

She hugged him, just like she had when they were children. It was the first time he felt forgiven.

'Tell you what though, you better come visit once in a while,' he said when she finally pulled away.

Droet wandered over at that moment. He looked between them, then took hold of their hands. 'In family, love is the oil that stops the squeaking, the glue that binds, and the arrow that shoots birds out of the sky when they hover. Got to watch those birds.' He tapped a knowing finger to his nose.

Tasia bit her lip and rested a hand on his shoulder. 'You get wiser by the day, Grandor.'

He laughed wildly before wandering off in the direction of the refreshment table.

Brom and Tasia went back to watching the dancing. Sarey and Charis were at the centre of it all, the sun low in the sky behind them. It was a Syrasan dance Sarey was struggling with, but what she lacked in skill, Charis made up for in enthusiasm. Their laughter rang out across the lawn. As much as Cora would miss her friend, he saw the warmth in his wife's expression as she watched them. She recognised love—even the inconvenient kind.

One of the servants exited the house to Brom's right, striding across the lawn towards Lord Yuri. He said something, causing Yuri to look in the direction of the house. Brom looked back just as Cora's mother stepped outside, taking in her surroundings. Her eyes landed on her daughter at the same time Cora looked up. Whether she admitted it or not, he knew his wife had missed her mother over the last year.

Sarey and Charis stopped dancing, the smiles falling from their faces as they looked between the two women.

'Mother and daughter,' Droet said nearby, staring up at the blue sky with a mouth full of tart. 'Nuts and salt.'

Brom walked over to greet Eldoris at the same time Tyron reached her. The men exchanged a knowing look.

'I thought you were not coming, Mother,' Tyron said, kissing her cheek.

She smiled at him, but she seemed nervous. 'There was a change in my circumstances.' She turned to Brom. 'Your Majesty.'

He exhaled. 'Just Brom, please. We're family.'

She gave him a tight-lipped smile.

'Mother' came Cora's voice. She stood just a few feet away, Lief wide awake in her arms.

Eldoris stared at the infant, her eyes immediately welling up. 'Oh, Cora. He is absolute perfection.'

Cora swallowed and closed the distance between them, holding him out for her to take. 'Do you want to hold your grandson?'

Eldoris gathered him close and breathed him in.

'I have seen that look before,' Tyron said. 'She has claimed him now.'

A few fat tears rolled down Eldoris's cheeks. Someone else sniffed nearby, and they all turned to see Hali crying. Aldara, who was standing with her, patted her friend's hand and offered an awkward smile.

'Please ignore us. She will be fine.'

'Sorry,' Hali said, brushing a tear off her cheek. 'It's just such a lovely moment.'

Cora touched a finger to her eye. 'Oh, for goodness' sake. You are going to start me off.'

Brom draped an arm around his wife's shoulders.

Eldoris looked back at her daughter. 'I am so sorry I did not come to Drake Castle after the birth.'

Cora lifted her chin. 'And I am sorry I never invited you.'

Eldoris waved the apology away. 'A mother does not need an invitation.'

When Cora opened her mouth to disagree, Brom gently increased the pressure of his arm. She closed her mouth and drew a slow breath.

'You know you are welcome anytime at Drake Castle, Mother.'

Brom eased his grip and kissed the top of her head. 'Come dance with me.'

She looked up at him. 'All right.'

It was an hour later when they finally sank down next to Eldoris. She was seated with Tyron, Aldara, and the children. Aldara was helping Zelia hold Lief.

A servant stepped forwards to pour wine, and Cora shook her head.

'Just tea, please.'

Everyone turned to look at her.

'I'll have the same,' Brom told the servant. His gaze met Cora's, and he winked. 'Your pain is my pain.'

Cora's eyes creased at the corners.

'You know, I think I shall have some tea also,' Aldara said, pushing her goblet away. 'Any more wine and I shall fall asleep in my food.'

Eldoris was staring at Cora like she did not recognise her. 'Yes. Tea sounds lovely.'

The young servant appeared lost for a moment. He looked down at the jar in his hand. 'Yes, Your Majesty.'

'And make it strong,' Cora added.

Brom laughed at that. 'You never do things by halves.'

'No, she does not,' Eldoris agreed.

Aldara took the baby from Zelia and returned him to Cora. 'You know, this one was fast work for a barren queen.' Her eyes shone with humour.

'I knew you could not be barren,' Eldoris said.

Tyron rubbed his forehead. 'Here we go.'

'You come from a long line of breeders,' Eldoris continued as though he had not spoken. 'Your body knew better than to bring a baby into that toxic marriage.'

'On second thought, perhaps I will have the wine,' Cora said.

Brom smiled down at his lap, then looked out to where Sarey and Charis were still dancing. 'They haven't stopped to draw breath all afternoon.'

Cora watched them for a moment, then turned to Aldara. 'Did Sarey tell you where they are to live?'

Aldara frowned. 'I thought she would have told you already.'

'She started to tell me earlier, but we got sidetracked.'

Eldoris looked up at that. 'That is Cora speak for she derailed the conversation.'

No one dared laugh.

'They intend to trade between the two kingdoms,' Aldara said, moving the conversation along. 'Charis has contacts in Veanor and Sarey from her village. They will be dividing their time between the two kingdoms.'

It was the best of both worlds. Neither would have to give anything up, plus Cora would see Sarey a lot more than if they remained in Veanor all year. 'That is… very sensible.'

'Yes.' Aldara gave her a knowing smile. 'Very sensible.'

Brom took Cora's elbow. 'Walk with me?'

Cora rose and pressed Lief to her chest. 'Excuse us.'

They strolled away from the noise and the people, across the green lawn to the path that led to the stables. As usual, Ida was protesting the food she had been given. She was more interested in sniffing the baby.

'Have you ever known a doting horse before?' Cora asked.

Brom leaned against the stall door, watching them. 'Glad she's not jealous. We'd be in trouble then.' He loved that expression on Cora's face: the warmth, the fascination, the way her eyes burned a little brighter when her curiosity was piqued. He reached up and ran a thumb over her cheek, then bent to kiss her. She tasted of the tea. 'I'm going to really enjoy making more babies with you.'

She purred into his mouth. 'You kings. Always wanting more.'

'Don't you want a daughter?'

She pulled away from him. 'That is a terrifying thought. What if she is like me?'

'Then she will be beautiful, smart, and fearless.'

'She might be a lot of other things too.'

'Perhaps she'll be more like me.'

'Is that supposed to be enticing?'

He laughed and leaned against the stall door again. 'Our children will be good people if *we're* good people.'

'No pressure.'

'And if they lose their way, we'll all suffer through it together.'

'Because their pain is our pain?' Her eyes smiled at him.

'Exactly.'

Her expression turned serious as she watched him. 'I am

going to do better, *be* better, every day until I finally deserve you both.'

Brom reached out and brushed some hair back from her face. 'And I'm going to spend every one of those days reminding you of your worth. What's a king without his queen?'

'A happy man, most would say.'

He could not help but grin. 'You know I can't rule without you.'

'And you know I cannot tolerate people without you.'

A low chuckle came from him.

'You laugh, but you know it is true.'

He took Lief from Cora, then drew her close. 'I see you, Ice Queen.' He brought his lips to her ear. 'There's no hiding from me now.'

Sarey stepped into sight at that moment, looking from them to Ida. Her hands went to her hips. 'Are you planning on spending the rest of the celebration with your horse?'

Cora shrugged. 'Probably.'

Sarey tilted her head. 'Charis wants to partner with someone who knows all of the traditional dances.'

'Then go find him someone,' Cora replied.

Brom gave her a gentle push in that direction. 'Cora would love to partner with your new husband.' He caught his wife's eye. 'Remember that big heart of yours.'

'I will certainly remember that big mouth of yours,' she whispered back at him.

Brom grinned as she turned away, gliding across the uneven path with all the grace and poise one expected of a queen. He watched her until she was out of sight. Then, with his son in his arms and his heart full, he followed after her.

ACKNOWLEDGMENTS

I would like to express my gratitude to the many people who contributed to this book. My biggest thanks goes to my readers. Without you guys, I wouldn't get to do what I love. Next, a huge thank you to my rock star husband who supports and encourages me even though my writing takes time away from him. I love you to bits. A big thank you to Joanna Walsh for your ongoing feedback and support. A big shout-out to my beta readers, who each brought a unique perspective. Thank you to Kristin and the team at Hot Tree Editing for polishing the manuscript into something beautiful, and to my proofreader Rebecca Fletcher for catching everything I missed. A round of applause for my cover designer, MiblArt, for another gorgeous cover. And finally, a huge thank you to my Launch Team for your encouragement, honest reviews, and being the final set of eyes on my work. You guys are amazing.

www.ingramcontent.com/pod-product-compliance
Lightning Source LLC
Chambersburg PA
CBHW021957130726
47903CB00014B/1619